GHOST NEXT DOOR

Helen Currie Foster

Alice MacDonald Greer Mystery Series

This is a work of fiction. All incidents (including conditions on Mt. Audubon), dialogue and characters, with the exception of some well-known public figures, are products of the author's imagination and not to be construed as real. Where real-life historical or public figures appear, the situations, incidents and dialogues concerning those persons are used fictitiously and are not intended to depict actual events or to change the entirely fictional nature of the work. Any legal issues and analyses are fictional and not intended as legal analysis or advice. Coffee County and Coffee Creek exist solely in the author's imagination, where they're located somewhere in the Texas Hill Country between Dripping Springs and Fredericksburg.

Design by Bill Carson Design
Library of Congress Control Number: 2018910369
ISBN-13: 978-0692168271

For Stuart Dickson Currie, who loved mysteries

OTHER BOOKS BY
HELEN CURRIE FOSTER

Ghost Cave
Ghost Dog
Ghost Letter
Ghost Dagger

Chapter One

"I've Got My Eyes on You"

Alice, barefoot in her nightie in the early sun, pinched open the last clothespin and clipped the wet towel onto the line strung around the posts of the pole barn where she parked her truck. As she often did, Alice smugly reminded herself that one joy of living alone on a small ranch at the end of a long gravel road was doing outdoor chores in only some, or no, clothes. No one could get halfway down her road without giving her plenty of warning. Brushing hair away from her eyes, she stepped back on the limestone ledge that bordered the pole barn, surveying with satisfaction the week's wash.

The pole barn sat uphill from the stone ranch house she and her late husband had bought as a weekend retreat before his helicopter disappeared over four years earlier. Alice had then surprised herself and everyone else by moving her life and law practice from Austin to little Coffee Creek in the Texas Hill Country, with the ranch her new center of gravity, her sanctuary.

The ledge felt cold to her bare feet, but the rising sun promised late September's bright blue weather. A perfect day. Then Alice heard it. A small mechanical hum, far above. An annoying little hum. She stepped farther back and peered over the roof. At first she saw nothing. Then she focused on a buzzard that was not a buzzard. A small—machine? Yes. A drone, hovering above her pole barn. Hovering above her property. Hovering above her.

A wave of rage. Alice yanked open the truck door, groped under the seat for the flare gun. She slammed a flare into the breech. Who dared invade her solitary domain?

Propelled by fury, she stepped back, pointed the flare gun, stared up at the hovering drone. It didn't budge. She thumbed the hammer, fired. A satisfying kick followed by the red fireworks. She didn't expect success—but she wanted to send a message.

A scrambling crash on the pole barn roof, then a *thunk* on the gravel drive. Propellers still whirling, the wounded drone staggered round and round in circles on the gravel. Now what?

She crept up to the wounded whirling dervish. It lurched in the gravel and a rotor lashed at her bare foot, causing her to leap backward. Should she run it over with the truck? Instead she tugged a wet towel off the clothesline and flung it on the drone. It wriggled for a moment, then, terry cloth now caught in the rotors, it lay whining, whining. Alice cautiously picked up the wet, vibrating bundle, careful to keep towel between her and the camera that hung from the gimbal underneath. She pushed the bundle under the tarp in the back of her truck. She limped down the limestone walkway back into her house, the Saltillo tiles cool under her feet, and hobbled into the bathroom to dab antiseptic on the scratches across her foot. Band-Aids and socks under her boots today.

Then she stopped short, a disturbing thought blasting into her consciousness. Who sent that drone? Was the camera on? Was it taking pictures? Did someone see her shoot it down? Would that someone come retrieve it? Did she have the *right* to shoot it down? As a lawyer, she was an officer of the court: had she broken the law? Her stomach churned.

In the nook off the kitchen, she stared into her laptop screen, scrolling through Texas statutes. What was this nameless tune teasing her brain? Okay, Use of Unmanned Aircraft. Taking pictures above private property was forbidden except for a host of exceptions: licensed real estate brokers . . . surveyors . . . pipeline inspectors. But look, the act made it a misdemeanor to take photographs of an individual without consent. She sure as hell had not consented. And she could get damages. Not much, though, and she'd have to prove the violation.

She walked back to the truck, peered at the drone's model number. Back inside she looked up Phantom drones on the Internet. Horrified, she read the cost: well over a thousand bucks. Not a cheap toy; someone should want it back. Its flying range was seven kilometers. What was that, about four miles? Then whose was it? It could be someone on the road past the end of her drive, but surely her neighbors weren't sending a drone over her property. Out here people didn't trespass on their neighbor's land: real property was sacrosanct, right? Oh, but she'd shot down someone's personal property, hadn't she?

Before she left the laptop, Alice finally identified the song lyrics jangling her brain: "I've got my eyes on you . . ." Cole Porter, of course.

* * * * *

Alice called her law buddy, Tyler Junkin. She assumed his criminal defense practice—unlike her property and estate law practice—gave him some knowledge of drones. "Glad to help my fellow lawyer, Alice," he said. "Come on by."

She pulled on boots, careful not to disturb her Band-Aids, and headed out the gravel drive toward the two-lane blacktop everyone called "the creek road," which ran south along Coffee Creek and into the town of that name. Vermilion and orange berries glowed on possum haw trees in the bar ditches. Small golden cedar elm leaves fluttered across the road. Otherwise, fall in the Texas Hill Country on the limestone plateau west of Austin offered just a few colors: straw-colored grass, the resinous yellow green of cedars, the darker green of live oak mottes atop the hills, the creamy white interruptions of limestone outcrops, and hidden blue-green creeks in an otherwise unpromising landscape. A Hill Country fall couldn't compete with fall in New England, but felt beautiful in its own spare way. She'd proudly shown this landscape to her college roomie, visiting from Manhattan, who'd said, "It's a little scruffy, isn't it?" Scruffy. But with the deepest fiber of her being Alice loved it. Though Alice admitted the poet must have been thinking of Greece, she thought W. H. Auden got it right: limestone creates the one landscape humans "are consistently homesick for."

Turning her truck toward Coffee Creek, she surveyed with suspicion the only vehicle parked along the road near her small ranch —maybe the drone owner? No, the Coffee Creek Electric Co-op repairman, for the third time this month.

She pulled up in front of Tyler Junkin's office, which, like hers, was a renovated 1940s limestone cottage in downtown Coffee Creek. His was located a block east of the courthouse square; hers, a block west. Tyler stood waiting at the open door. His looks—shrewd blue eyes, mouth ready to laugh—always reminded her of a Brooklyn bartender, standing behind the bar, wiping glasses, sizing up patrons. But then came his West Texas twang. "Hey, Alice! Come in! Want some coffee? Are you limping? What'd you do to your foot?"

Alice used any excuse to visit Tyler's office, decorated in Hill Country–masculine lawyer style, including a hint of mordant humor. She was especially intrigued by the fanged stuffed trout mounted on the wall of the ladies' bathroom. As usual Tyler had music going. The hectic rhythm of a boogie-woogie piano matched her anxiety level. "What's that, Tyler?"

"'Panic Street.' Memphis Slim," he answered.

Appropriate, Alice thought.

"A little coffee, a little fast boogie, maybe I'll wake up," Tyler said, leading her into the kitchen. "What's going on?" She noted he'd added a jackalope to the taxidermy collection mounted above the kitchen sink. He poured a mug of coffee for her and topped up his own cup, sighing with relief after the first sip.

"Tyler. There was a drone over my house. Hovering."

"Yeah?"

"I was hanging out laundry."

"And?"

"It made me really angry. So I got the flare gun."

He stared at her.

"It's out in the truck," she said. "The drone, I mean."

They walked outside. Tyler peered under the tarp, lifted the damp towel. The little monster lay silent, blades entangled in wet terry cloth.

"Whoa, that's a nice little Phantom," he said. "An older model, though. Let's take it inside."

So he already knew the model.

"How'd you know that?"

He gave her a "You are so out of it" look, then placed the bundle on the conference room table and hung the wet towel over a chair. "Max wanted one for Christmas. He's addicted." Tyler's entrepreneurial twelve-year-old son had started a business mowing office yards in Coffee Creek—including Alice's office. "Max knows everything about drones. But criminal defense lawyers also need to know about drones and drone law anyway, now that law enforcement's using them."

"I don't want to be the subject of law enforcement for shooting this sucker down."

"You're probably okay."

"Just probably?"

"But it's a shame you damaged this one—it's a nice model. And it's been retrofitted with a seriously fine camera—this one can look sideways, all directions."

Alice thought. "You mean it can photograph across property lines? Hover above my neighbor, but photograph me?"

"Sure. Not saying legally, of course."

Damn.

"Alice, I understand you were outraged, out there in your—what?"

"Nightgown." She took a deep breath. "Not a Mother Hubbard, either."

He grinned, shook his head. "Okay. The common law used to say landowners owned from the heavens to the depths. *Usque ad coelum et ad inferos.* But the Texas Supreme Court hasn't necessarily agreed. I don't know of any cases offhand. I suppose in theory the drone owner could want you charged with criminal mischief—provided the drone owner didn't violate drone law. I'd say—unlikely. On the other hand, if this drone was conducting surveillance on you and has pictures of you and you didn't consent, maybe you could have the drone owner charged. With a Class C misdemeanor."

"Big whoop."

"Of course, maybe it was a licensed real estate broker looking at your property? Or an oil and gas pipeline? Or a utility? They'd meet the exception, if they don't take pictures of individuals."

"Tyler, the damn thing was hovering over me and my laundry!" she retorted. She shook her head. "Who's standing up for the poor property owner? I don't want a drone hovering over me!"

"I hear you. And so did the drone, this morning. I'd like to see what's in this camera, though." He picked up the drone, examined the little camera on the gimbal. "I'm wondering if we can download the images to any computer or phone but the owner's. I'll have to ask Max."

Roller-coaster morning, thought Alice. Her rage at the camera had quickly given way to the notion that she as an officer of the court might have committed criminal mischief. Tyler had allayed that notion, and even if so—well, she thought surely there'd be a wave of support. No one wanted their property surveilled from above, from an eye in the sky. On the other hand, a small-town lawyer needed to avoid certain types of publicity. For a moment Ben Kinsear's face flashed before her, with that elevated eyebrow that usually meant her current beau was just about to say something like, *Alice, Alice. Always count to ten, or at least three, before firing a shot in anger.*

"Thanks, Tyler." Back to her truck. She pulled into the drive on Live Oak Street by the limestone cottage she called her office. Its wooden sign read "Alice MacDonald Greer, Attorney." Alice sped up the steps, ready for whatever awaited.

Bled Out, Right There in the Field

Alice had barely reached her desk before Silla swooped around Alice's office door, red ponytail swinging. "You're just in time," she said. "You've got to get these clients dealt with so you can make it to the mayor's press conference. She'll have a fit if you don't show."

Alice nodded. At high noon on this last Friday in September, Mayor Betty Wilson would officially open the weekend's major event: the First Annual Coffee Creek Barbecue Competition.

Silla went on. "You're meeting with Caswell Bond, that Colorado guy, at eight thirty and with the Llano history man about his will and medical directive at nine thirty. Then the Colorado guy's closing's at ten thirty at Olson Title." She dropped their files on Alice's desk and whirled out. Silla, twentysomething, an Oklahoma barrel racer, played hard and worked harder. She loved her horse, her dog, and her serial relationships. Alice needed Silla, who livened up the office and goaded Alice back into the world when she retreated too far into her introverted self.

Alice thought that two pieces of good luck for her law practice in Coffee Creek were Silla, and this old house. Its front door opened to an entry hall that ran, shotgun style, all the way to the rear porch. Alice had seized the living room, which opened to the right off the entry, for her office; it stuck out to the side of the house and had windows on all three sides. Silla used the old dining room, left of the entry, as her workspace. Behind the dining room was the kitchen. Two former bedrooms opening to the right off the rear part of the hallway now served as the large and small conference rooms

Sitting behind her antique partner's desk, an effective barricade against surprises, Alice surveyed her office. No fanged trout on the walls: on her desk, pictures of her two children, off at college; over by a window, the Scottish tea table her late husband Jordie had given her.

Time to work.

She picked up Caswell Bond's file. Alice enjoyed Caswell. He'd bounded in for his first appointment in what she learned was his uniform: cargo shorts, river sandals, clean but rumpled T-shirt, and a navy Colorado School of Mines ball cap. He stood about five nine, a wiry mass of energy, with shiny brown hair and alert brown eyes.

Today at ten thirty he and his mother were closing on the Tindall property, a ranch north of Coffee Creek in Llano County that included nearly a half mile of a creek draining off the pink granite uplift that formed Enchanted Rock. Coffee County basically sat atop limestone, but Llano County sat atop ancient pink magma that bulged up in pastures. Aerial shots of the Tindall ranch confirmed reports of its beauty, with tree-covered ridges on the west sloping down to pastures where the creek revealed pink granite outcrops.

Alice knew that Caswell had his own lab in Palo Alto but was spending a sabbatical year in the Colorado mountains at his mother's place. She'd wondered how a Stanford professor got enough income to buy a premium Hill Country ranch, with water, for well over three million dollars. True, there was a small loan for part of the price. But still. Curious, she'd gone to his online bio and looked with interest at the list of patents. The most recent involved "enhanced audio-magnetotelluric" devices. Must be pretty lucrative, whatever they were.

Alice was bemused by three things about this deal. First, "that Colorado guy" and his mother had deep roots in Texas. Caswell's dad was dead; his mother now owned his dad's half of the Black ranch, an old settler ranch that abutted the Tindall property. Her dead husband's brother, a Coffee Creek banker named Clay Black, owned the other half of the Black ranch; Alice was familiar with Clay, most recently from serving with him on the Rules Committee of the upcoming barbecue competition. Yet Caswell had insisted on maximum secrecy for the purchase, claiming that his mother—despite (or because of) her Coffee Creek connections—didn't want her name on record. Caswell's broker had made a private offer to the Tindalls' broker that included a bonus at closing if the owners refrained from listing the property. The Tindalls leaped at the offer, readily agreeing to secrecy.

Second, Alice had never represented clients who'd changed their names. The title company required name-change affidavits from the buyers because in 1970, the mother, then Valentine Martina Black, had changed her name to Valentine Granite Bond, and changed her son's name from Caswell John Black Jr. to Caswell Hawk Bond. For further privacy Alice created a limited liability company to own the ranch, which the son dubbed Granite-Hawk LLC.

A third puzzling aspect of this transaction was Caswell's repeated insistence on securing all mineral rights. Alice agreed in principle, of course, and was accustomed to clients who obsessed about mineral rights in the hope of shale oil riches, but Alice knew of no shale drilling yet in the pink granite of Llano County. She'd double-checked the deeds and badgered her friend Jane Ann Olson at Olson Title to confirm that all mineral rights were secure.

From her office window she saw Caswell climbing out of a white Subaru, which she'd heard some people call the state car of Colorado. Its dusty rear window bore decals from Rocky Mountain National Park and Colorado School of Mines. Caswell had said it was his mother's car. They'd driven down from Estes Park, where she ran, he claimed, a well-regarded restaurant. Alice hadn't yet met his mother. Jane Ann was handling the closing this morning, and only Caswell's signature was required on the closing documents. Alice planned to drop by Olson Title later, partly to be sure the sale went smoothly but partly from pure curiosity, in case Caswell's mother dropped by.

Caswell Bond bounded into her office, in his usual uniform. He yanked off his navy ball cap, running one hand through his short hair. Brown eyes assessed her. "Good morning!" He stopped short, waiting for a welcome, looking slightly anxious.

She got it. "How about some coffee? Silla makes a pretty good cup."

He sighed in relief. "Thanks. I got absorbed in a project this morning and forgot that second critical cup. My brain's not quite working yet."

She doubted that, remembering his online bio. Undergrad, Colorado School of Mines. PhD, Stanford, in physics and metallurgy. Those multiple patents. He reminded her of an exceptionally bright squirrel, one that might begin spouting equations and theories of the universe at any moment while leaping from branch to branch, then stopping and staring at her, bushy tail poised, waiting for her to grasp, oh, string theory. Whatever that was.

Suddenly a smaller body hurtled through the front door. "Dad!" A little boy, also wiry, with his dad's brown hair and brown eyes, and a face pink with excitement. "Drone competition! The sign by the courthouse says there's one Saturday morning. Acrobatics!"

"Ah!" Caswell grinned. "Davie's hooked on drones. You're pretty good on drone acrobatics, aren't you, Davie? But hang on, son. Come meet Ms. Greer. Ms. Greer, this is Davie."

The small pink face grew solemn. Davie looked at his feet, took a deep breath, then extended a small hand to Alice. "How do you do?" he said, wide eyes anxious.

She smiled, taking the small sticky hand and pumping it twice. Davie was wearing a faded red bandana around his neck. He reminded her of her own John, so shy at that age. She remembered Jordie telling him, "Son, you must look people in the eye and give them a firm handshake. Like this." She knew that for John it was scary, so scary, to stare up at a grown-up that way, to stick out your hand to a big stranger. But he'd managed.

Davie released her hand and backed away to stand close to his father.

"Davie," Alice said, "I like that bandana. It looks like it has a history."

His face grew pinker. "It's Dad's dad's. My granddad." He pulled two small brown plastic cowboy figures from his pocket and held them out to show. "And these were my granddad's when he was little. My grandmama gave them to me."

"The sheriff and the rustler," Caswell said. Alice smiled to herself, remembering John and the toys still hiding in his bedroom. "Davie's gotten hooked on old Westerns, especially *High Noon*."

Silla appeared, crouched next to Davie and said, "Hi! I've got paper, pens, and markers." She held them out. "Want to come join me in the conference room? Your dad'll come get you in just a minute." The child's brown head turned to follow the irresistible Silla, with one backward glance at his dad.

"Silla's got your closing documents laid out in the conference room," Alice said. "You might want to pay particular attention to the deed and title policy and the final version of the contract."

He nodded. "Everything in order?"

"Yes," she said. "The title commitment looks good to me. And if you're satisfied, I'll call Jane Ann at the title company to tell her we can close as scheduled. The closing will be at her office, at Olson Title. It's just two blocks away, on the north side of the courthouse. Jane Ann will have you sign at ten thirty. The sellers will sign separately."

"We won't meet the sellers, right?"

"Right, not unless you want to." She watched his face. He hadn't explained why the secrecy, why he didn't choose to meet the sellers. And she felt quite curious about his mother.

"Is your mother enjoying her visit?"

"Yes. She admitted she's surprised by how much she's enjoying being back here in the Hill Country. I had to work hard to pry her out of her mountains."

"And wherever you're staying, it's okay?"

"Oh, yes. We're staying with a college friend of Mom's. Very convenient."

"Well, make sure you're happy with the documents, and then I'll see you at ten thirty at Olson Title. Or if you want, meet me here and we'll walk over together."

"I need to get Davie back to his grandmother first, so how about I just meet you there? And, just checking—I know I've asked: we do get all the mineral interests?"

"The title company thinks so and I do too. Take your time looking at the documents to be sure you're happy. Silla's made you a set. They're all in the conference room."

Ten uninterrupted minutes of blessed silence, broken only by faint voices from the conference room. Alice picked up her calculator and, one last time, checked the closing statement.

Davie and Caswell Bond reappeared in her doorway.

"Okay. I'm happy," Caswell said. "You know, I drove up to the property yesterday morning and walked around a little. It looks great. I'm really getting excited. See you in an hour, then?"

"Oh, Dr. Bond?" Silla had reappeared, holding out a stack of clipped papers.

"Please call me Caswell." He grinned at her.

Silla smiled back. "Don't forget your set of the documents. After closing Jane Ann will give you a folder with all the signatures—yours and the sellers'."

* * * * *

Father and son said goodbye and left. Silla turned to Alice. "Lloyd Neighbors got here early so I put him in the little conference room. He's looking over his documents."

Alice picked up the Neighbors file, embellished by sticky notes on the pages she wanted to mention to him. Lloyd Neighbors lived an hour north, in Llano County. But especially where wills and trusts were involved, small-town clients often preferred to use lawyers in another town, another county, to keep the force field of privacy strong.

Lloyd Neighbors stood at the conference room table, extending a hand. He'd asked Alice to revamp his medical directives and will. "After my wife died I decided I'd be really, really specific on my medical directives," he'd told her. She'd liked him the minute she saw him: attentive eyes, strong handshake, a way of looking at you that made you feel attention was being paid. He had the leathery face and strong hands of a man who'd repaired fence and chased stock much of his life . . . but who still found time to write, to read, to write more. Today he was dressed for town: bolo tie, heavy-starch jeans, leather jacket. Neighbors kept his slight limp well disguised as he made his way back to his chair.

"Maybe I shouldn't ask, but did I hear the name Caswell just now?" he asked. "That's a name I don't forget. It reminds me of one of the saddest deaths I've ever known."

She raised one eyebrow, interested, and he went on. "Of course growing up I knew both Caswell Black and his older brother, Clay. Caswell went Army, wound up in Vietnam like I did. Clay was Air Force Reserve, didn't go. Anyway, back in August 1969, Caswell had just gotten back home. Purple Heart. I'd gotten back too, just a month earlier. You'd think we would have buddied up, but in sixty-nine it was different; we didn't talk about the war much, didn't go seek each other out. I'd seen him once in downtown Llano, knew he and his wife were living out on their half of the family ranch, with their little boy. He seemed really happy about it. I've never forgotten what he said and how he said it. 'I love the quiet out there. It's so restful.' I knew just what he meant. Back then I flinched every time I heard a chopper fly over. Actually, I still do. Anyway, it was tragic, what happened."

"Tragic?"

"Yeah. I heard he'd had an accident with some equipment, post-hole auger, something like that, bled out, right there in the field. His wife found him." Neighbors shook his head. "She left—with the boy—and I never heard where they went. Sold out, maybe?"

"I think the name you heard here was Caswell Bond, not Black." Alice couldn't and wouldn't share client information with him, wouldn't tell him that the dead veteran's wife still owned her half of the Black ranch and was a member of Granite-Hawk LLC, which was now buying another ranch just to the south. "Did you mention Caswell Black in the county history you wrote?"

"Actually, yes. A very brief mention, in the chapter on county folks involved in the military—from Texas independence on. Oh well. Ancient history." He pointed to the documents on the table. "I like what you've done here. I don't have any changes."

Just to be sure, Alice turned to the sticky notes on her copies, mentioning the reasons she'd made specific changes. "So, no questions?" she asked.

"Nope."

"Silla will set up an appointment so you can sign with the requisite witnesses."

Neighbors stood. He slipped his papers into a leather folder, picked up his hat, and gave Alice a warm smile and handshake. "I like working with you, madam lawyer."

"Thank you. It's been an honor." She smiled back at the intelligent face, the steady brown eyes. "How would I get a copy of your book?"

"Llano Historical Museum. They keep a few behind the information desk."

She'd ask Silla to order it. She stood in the entry hall as, limping just slightly, Neighbors headed out the front door. She walked back to her desk, thinking. "Bled out, right there in the field," he'd said. She couldn't shake the image. How sad for that little boy, Caswell Black Jr.—now Caswell Bond. He would have been—not quite five? But he'd survived the loss, as people somehow did. And now he had his own little boy.

She shivered. Her own children, John and Ann, had suffered that loss when their father's helicopter vanished in the North Sea. They'd be home from college for Thanksgiving break in a few weeks. She hoped they would thrive, would achieve, would survive as well as Caswell Bond apparently had.

Silla popped her head around Alice's door. "Interesting clients this morning."

Alice waited.

"Well, that little Davie. Do you know what he was asking his dad in the conference room? 'Dad, when a subduction plate moves down under another plate, like the San Andreas Fault, what makes that happen?' Then he asked, 'Dad, when there were dinosaurs, were the seasons exactly the same as now? Even when the North Pole wobbled?' Good heavens. What makes him think up those questions? Furthermore, his dad had answers for him." She swished out.

I'd like to know those answers too, Alice thought. Davie: a shy little boy. She tried to imagine him in a normal fourth-grade class. Was he so smart that only his parents could keep up with his mind? Yet he was still a little boy, anxious enough that maybe nightmares sent him creeping in to sleep on the floor by his parents' bed.

* * * * *

"Ten twenty!" Silla sang out from her workroom. Alice dutifully grabbed her jacket and headed out the front door to the title company, planning to stay only long enough to be sure no problems had arisen. None had. Jane Ann had already handled the seller signatures. Caswell sat signing his stack. Jane Ann told Alice the wire transfer was rolling.

"Caswell, no need for me to be here," Alice said. "Jane Ann's got it under control. She'll let me know when the lender says we're done and you've got your ranch."

Chapter Three

Can't Agree on Anything!

Back at her desk Alice noticed a steady rumble outside. A gleaming black RV passed her window, towing a ten-foot-long iron smoker labeled "Hot Streak" in tall silver letters. "Here they come," she said to Silla.

"Oh, a dozen barbecue rigs are already parked around City Park," Silla said. "They're jockeying for space, setting up the smokers, putting up their banners. I heard one of the pork ribs guys complaining at the Camellia Diner that the brisket boys got better slots than they did. He said we're discriminating against pork."

Alice hoped no one would bring that particular complaint to the attention of the Rules Committee, which she'd agreed to chair at the repeated insistence of Mayor Betty Wilson. "Alice, I need you on that committee," the mayor has insisted, peering at Alice over her trademark purple cat-eye reading glasses. "You and Jane Ann will do good solid work, unlike those other yahoos on the committee. Clay Black thinks he should run everything in town just because he's president of Cowman's Bank. I predict he'll find out otherwise now that Cowman's is being bought. Anyway, you've got to do this for me, Alice. City council wants this competition to be flawless. We want Coffee Creek to look sophisticated and up-and-coming."

Alice wasn't sure she approved of the council's ambition to be "sophisticated and up-and-coming"—she liked Coffee Creek the way it was, the way it had been, a small Hill Country town surrounded by ranches, a refuge from Austin's big-city traffic and same-same suburbs. Coffee Creek felt real. She'd grown up in Austin, loved its combination of university influences and oddball music, loved the icy spring-fed waters of Barton Springs, loved the funky clothing, loved the low-key Tex-Mex food, with mariachi music in the air. But she feared that Austin's indigenous flavor might be overpowered by big money and the rapid-fire development being force-fed to the city—the skyline, dotted with construction cranes, changed every time she drove into Austin—and by people crowding into burgeoning suburbs.

Still, she couldn't turn down the mayor. A small-town lawyer like Alice, trying to make a living, had to take on civic tasks when asked. And unlike the little Dutch boy with his finger in the dam, she couldn't stave off the problem. There was no way to keep Austin development from invading the Hill Country. The invasion had already begun. New subdivisions . . . new distilleries and wineries . . . artisanal pizza . . . all creeping westward. So she'd dutifully examined barbecue competition rules from across Texas and beyond—Kansas City, Virginia, North Carolina, Alabama; yes, even states touting vinegar- and mustard-based sauces—to develop the official rules for the First Annual Coffee Creek Barbecue Competition.

Silla stood at her door. "Alice! You've got five minutes before the mayor's press conference! Hurry! She's introducing the judges!"

Alice grabbed her keys and raced to her truck. City hall was only three blocks west, but she couldn't be late for kickoff.

* * * * *

The First Annual Coffee Creek Barbecue Competition was unfolding at Coffee Creek City Park, created at the turn of the previous century between Travis Street, on the south, and Live Oak Street, on the north. A sidewalk rimmed the entire park. On the east side of the park, with city hall just across Travis Street, stood the Victorian-style gazebo-bandstand fronted by a wide grassy "festival area," where the Mini-Pianorama would play tonight to a big crowd. The children's playground lay roughly in the middle. The west half of the park was less manicured. On a slight rise stood the town arborist's pride and joy, Founders' Grove, a motte of wide-branched live oaks dominated by an ancient tree with sinuous branches bent nearly to the ground. The live oaks provided deep shade for lovers, children playing hide-and-seek, solitary readers curled up at the trunk of a tree. Every year someone (not the arborist) proposed to thin or at least prune Founders' Grove; every year Coffee Creekers descended on city council to protest any change.

For the barbecue competition, a white judges' tent had been erected on Live Oak Street at the corner of the park closest to Alice's office. The air rumbled with the sound of big trucks hauling big smokers on flatbed trailers.

Alice finally found a parking space and rushed to join the small crowd on the sidewalk in front of city hall. The mayor stood atop the limestone steps, silver curls fluffed and gleaming, jaw jutting, purple reading glasses glinting in the sun, eyes scanning the crowd. She smiled down at two reporters at center front, then glanced at each of the two men standing to her right and left, as if to say, *Man up! You'd better be ready!*

She lifted the handheld mike. "Folks, it's almost noon." She narrowed her eyes at council vice president Josh Hinojosa, who obediently lifted high a black wrought-iron triangle. "At the stroke of noon, when Councilman Hinojosa rings the triangle, the First Annual Coffee Creek Barbecue Competition begins. And tomorrow, Saturday, at the stroke of noon, the judging will begin!" Cheers and applause. "Our five judges will decide the winners for brisket, pork butt, ribs, and sausage. Big decisions! Chairing the judges' committee is our own Judge Bernie Sandoval. He can't be here right now because he's still tied up at the courthouse. Figuratively speaking." Alice was pleased about Sandoval chairing the committee. She liked the portly judge, whose keen judgment and courtroom demeanor had won her respect during several of her probate cases.

The mayor went on. "Two more of our judges can't be here today because of their day jobs—Jennie Hardin, culinary arts professor at the community college, and Earl Stark, who runs our campfire cooking school. But now let me present our two guest judges! They've already won big reputations as chefs nationwide, not just in Austin." She turned to her left. "We are fortunate to have with us Johnny Tan, head chef at Spring." Applause. The young man, slim in designer jeans and a hip chef's tie-back cap, face slightly bored, slightly discontented, nodded once and started to pull his phone from his pocket, then refrained at the last minute when the mayor noticed and gave him a warning look. Come on, Tan, thought Alice. Show a little more enthusiasm for this little town. We're not that far from Austin.

With Tan now standing at attention, the mayor turned quickly to the sturdy man on her right, wearing his white chef's jacket and clogs. "And from Soleil, please welcome Danny Robicheaux!" Classic Cajun coloring, thought Alice: blue eyes, black hair. Robicheaux grinned, lifted a clenched fist, punched the air. The crowd applauded, appreciating his enthusiasm.

Alice watched both men with interest. She'd enjoyed dinner at Spring, a stripped-down new venue off Seventh Street in fast-gentrifying East Austin, and also at Soleil, a renovated highway café on South Congress, with Ben Kinsear, a former law-school beau. Kinsear, tall, dark haired, bespectacled, pursued good food and wine—and Alice—with intensity and imagination. He preferred Soleil for its étouffée; she was intrigued by the experimental menu and lively nighttime atmosphere at Spring. He'd get a kick out of this press conference, Alice thought.

The mayor looked at her watch. "And now, ladies and gentlemen, it's high noon. I hereby declare the competition open!" Hinojosa attacked the triangle and the air rang.

"Question, mayor." Everyone looked at the interrupter waving his hand, a thirtysomething man who'd edged to the front of the crowd. He was wiry, not quite five ten, Alice guessed, sporting cargo shorts with a navy "CIA in Texas" ball cap and a blue T-shirt. The waving arm bore a conspicuous sport watch. "I'm John Pine, food writer for *Austin Fine Eats*," he announced.

The mayor lowered her chin and glared down over her glasses. Alice frowned. Pine's weekly column—full of culinary gossip—mixed snarky but often dead-on reviews with repeated reminders that Pine had graduated from culinary school. He'd grown up in Westlake, a bastion of prosperity just west of Austin. One snippy exposé pointed out he'd never made it in Austin as a chef or even sous-chef, so despite his credentials Alice was skeptical as to whether he personally had culinary skill. But maybe he's just too obnoxious to get along with kitchen staff, Alice speculated. She tensed, expecting Pine to mock Coffee Creek's first attempt at the barbecue big-time.

The crowd quieted to listen. Pine asked, "Mayor, how confident are you that these two chefs can reach a joint decision? My understanding is that Tan and Robicheaux can't agree on anything!"

The two chefs had publicly dissed each other. Silla had shown Alice some clippings on the dispute, which Alice read in dismay. Tan disparaged Robicheaux's famous Cajun roux—"Swamp water, thickened." Robicheaux had swung back: "Spring? Chichi bits dressed up in foam. No substance." John Pine had poured gasoline on the flames: "Are Tan and Robicheaux losing not only their tempers but their glossy reps? Apparently these two wannabes nearly came to blows after neither was named best chef at the Austin Food Fair. Time to declare they're both, as we say around here, all hat and no cattle?"

Now both chefs glared at Pine with narrowed eyes. The mayor jumped in. "We're delighted to have two acclaimed chefs, both with national recognition, helping judge this competition. Both demonstrate great skill and imagination. We appreciate their traveling out to Coffee Creek for this press conference. And now, no further questions: it's Friday and they've got fully booked restaurants demanding their attention tonight. They'll be back in the judges' tent tomorrow morning. Right, boys?" Tan and Robicheaux nodded. "Okay, folks," said the mayor. "Thank you all for attending." Loud whoops and cheers and yee-haws from the crowd. And then she swept both chefs back toward city hall.

The mayor can handle them, Alice thought. Nevertheless, the two chefs studiously ignored each other as they exited.

Pine turned to a photographer. "No love lost there!"

"They don't like you either," said the photographer, repacking his camera. "I wouldn't want anyone looking back at me like that."

"Did you get a picture of them giving me the stink eye?" demanded Pine.

The photographer looked at him. "That wasn't the news, Pine. You aren't the story."

"I make the news," Pine said. The photographer rolled his eyes and left. Pine scanned the crowd, saw Alice watching him, stepped quickly over to her. "Aren't you Alice Greer?"

She smiled, admitted she was, and turned to leave.

He moved in front of her. "Aren't you on the Rules Committee? What qualified you for that?"

Oh boy. Don't get mad, answer only the questions you want to answer. And question back. "Why are you wearing a CIA cap? Are you a grad?" she countered.

"Because I graduated from the Culinary Institute of America, in San Antonio!" he smirked.

"Ah. And I love barbecue. Sorry, work to do. Gotta go." She

handed him a card, said, "Call me later if you have questions about the competition." He hesitated, then nodded and disappeared into the crowd. As she started off toward her truck she caught sight of Clay Black. He'd just crossed the street and was walking up the sidewalk toward her, in boots, heavily starched jeans, white dress cowboy shirt with a bolo tie, and a black leather vest. Alice noted he was also wearing his white hair longer these days, curling a bit over his neck. Copying Guy Clark? Alice thought uncharitably. Trying to show that bank presidents aren't always stuffy?

"Alice! Did I miss the kickoff?" Clay, Rotary's representative on the Rules Committee, had missed most of the meetings and all of the actual work. "I had a meeting, had a significant new client come by the bank to talk. Gotta take care of clients, right? This client probably uses Austin counsel, though. That much money and all, you know how it is."

Alice ignored this jab at small-town lawyers. Clay would be stunned to know that her clients included ranchers with what her banker friend Miranda called "very high net worth." She'd watched Clay look past and talk over the women Rotary members. No surprise that Coffee Creek businesswomen drove past Cowman's Bank and parked next door to do business instead with Miranda at Madrone Bank.

Clay lowered his voice. "Hey, Alice, I heard someone bought the Tindall property, just south of my place up in Llano County. You know anything about that?"

Alice kept her face impassive. "Were you interested in that property?"

"Of course. I grew up here in Coffee Creek, but we also had our ranch up in Llano County. My parents divided our ranch between me and my brother. And after my brother died I, um, wanted to buy his half out of his estate. Wanted to keep it in the family, you know."

Ah, his brother—meaning the dead father of her client Caswell. "Wasn't it already in the family?" Alice noticed Clay rubbing with his right thumb the heavy gold ring, bearing one large diamond, on his right ring finger. The diamond winked in the sun.

"Oh. Well, yes, of course," he said. "But I guess his widow wasn't interested in working the ranch, so that half is just leased for grazing.

I'd like to have it back. The Tindall ranch backs up to both halves of our ranch, my brother's and mine. It's higher, too. Kind of overlooks mine. I've always thought the Tindall ranch would really complement my property. What bothers me is, I don't know how come I never heard about the Tindalls putting their ranch up for sale. I'd have liked to consolidate the land, expand my deer leasing business. You know I've got some serious trophy bucks out there."

Alice nodded noncommittally.

A massive diesel pickup hauling an equally massive black iron smoker crept past. Ornate pink lettering on the driver's door announced "The Houston Hotties!" The driver, a pink bandana around her neck and a straw Stetson atop her exuberant hair, smiled and waved from her perch behind the wheel. Her three fellow cooks waved and whooped from the front and back seats. "Hotties reign!" crowed one of the women. "Bring it on!"

"Well," Clay said, "here come the rigs! I think I'll head on over to the park for a walk-around, be sure all the contestants are happy with the setup and the rules."

Uh-oh, Alice thought. "Just remember, Clay," she said, "if there is any alleged rules violation, each committee member must call me right away so we can convene the full committee. And we want to be helpful, of course"—he had puffed himself up—"but the fewer *rules* issues we run into, the better. We want the *rules* to go unchallenged, so that the outcome will be unchallenged and our first annual barbecue competition will be a success." She watched him absorb this thought. "A *big* success for Coffee Creek."

Apparently he hadn't thought of it that way. He ached for limelight, for personal publicity, but success demanded . . . no rules issues? He hesitated, then perked up. "Well, I just want to make sure that all the contestants have been properly welcomed and feel well situated."

"Excellent. And if not," she said, "that's a problem for Rotary, which is in charge of designating the locations. Not for the Rules Committee."

His face cleared. "You are right. I'll be wearing my Rotary hat."

"Right."

"I'd better get on it." With an offhand "Thanks, Alice," shoulders erect, he turned and scanned the crowd.

Alice sighed. She'd heard the mayor grumble that Clay Black was less likely to pour oil on troubled waters than to create a problem just so he could devise and announce a solution. Clay Black couldn't stand not to be involved, couldn't stand not to be important, she'd said.

Again Alice puzzled about the fact that he was uncle to Caswell Bond. Why had her client avoided him so assiduously? As she watched Clay leave, his dark-haired wife, Annette, in boots, flounced denim skirt, and an elaborate squash-blossom necklace, surged up out of the crowd and grabbed his hand. He brightened, and they left. Annette greeted everyone she saw, turning her saunter down the sidewalk into a sort of royal procession with the president of Cowman's Bank.

Alice watched, thinking of Jordie. If I'd acted like that, she thought, treating Jordie like some sort of prize bull, born for royalty—Jordie would have rolled his eyes. But of course Jordie was different. Big, watchful, hilarious, confident, and totally comfortable in his skin. He was the least needy person she'd ever met. And yet he was devoted, powerfully devoted, to those he loved.

And gone.

But sometimes still here in her head.

Chapter Four

See What Was Coming

Friday afternoon, but still work to finish. Inside Alice's office it was dead quiet: Silla had left early to check out a used horse trailer.

Alice stalked to her desk and turned on the computer, eyeing with distaste the stack of manila folders awaiting her attention. First, she thought, I just want to see Clay's ranch. See what he's talking about. Caswell had told her that to get to the three ranches—Clay's place, the old Caswell Black property, and the Tindall ranch—he drove north of Fredericksburg, turned west toward the ridges stretching north of the pink granite bulge of Enchanted Rock, and then turned left on a gravel road.

She found the Llano County appraisal website and scribbled down the coordinates of the three ranches. Curiosity rising, she pulled the area up on satellite view on her computer. The screen showed that the Caswell Black property was mostly pasture, with a plain metal ranch gate, barn, windmills, and stock pens. In a grove of trees Alice spotted an old stone chimney and the limestone walls of a small house. Its roof had fallen in. Maybe that's the original ranch house, she thought.

Across the gravel road from the Caswell Black property stood the gate into Clay Black's half of the family ranch. She could see that his gate was flanked by stone pillars; the drive meandered uphill to the house and what looked like a bunkhouse. For his hunters, she guessed. She scrolled further down, following the gravel road until it dead-ended at the gate into the Tindall ranch. She could see the white streak of a caliche driveway that turned right after leaving the gate and ran uphill to the Tindall house and barn. The Tindall ranch encompassed a thousand acres. Half adjoined the south side of the Caswell Black property; half adjoined the south side of Clay's.

Zooming further out on the satellite image she could see that the three ranches lay amid spectacular scenery, with rolling hills rising progressively higher as one drove west, climaxing in the sharp folded ridges that rose to the west of the three ranches. According to the satellite map, the tallest of these was called Turkey Ridge. A creek—labeled Quartz Creek on Alice's satellite map—began life on the slopes of Turkey Ridge, ran onto the Tindall ranch, then curved its way past the tall oak-covered hilltop that dominated the west end of the ranch and out through the pastures. The metal roof of the Tindall house and outbuildings glinted below those hilltop oaks. Now she understood Clay's complaint that the Tindall ranch overlooked his place. The Caswell Black property sat lowest, its gentle rises looking across the gravel road and up the long drive to the hilltop where Clay's house sat. Clay's hilltop, in turn, sat lower than and was overlooked by the hilltop where the Tindalls had built.

Alice zoomed in closer on the Tindall ranch. Caswell had told Alice he particularly wanted it because of Quartz Creek. "I want water," he'd said. He'd heard from his mother that his dad once tried to buy some stream frontage from the Tindalls, but they'd said no. "It's the creek I'm after," Caswell had said. "I've always wanted that creek."

Now Caswell had his creek.

Then Clay's face rose before her, his tight mouth, his apparent anxiety, his barely suppressed anger over the Tindall sale. Was it over the sale itself, or not being in the know, or both? Then she wondered if, once Clay learned who'd bought the Tindall ranch, he'd feel surrounded. His brother's wife and son now owned property on two sides of his ranch. Furthermore, when they stood atop the Tindall hilltop, they could see most of Clay's ranch.

She thought about how that could feel. In France, she'd stood atop the castle at Beynac, looking out over the sweet curves of the Dordogne, the river lined with barns, rich pastures, farmyards with chickens, ducks, geese. She'd stood atop the castle and realized she could see what was happening on almost every farm along the banks. And just so, she imagined, had the lord of the castle, in his feudal police state, kept track of every peasant, every cow, every new clutch of ducklings, every shock of hay to be taxed, every pig to be confiscated.

And Alice herself? She treasured, was even smug about, the privacy of her cliffside house, perched above her creek; no one could overlook her there. Indeed, every house she'd ever bought had been on a hill, if only a small one, with elbow room between her and any neighbors. Then she remembered the damned hovering drone over her pole barn. Based merely on her reaction to the drone, if anyone could overlook her house—well, she wouldn't be able to stand it. She knew that.

Which made total sense. Why else did early people gravitate to cliffside shelters where they could survey the countryside, see what was coming?

Alice always wanted to see what was coming. She hated not knowing what came next.

With a sigh she turned back to the menacing stack of manila folders Silla had slapped on the corner of her desk. Time to work. The lot of a small-town lawyer, she thought; sometimes feast, where she was madly trying to solve problems for several clients at once; then famine, where she stared at the phone, afraid it would never ring again. Joys came—a stout victory like she'd won recently for a client who'd been done out of his inheritance; or the conservation easement for a ranch, all the heirs and beneficiaries finally coming to agreement—but no matter how long the project took, at its completion the joyful sense of success lasted only a minute. Really, she thought, shouldn't it last at least an hour? But after a minute of self-congratulation, of satisfaction, she always began worrying about an unfinished case, or the lack of a new one.

Maybe she needed more yoga. More meditation. More weekends with Kinsear? After Jordie's death and several years utterly devoid of romance, during which Alice flatly rejected any efforts by friends to change her solitary life, she'd run into her old law-school beau Ben Kinsear, a pre-Jordie flame, now a widower with two teenage daughters. Kinsear had made it large in New York as counsel to a hedge fund, then returned to his ranch in Fredericksburg and opened a bookstore, The Real Story. He was back in New York this week but had promised to join her tomorrow for the Pianorama at the Beer Barn, which would mark the end of the barbecue festival. The Beer Barons, the three owners of the Beer Barn, who were also her clients, had worked for weeks to organize a fierce collaboration-cum-competition showcasing Austin's masters of blues, classic boogie-woogie, and stride piano.

Kinsear had been vague about his New York trip. What was the man doing? Why was she still so cautious about him? For one thing, she steadfastly avoided spending any nights with him in Fredericksburg. His daughters had lost their mother a couple of years earlier when she broke her neck jumping her horse. Alice suspected they weren't ready to contemplate the idea of their father bringing another woman into their lives. She couldn't blame them.

Her own kids had adored their father. But they'd managed to welcome Kinsear with firm handshakes on the few occasions when they'd met him.

They know they won't lose Jordie, she thought. His pictures would never disappear from walls or tables. She and the kids would never quit quoting his Scots sayings, would never quit laughing about Jordie's fiercely competitive nature, would never quit feeling the invisible safety net of his approval.

The future with Kinsear? He, not Alice, was the one who on several occasions had broached the subject of their future, stepping right up to the edge but not uttering the M-word. If ever he did ask her to marry—what would she say? She brushed that thought away, because she honestly didn't know. Different towns, different lives. What was wrong with their current arrangement? On the other hand, what could be wrong with replacing chronic late-night loneliness interrupted by occasional trysts with the profound comfort of sleeping and waking together?

Alice walked to the kitchen and poured the last cup of coffee from the office coffee pot, grimaced at the bitter taste, dumped it out. She thumped back down in her chair and attacked the draft in the first folder. She toiled away, trying to ignore the growing smell of smoke that infiltrated her office from all the little fires—charcoal, hickory, pecan, and oak—in all the rigs, big and small, lined up around City Park.

Chapter Five

Just Wait Until Tomorrow!

At five thirty Alice threw down her pen. Late sun slanting across the window turned the room orange. The sun would set a little after seven. Time for the Rules Committee chair to make a precautionary tour of the rigs. Did she look festive enough? She checked the full-length mirror behind her office door. What did people see when they looked at her? Medium everything, thought Alice: medium height; brownish-blond hair highlighted by her talented Austin hairdresser; and her face, the one Kinsear kissed. Lipstick needed, and mascara. Today she'd worn jeans, her beloved handmade Goodson Kells boots, and the over-the-top jacket embroidered with yellow roses.

Men had it easier, she thought, applying lipstick. Blazer and extra shirt and tie on the back of the office door in case of a court appearance. Certainly no mascara, at least in Coffee Creek. Probably only a small, not a full-length, mirror. Just a glance, a comb through the hair, a check for any recession of hairline, any diminution of testosterone, any unacceptable variation of the male lawyer uniform. Whereas here she was, spending too much time staring in the mirror. Wait, what was too much time? Without a doubt, people at the courthouse did make instant judgments based on appearances. That was reality. Shaking her head at her own thoughts, she set the office alarm and locked the door behind her. She'd walk to the park this time, leave the truck here.

On the short walk down Live Oak Street toward the park, she joined a throng emerging from their vehicles, strolling down the middle of the street, toting lawn chairs, coolers, blankets, heading for the east side of the park, where the Mini-Pianorama should be cranking up soon in the gazebo. The mayor had prohibited street parking around the park except for barbecue rigs and food trucks. Food trucks were clustered on the east side. Contestants had to set up their rigs in assigned parking spots around the rest of the park: brisket on the north and west side; pork butt, ribs, and sausage on the south.

Looks like our plan is working, Alice thought with relief. The food trucks—tacos, sushi, banh mi, muffulettas—were doing brisk business on the east side. The Friends of the Library were selling paper bowls of homemade blackberry cobbler from card tables on the corner. Josie's, a new bakery-cum-café on the main highway through town, offered ham and chicken croissants and fruit pastry. Though she considered Josie's another sign of the apocalypse, another sign of the invasion of Austin chic, Alice liked Josie's cortados, which could jolt you awake in a minute. Already Josie's patrons bragged about spending long mornings in the café, reading, writing, and emailing, sustained by lattes and almond croissants—not the traditional morning coffee and biscuits at the Camellia Diner, a frozen-in-the-1950s establishment across from the courthouse and a favorite haunt of Alice's. Reportedly the diner was considering installing Wi-Fi. Heavens, Alice thought.

People surged around her, munching banh mi, muffulettas, fried pies. But the crowd's mind was clearly on barbecue. Though none would be sold until Saturday afternoon, after the judging, the compelling smell of smoke drew them like a magnet. The crowd sauntered along the sidewalk bordering the park, calling out to the contestants at their rigs. Some contestants had already fired up their smokers. The meat inspectors had come by to check and tag their pieces of raw meat. One eager beaver already had his brisket out and spiced and was looking at his watch. Rules forbade putting brisket on the grill before 6:00 p.m. Alice thought six would be jumping the gun. Timing and temperature were critical, and a huge source of argument. Every contestant held strong opinions: some would start their briskets early, let them sit, then reintroduce them to the smoke, perhaps even encasing the brisket in aluminum foil while it sat. Others ridiculed both notions. Alice had heard otherwise mild-mannered amateur barbecuers sling scorn at each other over such issues. She just hoped no contestants would actually come to blows.

The winner could afford no mistakes on timing, or temperature, or seasoning. Briskets would be on before midnight, pork butt just afterward, and not until predawn hours would the pork ribs go on, followed by homemade sausages. At the stroke of noon tomorrow, the five judges would begin scrutinizing each carefully arranged "turn-in box," the ticketed plastic-foam container presented by hopeful contestants: sausage at noon, ribs at twelve thirty, pork butts at one, and finally briskets at one thirty. Hours of smoke, spice, and heat would be judged by five judges who had their own strong prejudices about barbecue.

Alice waved at the cobbler sellers and acquired a program and a bottle of water from two pony-tailed Girl Scouts. Then she headed into the large white judges' tent, where the judges would taste every entry while the contestants looked on. Her Rules Committee was allotted three plastic chairs plus a small table in the corner stacked with copies of the rules and judging forms. Satisfied, she started back out of the tent but stopped dead when she saw Clay Black buttonholing Lloyd Neighbors, right in her path. "But was it Caswell *Black* you saw?" Black asked.

"Alice said Caswell *Bond*, not Black," said Neighbors. "I did run into the Tindalls at the taco truck just now. All they would say was that the buyer was some company named Granite-Hawk."

Alice moved forward. Clay Black turned. "Alice! Glad I ran into you again. Was that Caswell Black Jr. in your office this morning?"

Neighbors was blushing.

"Lloyd knows we lawyers sometimes can't talk about our clients." Alice smiled at Neighbors.

"But the thing is," Clay said, "I have a right to know who's buying land right next to me. The Tindalls' place runs all the way across my south fence line! I've asked all around the park this afternoon and no one knew about the sale. Yesterday morning early I saw someone out there, walking around in a T-shirt and a ball cap. Damn! I wish the Tindalls had let me know they were interested in selling. They never said a word. Even though it's hilly and worthless"—sour grapes, Alice thought—"I'd have bought it just to enhance my privacy. And who or what the heck is Granite-Hawk?"

Alice certainly couldn't tell him. She just smiled and shook her head. But she couldn't help considering the matter from his viewpoint.

He couldn't leave it. "My brother was named Caswell. Caswell Black. And so was his son, Caswell Jr. It's an old family name. There aren't many folks named Caswell." He stood for a moment, face painted orange by the sun, which now touched the tops of the live oaks.

"Your brother died right there across the road from you?" Alice asked. She glanced at Neighbors for confirmation.

"Right out in the field, didn't he, Clay?" Neighbors asked. "What I heard was they had some fence down near the front gate and a truckload of cattle due." He shook his head. "I saw some things like that in Vietnam. Man, those are the memories that don't go away, trying to reach someone in time to help."

"Yes. I was at my place that day but not in time. I wasn't where I could see him." He looked down at the ground.

"But if he was out by the front gate—you must think about it every time you drive out your own gate," Alice said, then wished she hadn't.

Clay stared off into the distance, eyebrows lifted slightly. Change the subject! she thought. "Are you still in touch with your brother's family?"

He shook his head no. "We tried—Annette was very fond of that little boy. But her letters came back in the mail. We never heard where they'd gone."

"I'm sure you'll meet the new folks," Neighbors said. "Ask 'em over for a drink."

Clay didn't answer, just kept staring into the distance. "Someone damn well should've told me," he muttered.

"Darling! Found you!" Annette Black reappeared, sunglasses perched on perfect hair, and slipped her arm into Clay's. She smiled at Neighbors and Alice. "Isn't this barbecue competition just the best? I'm thrilled about the turnout. Clay says you have fifty entrants!"

Alice nodded. She'd sat through long library board meetings where she'd found Annette irritating, with her chronically sweet expression, her relentlessly positive comments. Yet she knew Annette, a retired surgical nurse, must be smart.

Annette rushed on. "The whole thing was Clay's idea, you know. He pushed it from the beginning." Clay's forehead slowly turned pink.

Alice allowed herself to lift one eyebrow; she knew that the mayor herself had come up with the project, because Alice had been present when the mayor and Alice's friends Red and Miranda had brainstormed about a fall crowd-pleaser to boost downtown Coffee Creek. Miranda had proposed Oktoberfest ("Too much like New Braunfels," sniffed the mayor. "We'll do it the last weekend in September"). Red had suggested a home tour ("Too fancy-dancy and not enough homes worth touring," retorted the mayor). Alice, in desperation, offered up a book fair. The mayor just scowled over her glasses. "We could have a Pianorama or blues or music fest," Alice said. "With food trucks."

"We definitely need food," the mayor said, "and I would favor barbecue. And let's think big." The four women had looked at each other, and before them rose a vision of smoke and heat, spice and meat.

Clay Black had been nowhere near this vision.

"I think the mayor gets the big credit on this," Alice said.

"Oh," Annette said, "she does enjoy the limelight. I sometimes think people have no idea how much Clay does for this town, though. I'm so proud of him." She squeezed his arm and smiled up at his face.

Clay smiled down at her.

Does she really believe that, wondered Alice, or is this part of a long-running PR act?

Annette went on. "We're usually out at the ranch on weekends, but I think we'll stay in town tonight. I'm going over to the gazebo to hear a little music while Clay checks out the rigs. He has to confirm that the rules are being followed." She didn't seem to know that Alice headed the Rules Committee. "Actually," Annette added, "Clay would have loved to enter. His brisket is to die for. He's got a big pellet smoker—honestly, it's almost as big as a truck—and he can smoke five briskets at once. He's so exacting, so keen to get the temperature just so. He checks it digitally and keeps a record. The pellet smoker's so precise, isn't it, Clay?" He nodded and she went on. "And his venison sausage is so good! People beg for it at Christmas. That's all from our own deer, of course, up at the ranch."

"Your hunters share some of what they shoot?" Alice knew that Clay had high-fenced his ranch and leased it for deer hunting.

"Oh, no," Clay said. "It's only from what I take, personally. And I'm a pretty good marksman."

Annette chimed back in: "Clay is a superb shot."

Clay smiled at her. "But lately, on my own land, I prefer to bow-hunt," he said. "More challenge, to my mind. Bowhunting takes a bigger skill set. I prefer stalking, whether with a bow or a rifle, for as long as it may take, to sitting on a stool in a blind. And stalking requires silence, which of course takes patience and skill. Using a bow levels the playing field a little more with the deer. But that's just my own view. Of course I leave the trophy antlers to my hunters." He nodded slightly and said, "You know, hunting's like the banking business. You have your long-term strategies, stalking your target—but if an opportunity knocks, you zero in for the kill."

Stalking, thought Alice, envisioning the hunter crouching, slipping behind trees, eyes on the unwary prey, waiting for the perfect moment. She mentally shook her head and reached for a copy of the competition schedule. Clay peered over her shoulder. Music until nine, when the mayor would announce the fireworks. It did get dark early these days.

Alice excused herself, left the judges' tent, and walked partway across the big grassy area toward the gazebo on the city hall end of the park. The Mini-Pianorama piano duel had cranked up. A crowd was gathering to hear blues hero Johnny Nicholas, tall and lanky, trading licks with piano favorite Floyd Domino, smiling in his trademark cowboy hat. Domino looked at Nicholas and said into the mike, "How about that Freddie Slack tune 'Down the Road a Piece'?" The two men nodded their heads, feeling the count. Domino started on piano and Nicholas chimed in with the intro vocals, then jumped in on piano as well. Back and forth they went. Domino tilted his head whenever he tossed the lead back to Nicholas. Alice stood watching from a distance, loath to leave, mesmerized by the dueling riffs, the steady beat of the left hands, the riotous right hand runs tumbling in her ears.

Duty called. She retraced her steps back past the judges' tent and started down the sidewalk into brisket-land to check out the contestants. She still puzzled a bit over Clay Black. Even if it overlooks my land, wouldn't I be excited if a long-lost relative bought land next to me? she wondered. Well, maybe, and then again, maybe not.

Alice reached the first parking bay for the brisket contestants, where a huge cooker bearing the name "Silver Streak," in fancy silver paint, loomed over the street.

"Howdy, ma'am!" called a burly man with his cowboy hat pushed back. "CCBC Chief Cook," announced his T-shirt. Under the rules, only the chief cook for each team could sport the official "Chief Cook" T-shirt. "We won best brisket in Junction, two years running! Watch out!" He turned and began loading firewood into the firebox.

"Yeah, but we won first last year in Brady!" retorted a twentysomething in the next bay, wiping sweat from his forehead. He finished manhandling his rig into place and started loading the firebox.

"Brady? Hey, Brady! Sure you don't have any goat in that rig?" called the Silver Streak chief cook. The town of Brady held an annual barbecued goat festival. Alice hadn't ever attended, due to mild prejudice against goat meat. As justification she cited the French: they produced superb goat yogurt, superb goat cheese, but did they cook goat? She thought not. Lamb, veal, rabbit, beef—but no goat. And there'd be no goat here: the meat inspectors had walked around to check each rig starting at noon. No nonqualifying or precooked meat allowed.

"You just wait until tomorrow," called the twentysomething. "Our secret rub's gonna take it all!"

Chapter   Six

Land's a Good Investment

Alice continued west along Live Oak. Brisket entrants brought the biggest rigs and generated the most publicity, though the Czech and German sausage-makers maintained a hot competition. She sauntered on, past the Houston Hottie rig, the Seguin Slow Burn and Frio Firebomb rigs. Each had a chief cook and team not exceeding a total of four, per the rules. She turned the corner, passing the Hondo Hot Time Honeys, all women, then the Harper Hot Licks. Further down the block she saw a gap—no rig parked out front. Where was the contestant? She heard the chief cook of the Harper Hot Licks say, staring toward the gap, "Can you believe those women?"

Alice glanced down at the program. The program listed the team for that assigned spot as the Coffee Creek Revival and listed Marguerite Amaryllis Ellison as chief cook. Marguerite Amaryllis: Was it possible? There could only be one Marguerite Amaryllis. Alice quickened her pace, passing the black smoke-stacked Bandera Brisketvagen. Its chief cook, grinning, shaking his head, stared at the vintage gold Cadillac station wagon backed partway up the parking spot next to him, rear door open. Next to the sidewalk, no rig: instead, three Weber kettle grills lined up on the asphalt. Just ordinary kettles, too, the kind you could buy at any hardware store. And there, holding a Dos Equis and staring down the Bandera Brisketvagen's chief cook, a sardonic grin on her face, stood M.A. Ellison herself. She wore her usual outfit: chinos, boots, and a flowered lawn shirt. Two folding chairs sat in the grass by the curb. In one lounged a striking white-haired woman, deeply tanned. On the lawn behind her chair jiggled a green tent, only partway up. Someone was thrashing inside.

"M.A.!" Alice couldn't control her grin. "Marguerite Amaryllis!" Alice had drafted M.A.'s will. She knew M.A.'s reputation for devilled eggs and pimento cheese—legendary. But *brisket*?

"Have a seat," barked M.A. "Meet my friends!"

Out of the tent crawled Caswell Bond, followed by Davie. "It's up, Gran!" called Davie triumphantly. "You can sleep in it now!"

"Alice!" said Caswell, face brightening. "I want you to meet Mom!"

Great heavens, thought Alice, glancing at the quiet woman in the lawn chair.

"They're staying with me," M.A. explained. "Val and I go way back. We roomed together at SRD back in the sixties." Alice knew that SRD was shorthand for the Scottish Rite Dormitory at UT–Austin.

M.A. went on: "Alice, you've done some hiking in the Rockies; get Val to tell you about her adventures climbing the big ones back in the seventies when she first went out there."

"Hello," Alice said, gazing at Caswell's mother. She'd signed the LLC document as "Valentine Granite Bond, Member." Alice couldn't take her eyes off her: she had the cheekbones of a Greek goddess, a broad forehead with a widow's peak curving up into nearly white hair, and deep-set eyes that looked straight at Alice. Like Ingrid Bergman in *Casablanca*, Alice thought, except for the tanned cheeks and smile wrinkles around her eyes, reflecting years above timberline.

"Hello, Alice. I'm so glad to meet you. Thanks for your help on the Tindall ranch," said the quiet-voiced woman. "Please call me Val. No one calls me Valentine these days."

"And you should explain your name change," M.A. interrupted. "Alice wants to know why you're 'Bond' now."

Yes, indeed I do, thought Alice.

"Well, as you saw from our name affidavits, I changed my name to Valentine Granite Bond when—well, a long while back. I'd always hated 'Martina' so I dropped it. I started using Val for short when I got my first job as a chef. I hoped it sounded crisp and professional."

"Everybody should get to pick a name," Caswell put in. "I've been Caswell Hawk Bond since I was five. She let me pick 'Hawk.'" He turned to his son, who'd climbed into the tailgate of the Caddy. "Okay, Davie. Let's go check out the music. And see when the fireworks start. Maybe the drone will get some great pics."

The boy climbed out of the Caddy, drone in one hand, controller in the other. "Is there popcorn, Dad? And can we watch the guy set up the soundboard for the band?" Val made both put on fleece jackets. Caswell took the controller. Alice saw Davie slip his hand into his father's other hand, and the two set out toward the gazebo.

Alice turned back to M.A. and the long-limbed woman quietly

watching Alice's face from the lawn chair. Val had given only a partial answer. She and Caswell had left behind not only their names but their ranch and the state of Texas. Why?

M.A. groped in the pocket of her chinos for her wallet, pulled out a photograph, showed it to Alice. "Here we are on the steps at SRD, sophomore year," she said. Both girls were laughing, very hip with their long 1960s hair and bell-bottoms. M.A. was . . . M.A.: energetic, good-humored, pretty. Val was jaw-droppingly gorgeous. Alice handed back the photo, shaking her head at the cheekbones, the eyes. What beauty.

"Okay, ladies!" M.A. beckoned. Val got up. She and Alice helped haul an ancient folding table out of the back of the Caddy and set it up in front of the three Webers. M.A. grabbed a wooden box and removed the lid. "Okay, Val. Silicone gloves." M.A. plopped a few pairs on the table. "Spatulas. Tongs. Heavy-duty foil. Basting brush. Official turn-in box, cutting board, platter, and knives are in the back of the car. What else, Val?"

Val pointed to the Caddy. "The mop and the rub are in the cooler in the back." Alice knew that "mop" meant the mysterious basting liquid created for the briskets; the "rub" meant the secret dry spice mixture that went on the meat before it hit the grill. "Where's your digital thermometer?" Val asked M.A.

M.A. reached into the collar of her flowered blouse. "Aha." She removed the red plastic pen-shaped contraption hanging by its black cord around her neck. She pulled off the top and menaced Alice with the six-inch needle. Then she squinted at a small window on its barrel. "It's set on 'off' so the battery should last." She laid it on the table by the basting brush and opened the cooler for another beer.

She and Val sat back down in their chairs.

"So, how d'you like our setup?" M.A. asked Alice, motioning with a grandiose sweep of her arm to the three stolid Webers, sitting in a row. "Some of these guys around here aren't so crazy about it." She raised her voice, grinning. "I begin to suspect they don't take me seriously! Isn't that right, Harvey?"

She waved at the chief cook next door. He grinned and waved back, pointing at the Webers and shaking his head.

M.A. turned back to Alice. "You've never had my brisket, have you, Alice?"

"Nope."

"You got to get that Kinsear boy back over here. He'll appreciate it." Kinsear shamelessly flattered M.A.'s cooking, trying to get her recipes.

"Absolutely. M.A., are these three grills enough?" Alice knew that M.A. needed to cook enough to serve five judges and have some reserved, just in case.

"Sure. Hey, honey, I've only been doing this for half a century. And my team includes a famous chef!" She grinned at Val.

Val smiled back. "I have nothing to do with this brisket adventure. Her secret's the rub. You won't guess what's in it, either."

Alice surveyed the Caddy, the three grills, the lawn chairs. "How are you planning to watch over your—your setup tonight? Just sit there in your lawn chairs?"

"No worries. Caswell's got our tent up. He and Davie are sleeping in the back of the Caddy. The city's put up some fancy porta-potty units where we can wash up, over by the war memorial. And at least one of us will stay awake. We old ladies are night owls."

Val nodded. "Especially from two to four a.m. That's when I worry. You know, about politics, restaurants, world peace."

Alice could relate to that, to waking at the darkest hour, thrashing in tangled sheets, sitting up suddenly to stare out the French doors, hearing scrabbling little feet on the deck, on the stone walk, on the outdoor staircase, feeling the weight of the moon's stare through her bedroom window as it neared full. Afterward, dreams always pursued her, dreams where she couldn't find the way through the airport, was lost in a strange dormitory, or was late to the hall where she was supposed to give a speech, still in her bathrobe and unable to make the words come out. And when she finally pushed herself awake, more mundane worries flashed into her mind and wouldn't leave, a list of unfulfilled obligations unfurling before her eyes, accusing, unforgiving.

Yes, Val and M.A. were right: better to sit in a lawn chair wrapped in a blanket, stoking the small fires in the grills, adjusting the vents, watching the stars wheel by. Far better.

The setting sun was gilding the faces of M.A. and Val. She smiled inside, watching the two friends lounging in their lawn chairs. But now M.A. and Val were staring past her, frozen in their seats. Val's face tightened. "Hello, Clay," she said.

Alice turned. Clay Black stood just behind her, his eyes glued to the tall woman in the chair. He moved up next to Alice. "Val," he said. "Val Black. You came back! You finally came back!"

Val didn't correct the name. "Clay. I'm only here for a day or so. You remember M.A.?" M.A. did not offer her usual smile, just nodded.

"Sure," Clay said automatically, barely conscious of M.A. He only had eyes for Val, sitting rigid in her "Assistant to Chief Cook" T-shirt. "You're in this competition?"

Val nodded.

"I'm on the Rules Committee!" he blurted. "With Alice here." Alice glanced down, saw him thumbing the ring on his right hand. Clay straightened his shoulders, gathered himself. He grinned down at the Webers, flanked by bags of charcoal, and took a step closer to the folding table. "Well, I see you've got all your paraphernalia spread out." He stared at the careful arrangement of tools.

"Yup," said M.A. "Less is more."

"Maybe so, maybe so." He didn't look at M.A. but kept his eyes on Val. "Hey, Val, was that your son I saw yesterday morning, out at the Tindall ranch next to me? Just walking around out in the pasture? Gray T-shirt, blue ball cap? Cargo shorts?"

"I don't know. He didn't mention it," Val said.

"Brown hair, vigorous, kind of?" Clay asked. Val didn't answer. "Is he out here too, tonight?"

Val nodded. "Yes. Somewhere."

"So, did you buy the old Tindall place? Is that why you're here? Someone mentioned to me that it got bought."

Silence. Val didn't speak. Damn it, thought Alice.

Clay pressed on. "Well, I'll take silence to mean it was you, or you and him, who bought," he said. "You must be Granite-Hawk." He went on, his sentences disjointed. "I wish you'd told me you were looking at the Tindall place. I didn't even know it was for sale or I'd have made an offer." Pause. "You know I'm president of Cowman's Bank?" Another awkward pause. "Does this mean maybe you're coming back, Val? To live here?" He looked almost thirsty, licking his lips slightly, staring at Val.

Alice couldn't define the intent look in his eyes.

Val shook her head no. "I'm happy where I am."

"Then I'm guessing your boy must think it's time he came back to Texas. He was walking that land like—like he owns it."

"He told me the memories just came rushing back when he got here," M.A. said, then stopped abruptly.

"Actually, he doesn't remember much about the ranch, Clay," Val said sharply. "Not much at all."

"But is he coming back? Will he be living here?" The questions came out in a rush. "I mean, any boy wants a ranch, right?"

"It's just an investment, I think."

Clay continued, fishing. "He sure looked busy, scanning the ground like he was looking for something."

"Land's a good investment," Val said, voice flat.

"The Tindall house is pretty nice. They remodeled, you know. They've invited me over, of course. Maybe once you spend some time there you'll decide to stay there some."

Val looked at him, and her voice changed, suddenly dark, suddenly final. "We could, couldn't we. Yes, we could go to the same church you go to, get close to all your friends."

And to Alice that sounded like a threat. Clay looked taken aback.

"Attention!" Loud static crackled from the public address system. They all jumped, Val and M.A. turning around in their chairs to stare into the park. Clay moved closer to the folding table, head up, listening. *"Attention!"* Alice, lifting her head to listen, recognized the mayor's voice. "At the bandstand we have a young man—how old are you, son?—a young man of four named Frank who is looking for his parents. Red T-shirt with a dinosaur. Will Frank's parents please come to the bandstand."

"Poor little rascal," said M.A.

"Well, I'll be going," Clay said with a one-sided smile. "Got to get home to Annette! Although she might still be here listening to the music. She fusses when I'm not around. But she knows I've got responsibilities to attend to."

Silence hung heavy for several seconds; then Val leaned forward in her lawn chair—slowly, so it looked like an enormous effort. Then she said, "Please tell Annette I said hello."

"Sure. Well, good luck tomorrow. We'll be here for the judging, won't we, Alice?" He glanced at Alice, then looked back at the two women. "Got to be sure the rules are followed!" He nodded. "See you tomorrow."

Alice exhaled once he was gone, only then realizing she'd been holding her breath. Rarely had she been part of a conversation at once as mundane and as fraught with discomfort as this one.

"Good Lord," said M.A.

"Yes. I just felt trapped in this chair, like I couldn't stand up," said Val.

"Yeah." M.A. blew out a long breath.

They both looked up at Alice. "Don't mind me," Alice said. "Listen, Val, I think Lloyd Neighbors might have heard Caswell's name when he was at the office today. We told him it was Caswell *Bond*, not Black. But I suppose he may have mentioned that to Clay, who put two and two together."

"It's all right. I mean, I'm sitting here in front of God and everybody, smack-dab in the middle of Coffee Creek. At City Park. With a town notable. That's you, M.A. I knew we couldn't keep it secret. I can't expect to be invisible." Val looked around. "Where are those boys?"

"I'm glad they weren't here," said M.A.

"Well, that's right."

Alice couldn't read the look that passed between the two women.

"Okay," said Alice, "I think I'll finish my rounds. See you in a bit. I'll bring us some supper. After I get past pork." She turned to leave.

Chapter Seven

When It Looks Done, Smells Done, Feels Done

"**L**adies!" John Pine strode out of the deep shade under the live oaks behind the tent. "Ladies! You're the talk of the competition. How about a few words for *Austin Fine Eats*?"

M.A. slowly climbed to her feet again, one eyebrow lifted as she confronted the interloper. Val stayed in her lawn chair, gazing down at her lap. Alice stopped in her tracks, trying not to grin. This could be worth staying for.

M.A. said, "Your name again, young man?"

"John Pine. You've probably seen my column."

"You know, I don't believe I have. Where did you go to high school?"

"Westlake."

"Who'd you have for English?"

He was startled. "Mrs. Crider."

"Oh, Mrs. Crider. How'd you do in her class?"

"Hey, I'm supposed to be interviewing you!"

"Well, of course, I don't want to be misquoted. So I have to check you out."

"Look, I just want to find out how you think you can compete with three kettle grills against the experienced guys with the big rigs."

"Easily."

"*Easily?*"

"It's just heat and smoke and timing, young man. Nobody's got a monopoly on that. How long do you smoke your own brisket, for instance?"

"Umm . . ."

"You've never smoked one, have you?"

His eyes flicked left, right, trying to find an out. He regrouped. "Of course I can cook. But you don't have to grill a brisket to know how one should taste."

"Isn't that the truth! So as far as you know, the size of the rig has nothing to do with heat, smoke, or timing, does it?"

"I can't say for sure. Now let me ask you some questions."

"Well, let's see what happens tomorrow, shall we? I'm still curious about you. Now, I think someone told me you went to culinary school?"

The sun had set. Pine colored, his face turning slightly darker in the fading pink light.

"Where in Austin have you cooked?"

A long, long pause. "My apartment," he said finally, with an unwilling smile.

M.A. laughed. "When in doubt, tell the truth. Okay, what do you want to know?"

Alice watched, mesmerized. Maybe this was how M.A. taught high school biology all those years—terrify the student, then hug him. "And, by the way, I'm recording our interview too," M.A. added, waving her hand. Sure enough, she was taping a video on her phone.

"Okay. Do you marinate your brisket? Or use a dry rub? Is there anything but salt, pepper, and paprika in your rub?"

"No to marinade. Yes to dry rub. Yes to 'anything but.' But don't ask what it is."

"Why three kettle grills? Just so you have enough to serve the judges?"

"Well, every brisket's different. Maybe one of these cows was more serene than the others."

"Do you rely on time? Temperature? What do these—these kettles measure?"

"There's no thermometer in these kettles."

He was shocked. "But all the big rigs—"

"I don't need a thermometer in these kettles. When it looks done, smells done, feels done, it's done. Oh, sometimes I might poke it with a digital thermometer."

"What do you mean, 'looks done, smells done, feels done'?"

M.A. cocked her head, gave him a long look. "Mahogany brown, with a good crust, and with the brisket beginning to curl but not anywhere near dried out. Smell? Hard to describe, but from experience you'll learn you're looking for a specific smell. Feels done? Poke it with your finger. If it's too dry you'll feel instant regret that you waited too long. If it's just right it'll still have some give but feel tender." She gave him a sympathetic look. "Hey, son. Do you want to come back in the morning? I'll show you the 'looks done, smells done, feels done' routine."

"Well—you know, I'd like that. What time? Nine thirty?"

M.A. nodded.

"I might come back around tonight, too. Now I've got to catch a couple of the pork people. I speak a little pork." Pine walked off toward pork.

* * * * *

M.A. clicked off the video she'd been making of Pine and put away her phone. She shook her head. "He reminds me of the class wannabe, the kid who wants to be cool, thinks that means being sarcastic, lobbing disruptive comments around. Sometimes a kid like that needs—oh, a little love. And sometimes, a verbal spank."

The sunset was gone, the western sky fading into pale green. M.A. lit a Coleman camp lantern and set it beside the three Weber grills. "So we can see if anyone prowls around tonight," she said.

"There she is!" And around the Brisketvagen trotted a group of middle-aged women who swarmed around M.A. M.A. turned back to Val and called, "Hey, come meet my church book club!"

One of the women stared intently at Val, who slowly unfolded herself from her chair and stood. The woman took a tentative step forward and said, "Val? Val, do you remember me? We were in the same Girl Scout troop, remember?"

Exclamations erupted. "Val! Oh, honey!" Another book club member, arms wide, trotted toward Val, hugged her. So Val had to explain how Valentine Martina Black became Val Bond.

Alice watched the women for a moment, then backed quietly away. She wasn't part of this reunion, and she was starving. Tacos al pastor, she thought. But first, walk down pork alley, take a look at the pork?

M.A. slipped over to join her. "Okay if I tag along and visit the pork people with you, Alice? I need to stretch my legs. Besides, I want Val to spend a little time with those women, get the sense she could enjoy being here in Coffee Creek." She squinted at her phone. "Nearly eight thirty. At nine I'll be back to start up the grills."

Ruthlessly abandoning Val to the book club, Alice and M.A.

sauntered toward pork row. It seemed relatively quiet. Most pork butt contestants planned to put their meat on about 1:00 a.m., assuming they'd need nine or so hours, building in enough time to gussy up their presentation before the pork judging began. The pork rib contestants could sleep in until dawn.

From the bandstand on the gazebo Alice heard one of the piano players announce their last set: "A Tribute to Pork, a Texas Underdog," mixing Southern, Texas and Cajun music. The keyboards led off with "Right Place, Wrong Time," to enthusiastic applause, including from M.A. Alice was enjoying the twilight music, the slow stroll, the smell of smoked pork. She remembered driving down a dirt road in East Texas to take possession of a dark aromatic pork butt, carefully wrapped in foil. She thought of pigs, rooting for acorns in the oak and pine woods; pigs, left by the Spanish to fend for themselves on New World acorns, and create New World barbecue.

On that great note Alice's stomach growled. What about dinner? "M.A., I'm going to go get us all some tacos."

"Wonderful." Then M.A. looked at her watch. "Good honk, it's quarter till. I need to get back. But first I'm gonna go say howdy to those piano players before they quit." M.A. veered off toward the crowd in front of the gazebo, while Alice headed across the long park lawn toward the food trucks.

Alice had spied the planet Venus—the "wishing star"—and was considering what wishes she might make. How many could she get? For her children, Kinsear, the world? Around the park she saw the streetlights flickering on, adding their pumpkin-colored light to the deepening twilight. Coffee Creek had become a "dark skies" town ten years ago, opting for low-pressure sodium streetlights downtown. Alice, a stargazer, loved that Coffee Creekers cared about stars. She had to admit that the pumpkin-colored light made faces orange and blue jeans gray, but tonight everyone would be able to see the stars, and soon Orion, because fall was here. The late September air smelled of falling leaves, of chlorophyll shutting down, of earth readying for winter.

At the food trucks snugged up to the curb, crowds milled around—bikers, kids, parents, tourists. Alice stood in front of the banh mi and taco trucks, momentarily dithering. Down the block she saw Clay Black shaking hands briefly with a tall man with a ball cap pulled down over his eyes.

Sudden loud voices startled her. She spun around. Behind her in the street Johnny Tan stood stiff-legged, threatening John Pine.

"Creativity? What do you know about creativity? You've got no idea what creativity takes. You couldn't possibly know what it's like to spend sixteen to twenty hours a day on your feet, running a kitchen! You just sit around and copycat all the articles in *Bon Appétit*!" Tan, his face furious, voice raised, clenched his fists. Oh lord, Alice thought. Please let our judge not get into a fight.

John Pine lifted his chin, face shadowed by his baseball cap. Alice couldn't quite hear what he said—something like ". . . you got enough time to read *Bon Appétit*?"

Tan's eyes narrowed. "You little squirt." But a young woman scurried down from the banh mi truck and grabbed Tan's arm. She and Tan both climbed back into the truck.

"That's Tan's girlfriend," whispered a woman behind Alice to her companion. "She runs the banh mi truck."

Alice thought for two seconds, then walked over to Pine. "Hey, I'm getting in line for tacos. Come stand with me for a second." To her surprise, he came along, glancing inquiringly at her.

"I'm hoping our barbecue competition will be a success," she said. "That might be more likely if the judges can concentrate."

He snorted. "You could hope for that."

She tilted her head, appraising his face. "Have you thought about a different approach, like finding out what life is really like for some of these chefs? I understand you don't want to be too cozy, but it can't be an easy life for them. Might be some good stories that direction."

"Oh, yeah, there are indeed stories," he said. "I'm working right now on an exposé. 'Drugs in the Kitchen,' that's my working title. Yeah," he went on, watching Alice's face, "it's dark out there. Vanilla and elderflower—that's not all these guys use. They're equal opportunity in creative chemical use."

"Not our judges?" Alice asked. "You're not writing about them?"

He lifted an eyebrow. "Not saying. Just watch for my article two weeks out."

"Not ridiculing Coffee Creek, I hope?"

"No, no. Well, maybe a little. But you wait, you're gonna see some fireworks. This restaurant life, it's not just about the egos, or the competition. It's about money. For some, it's all about the money. So you want touchy-feely? That's not my style."

"I can tell that," she said. This felt like talking to a teenager. "You still might try a different approach now and then. Mix it up."

He nodded. "Yeah, yeah. Okay. Listen, remind your friend Marguerite Amaryllis or Tulip Daffodil or whatever it is that I'm taking her up on her offer. I'm coming by tomorrow morning to see how she tests her briskets."

With that, he wandered down the street past the banh mi truck, then jumped up on the curb and started back into the park.

Still waiting in the taco line, Alice watched Pine leave, hoping he might learn something from M.A. the next morning. In her peripheral vision she caught a glimpse of Clay Black gazing at her from half a block away. How long had he been watching? He stood alone, now scanning the crowd as if he were looking for someone. Maybe he's misplaced Annette, Alice thought. Or maybe she's already gone home.

Alice's turn: she stepped to the taco truck window and came away with a greasy aromatic bag of tacos and a wobbly cardboard tray holding three iced teas. Balancing the load, she stepped up onto the curb and started her journey into the park, then stopped. Which way?

Chapter Eight

Death Ray Boogie

The city could declare success over tonight's lineup. Music lovers had packed the big lawn in front of the gazebo, drawn by the battling pianos. Alice found herself nodding her head in time to the music streaming out across the lawn. "That was Pete Johnson's 'Death Ray Boogie,'" said the announcer. "Nearing time for fireworks, folks! This is the last set!" Meanwhile, more humans of all ages and conditions still streamed into the park and onto the lawn, searching for the perfect spot to watch fireworks. Alice herself longed to hear just a little more music; she wished she were out there on a blanket with Kinsear.

But she couldn't get close to the gazebo, given the mass of humanity, given these tacos, these teas, these responsibilities. Yes, she thought, and who's the one who volunteered to tote all this food? Feeling a little lonesome, a little sorry for herself, she decided she couldn't march straight across the lawn in the direction of M.A.'s grills. She'd take the indirect route, skirt around the back of the crowd by the playground, and then cut through Founders' Grove, the ancient live oaks that covered a third of the park. She began to weave her way past blankets, coolers, sleepy children, people entwined in growing darkness. The moon hadn't yet risen. The western sky was fading. The streetlights around the edges of the park gave only their dim pumpkin light.

In growing darkness she nearly stepped on a couple necking on a quilt, tripped on the electric cables running from the gazebo to the sound board, and finally bumped into the mayor, still on her tour of inspection.

"What do you think, Alice? Looks pretty good, doesn't it?" The mayor's silver hair glimmered as she surveyed the crowd.

"So far, so good. Fingers and toes crossed."

"I agree. Did you see that rascal John Pine swanning around? His column today was ridiculous. I just read it on my phone and I'm still mad. I'm going to speak to him about it when I find him!"

"What did he say?"

"He just had to make fun of Coffee Creek, I guess. Quote: 'Culinary arts in Coffee Creek? Something more than prefab chicken fry? Well, this little town is trying to convince you otherwise. Don't believe it yet.'" The mayor snorted in disgust. "The little twerp!"

Alice shook her head. "He's got a tin ear. He knows he'll lose credibility if he overhypes restaurants, so he gets too snarky. He hasn't figured how to hit it down the middle. Maybe he'll learn."

"But what does he mean, prefab chicken fry? That's pure libel! Camellia Diner hand-breads every cutlet and never uses frozen beef! I'm insulted on behalf of Coffee Creek! Where is the little jerk?"

They looked around. "He's wearing a T-shirt and blue ball cap. I saw him over at the food trucks, picking a fight with our judge Mr. Tan," Alice said. "He was headed this way."

"I'll track him down later. Right now I've got to announce fireworks."

The mayor moved off toward the gazebo, somehow sailing between blankets like Moses crossing the Red Sea. Alice heard the announcer say, "Okay, folks, we're winding up with something incredible. Our piano players will now present 'Boogie Woogie Dream'!"

Oh gosh, thought Alice, stopping in her tracks. Kinsear had introduced her to the fabled boogie duet between Albert Ammons and Pete Johnson. She stood listening. Tonight's version was at least as bold and hard-driving as the original. From here she could just see the piano players, faces intense, tossing the lead back and forth with impeccable timing, and finally a grand finale of crashing keys.

The crowd erupted, very happy. That's boogie-woogie, Alice thought.

Almost immediately Alice caught a faraway glimpse of silver curls arriving under the gazebo lights and heard the mayor's authoritative twang on the microphone, announcing that fireworks would start in exactly one minute, at nine o'clock. The crowd rearranged itself further, dragging lawn chairs, flicking open blankets, making room.

Once again Alice started toward M.A.'s setup. I'll have dinner with M.A. and Val, watch some fireworks, and head home, she thought; maybe Kinsear will call from New York, and I'll have a bubble bath with grapes and start that new mystery.

"Ohhh!" breathed the crowd. The first *whoosh* went up, then a pause, then the sudden *bang*. Red and green starbursts spangled the sky. *Bam!* The rockets' red glare, Alice thought. She edged past the back of the crowd, which reached almost to the playground. Moonlight splashed the ground, glinting on the metal supports for the slide, turning the swings' chains to silver as they hung motionless in the moonlight.

Now she'd reached the edge of the darkness beneath the heavy branches of Founders' Grove. The tangle of trunks and branches of ancient live oaks stretched beyond the playground and across the other side of the park, past M.A.'s grills. From here it should be a straight shot through the oaks, she thought. She decided to stay on course by training her eyes on her beacon, the faraway glimmer from the Coleman lantern M.A. had placed by her grills. She dodged tree trunks so she could keep the lantern in view. Somewhere to her right, in deeper darkness, she heard a few footsteps scuffle in the fallen oak leaves. Then silence fell.

Whoosh! Bang! "Aah," said the crowd.

Alice balanced the taco bag and the wobbly cardboard tray holding her three large teas, wishing for an extra hand to shine a light on the tree roots that snaked across the ground.

Suddenly she hurtled forward, nearly falling, two of the teas lurching away and splashing heavily on the ground as she hopped frantically to regain her balance.

Was it a tree root?

Too yielding.

Whoosh! More oohs and aahs from the crowd.

Alice set down the tacos and tea in the dry oak leaves and tugged her phone from her pocket, thumbing it on.

In the wavery light a man lay sprawled on his left side, face turned partly down toward the leaves, one arm and one leg flung out—the leg she'd stumbled over. His mouth was partly open. So was the one eye she could see. He did not move. On the ground she saw a "CIA in Texas" ball cap.

She stood frozen. The phone light turned itself off. She tried instead to turn on the phone flashlight, finally succeeded. Shining it down, she leaned over, made herself touch his shoulder, watching the open eye. "Hey?"

Silence. The eye didn't blink.

"John?" Tentatively, she touched his right wrist. Still warm. Still warm! But he was so still, so deeply still. She tried but couldn't feel a pulse. Leaning this close, she smelled the blood. She stared down at the black stain below his body.

She jumped back up, looking wildly around her, under the trees, then out toward the crowd. She saw no one, heard no one.

"Help!" Alice yelled. "Help!"

Whoosh. Aahs from the crowd. More fireworks.

"Help!"

No one could hear her.

She fumbled again with her phone, desperate, fingers trembling. She called 911. Breathless, stumbling through the words: "A man's hurt, here in the middle of the park, in Founders' Grove. He's on the ground and there's blood. I can't get him to respond at all."

"Where are you?"

She looked around, tried to judge. "In the middle of the Grove, not too far from the big lawn."

"We've got officers at the park. I'm calling them now. Just stay where you are, okay? Stay right there," the dispatcher told her. "Got a phone? Yes? Keep the light on so they can see you . . . Okay, I've got someone on the way." Alice waited, slowed her breathing. I've got to stand still, she thought. Not mess up this site. She played her phone flashlight over the ground around the body. Scuffed leaves, yes. But nothing else, except a couple of yards away, where she'd left the taco bag and the teas, two spilled, one forlorn in the carry tray. She turned slowly in a circle, shining the phone. Where were the police? A strong flashlight bounced toward her, blinded her. "Ma'am?" said the flashlight.

"This man," she said, pointing.

A Coffee County constable knelt down, shining the unforgiving brilliance of his Maglite on the body. He felt for a pulse, radioed for an ambulance. Had she heard him say "no pulse"? The white light moved slowly over the body, then stopped. Alice saw the spreading dark stain behind the body. The downhill side of his shirt was soaked; so was the hip of his cargo shorts. Oh, God. Alice shut her eyes, turned away, leaned on the nearby tree, took a deep breath, took another. The back of her neck turned wet, she felt faint, she didn't trust her stomach. She bent over, propped her hands on her knees, and breathed very slowly. Better. She stood.

The officer grunted and sat back on his heels. He pulled up his radio, turning away from Alice, and muttered into it. Then he turned back toward her. "Do you know this man?"

"He's a food writer from Austin named John Pine, I believe." She pointed at the ball cap. "That's what he was wearing earlier tonight."

He looked up at her inquiringly. He shone his light toward her while she talked, but not straight into her eyes.

"He had it on when he stopped by to interview the chief cook over at that rig." She pointed toward M.A.'s lantern. "And he still had it on not long ago, over at the food trucks."

He asked, "Just now, what happened? How did you find him?"

"I didn't find him. I tripped over his leg. I was carrying supper to my friends." She pointed at the cardboard tray and paper bag, sitting in the leaves. "Is he—?" But she knew the answer; the constable was standing up, brushing the dirt off his knees.

"I need your contact information."

She identified herself, pulled her license out of her back pocket, gave him a business card with her phone numbers. He shone his light on it, then looked up sharply at her face.

"You could call George Files. He knows me," she said. She'd met Files, a detective in the Coffee County Sheriff's Office, after someone murdered one of her favorite clients.

He nodded. "Okay. Tell me one more time, how do you know this guy?"

"The first time I ever saw him was today." She recounted the press conference. "I saw him around the food trucks a little while ago." Somehow she found herself not mentioning, yet, the confrontation with Tan. "And earlier, like I said, he was walking around the rigs." She pointed at the faint glimmer of the Coleman lantern off at the edge of the park.

Flashing lights, but no siren. An ambulance rumbled toward them across the playground. Doors slammed; men ran across with a gurney. The constable met them.

She couldn't hear the conversation from the men bending over the body. But now the EMTs moved more slowly, closed up their bags. Initial urgency had vanished. They wouldn't be using the gurney yet. Instead, someone would be stringing crime tape.

The constable muttered into his radio. "Files is coming," he said to Alice. "He says you can head home and he'll talk to you first thing in the morning. There'll be plenty to do here tonight."

"You know where to find me." She retrieved the one remaining tea and the bag of tacos, holding the bag and its once-appetizing smell off to the side. She headed slowly under the live oaks toward the flickering light of the Coleman lantern. John Pine! A snotty little brat. But a brat who had responded, perhaps, to M.A.'s teasing kindness.

The continuing rumble of fireworks and oohs from the crowd reminded her of the mayor. She'd need to know. Alice set down the food again and dialed her number. "What the hell is that ambulance doing by the playground?" demanded the mayor. Alice explained.

"Shit," said the mayor. "A murder at our first annual barbecue competition?" Then she said, "This is terrible. I will want to be in touch with his family at some point." Silence. The mayor was thinking it out. "Tomorrow morning, after the news hits," she said. And hung up.

* * * * *

Alice finally reached M.A.'s setup. "Hallelujah! We're starving, Alice!" said M.A., climbing out of her lawn chair. "Thought maybe a bear got you!" M.A. took the paper bag and began dealing the tacos out onto paper plates. Alice turned away, a stomach spasm bringing the acid taste of vomit to the back of her throat.

Val was watching Alice's face. "Alice, what happened?"

Alice told them. "Someone killed John Pine."

"Caswell and Davie!" Val jerked up out of her chair, staring toward the crowd. "They're back there!"

"I didn't see them," said Alice. "They're probably still watching the fireworks."

Accelerating booms, accelerating whooshes, a long string of twenty thousand firecrackers: time for the grand finale. The three women waited. The whooshes stopped; conversations started; people began to trickle out of the park. Val said nothing, lips pinched shut.

Suddenly a small boy raced out of the darkness, followed by Caswell. "Grandmama! I think I got the fireworks with my drone!" Davie clutched his drone to his chest. "Wait till you see!"

Val hugged him gently, avoiding the drone wings and propeller. Then she looked up at Caswell, and back at Alice. Caswell raised his eyebrows at Alice and walked over, face a question mark. Alice whispered briefly what had happened to the food writer. Caswell looked steadily at her. "And you found him? That's rough, Alice. Are you okay?"

She nodded, overcome by the thought that she wanted out of here. Right now. "What time do you put on the briskets, M.A.?"

"It's past nine thirty. I wanted to have them all on by ten. We've got the grills going. Want to stay, help us put on more rub? I can't give you a T-shirt; we can only have four people on the team. You can be honorary though." She looked hard at Alice. "I'll bet the thought of touching meat right now doesn't cut it."

God, the very idea. Alice shook her head. "Gotta go. I can't help, anyway. I'm on the Rules Committee. Lord knows that would be an ethical violation." She headed for the street, managed to say, "You all sleep tight; I'll see you in the morning."

She caught sight of Davie's questioning face.

"And I'll see you at the drone acrobatics, right?"

Relieved, he nodded.

Chapter Nine

Some Sort of Aphrodisiac?

Half-listening to the crowd of parents and children, to happy conversations about the fireworks, about bedtime, about watching out for cars, about why it was too late for ice cream, Alice trudged the three blocks back to her office. She tugged the front door to be sure it was locked, then walked slowly back to her old tan Toyota truck. No radio, tonight. She just wanted quiet. She backed out and headed out of town on the creek road, rolling down her window so she could hear the crickets, the tires on the asphalt, the wind.

Her phone rang. "Alice! Where are you?"

Kinsear.

"Driving home! What about you? Somewhere in Brooklyn?"

"Nope. I caught an early flight. I'm turning into your driveway. I was hoping you might put up a lonely traveler tonight."

"That could happen," Alice said.

She hung up, took a deep breath. And realized how relieved she felt. And not just relieved: she knew she'd be hugged, kissed, comforted, loved, held separate from death, after finding a body at her feet. Was murder some sort of aphrodisiac? Lord, she could not mention that to anyone. Life after death, but still?

Alice and Kinsear had dated intensely for a short time in law school at UT, until the summer internship in Houston when she met the big Scot, as she called Jordie. Once Jordie entered the picture Alice had buried deep the memories of her fling with Kinsear. So when he walked into the Fredericksburg beer garden, she'd felt panic, then dragged her feet, slow to allow herself to enjoy watching their relationship reheat. She'd still felt she was betraying Jordie. She'd felt anxious about the children. She'd felt protective of her new identity as a hardworking lawyer in Coffee Creek.

Face it, Alice, she said to herself. You worry about everything. Yeah, yeah, you think that's your job and that no one worries better than you do. You consider yourself the uncontested queen of worrying.

What about enjoying this very moment? What about enjoying just being alive, enjoying it like jumping off a rope swing over Cypress Creek, into Blue Hole? What about enjoying it like sliding down Andrews Glacier in the Rockies as a kid? Like racing down the river rapids in an inner tube at Schlitterbahn? Like taking the first sip of a velvety Napa cabernet, the one you can only afford once a year? Like riding the waves with the green sea turtles on the north shore of Maui? What about enjoying being alive like—like—well, she'd give it more thought, but right now she'd reached the point where she almost felt capable of enjoying Kinsear without worrying that he was about to press her to make a Decision.

Far down her driveway the front porch lights were on and Kinsear's ancient Land Cruiser sat vastly, heavily, on the gravel drive. Kinsear was standing in the moonlight by the pole barn where she parked the truck, wearing his old canvas barn coat. He kissed her, looked at her face, tilted his head appraisingly and looked hard into her eyes. "Okay, what happened?"

She told him.

"*You* stumbled over the body."

"Yup."

He sighed, shook his head, looked up at the moon. "Of all the gin joints . . . oh, wait, of all the barbecue competitions in Texas, yours has to be the one with a dead body. Found by you."

The vision of the still body rose before her. "I tripped on him. He was lying in his own blood." She burst into tears, felt her nose start to run. "And I spilled the iced teas," she sobbed, hiccupping. Kinsear tugged a bandana from his pocket, handed it to her, hugged her. She blotted her eyes and sniffed. "Well, it's probably a good thing it was me, and not some little kid running around watching the fireworks."

"Because you're experienced in the body-finding business and it wouldn't bother you?"

That was a sore point for Kinsear. Not that he wanted to compete in body finding, but he felt uneasy about Alice's propensity to find herself dealing with dead bodies.

"It did bother me. I'd just met this poor guy today. And now he's dead. Permanently." She was tugging open the passenger door of her truck, her rear to Kinsear, groping for her briefcase.

"He may be dead. We're not." From behind he wrapped his open barn coat around her, pulled her backward toward him. The warmth felt so good. She felt a hand snake under her T-shirt, move up, up,

75

ignoring her bra. The hand snaked down, under her jeans, popped the snap, slid down into her underwear. After a few moments she turned around, dropping the briefcase on the cement of the pole barn floor.

"Long time," he said into her hair, continuing his disturbing attentions.

They somehow made it down the walk and through her creaking front gate. He locked it against the burros, took off the barn coat, spread it on the grass in the moonlight.

"I do have a bedroom," she muttered.

"You look good outside, here in the fall moonlight. Let me just see . . ."

Moonlight. Giggling, they pulled off boots and jeans, fell on the barn coat. "I hope we don't wake up the fire ants," Alice breathed.

"Hush. I have missed you."

Later she wondered whether outdoor sex was a misdemeanor in Coffee County . . . whether drones were watching . . . whether the burros were looking through the fence . . . whether the stars were staring . . . whether moonlight was the reason every cell in her body felt electrified.

At 4:00 a.m. the gibbous moon was shining directly onto Alice's bed. She couldn't sleep in moonlight; she loved the moon, though not lying awake to watch it slide past her windows at three or four in the morning. But she couldn't make herself draw the curtains by the French doors, afraid that to miss a night of such moonlight would deprive her soul of a needed moment, maybe *the* needed moment, of beauty, and in a lifetime where such moments might rarely be vouchsafed, she could not sin by failing to open her eyes to the moon. She slipped out of bed, leaving Kinsear in a pile of pillows, and walked barefoot to the kitchen and out onto the deck, where she could stretch her arms up to the moon and let it wash over her, fill her eyes, fill her fingers, fill her outstretched hands.

She did not consider this pagan behavior. In the same way, she watched for the shadows of her mother and father, dancing (her mother) and reading (her father, walking, eyes on a Greek text) above the house. She felt they visited on occasion.

At five thirty she made coffee, muffling the grinder in a towel so it wouldn't wake Kinsear, and sipped it out on the chilly deck, watching the moon sink in the west and Orion tilt down into the valley below the deck where the creek whispered past the limestone bluff.

Then she crawled back into bed with Kinsear. Saturday morning, after all.

Chapter Ten

New Ones Are So Sharp

The wake-up call from Coffee County Detective George Files brought extra chill to the morning. "Sorry, Alice. Can you be here by eight thirty? We've got a lot of ground to cover."

Literally? Figuratively? She didn't ask, didn't think he had much morning sense of humor. And he'd probably been up all night.

Kinsear, sleepy in pajama bottoms, clutching a homemade latte, shook his head. "Discouraging way to be greeted, with you running off to that detective."

He told her he'd probably head back to Fredericksburg for a while to check on his bookstore, The Real Story. So he'd miss the drone competition and, at high noon, the ringing of the iron triangle, when Alice's Rules Committee had to be on hand for the judging. But he'd return that night to take Alice to the full-dress Pianorama at the Beer Barn.

However, he told her, looking at her over his latte, he'd probably have to go back to New York on Monday. "I've got to work through some issues for the hedge fund."

"What exactly is going on up there?" she asked.

"Oh," he said in an offhand voice, "well, they're in negotiations to get bought. They asked me to come help sort things out. Looks like a pretty good deal for them, potentially."

"They still like you enough to ask you to come help them get sold, hmm?"

He snorted. "They want me to keep an eye on their high-priced merger lawyers." Then he glanced at her. "Actually, they've asked me to come back. The buyer wants me on board too."

Her eyes widened, her stomach lurched.

"Come on, Alice, it's not the first time they've asked. But I've been telling them no, I'm happy down here."

She blinked. "Right." She leaned back, looked at him. "It's not tugging at you still?" She'd never worked in New York. She'd worked with New York lawyers on some cases and knew they craved the vibe, the energy, the fierceness, the same way she craved a big sky.

Would Kinsear want to go back to that life? She pressed her lips together, considering what that would mean, feeling the elevator drop of her stomach.

"Hey, stop that! I'll see you tonight." He held both her hands. "And do not, I repeat, do not walk under the shade of the oaks this afternoon while I'm gone. Do not carry tacos and tea beneath the fatal trees. I mean it. You know I try not to interfere, since you constantly insist on running around loose, but I'd really like to draw the line at more bodies."

She nodded. "I'm not in the mood to find any bodies. Of course, I can't always control what other people do."

"Alice, Alice." He kissed the top of her head. "I admire your passionate insistence on taking care of your clients. I'd like to think you can do that by spending more time in the office without putting your body at risk. I'm fond of this body." He was holding her shoulders.

"I'm sad about John Pine. He was only obnoxious, trying to make a name for himself." She thought for a moment, though, about how a new chef might feel, trying to make a name for himself, and reading an obnoxious review.

"It does seem like overkill, so to speak, to murder a food writer. But at a barbecue competition surely you'd find a few suspects?"

She nodded. "Maybe George Files will give me a hint as to who they are."

"Remind me again—who were your judges?" Kinsear asked.

"Judge Sandoval, our probate judge. Then Jennie Hardin, she's culinary arts professor at the community college, and Earl Stark, who runs our campfire cooking school. And also Johnny Tan from Spring and Danny Robicheaux from Soleil."

"Tan and Robicheaux. They're busy boys these days. I heard Robicheaux's supposed to be opening a restaurant in that fancy new hotel on Colorado Street in Austin. Houston backers, I hear. The price of oil goes up, fancy restaurants open."

"What will happen to Soleil if he's splitting time between two restaurants? Does he just quit sleeping?"

"Probably," Kinsear said. "Tan's busy too. I hear he's got a cookbook coming out. Okay, gotta go."

He kissed Alice, reminded her she'd promised to avoid trouble, and left.

The news that he'd repeatedly been invited to join a new Manhattan enterprise left Alice feeling uncertain, discombobulated. She stood up straight. She wouldn't think about it.

Instead she thought about M.A. and her friend, Val. She couldn't get Val's face out of her mind—the 1960s face of Val the coed, laughing, arm around M.A., and Val's face last night as she sat regally in a lawn chair, still beautiful despite the ravages of the cold dry wind in Colorado high country. What lay behind the somber look in those eyes? All three—M.A., Caswell, Val—knew something Alice didn't. And maybe—she hoped—Davie didn't. What was it?

Then there was John Pine, dead in the oak leaves. She wondered what drove someone to terminate his life with such deliberate, pointed violence. A bare bodkin; Hamlet's quietus. She shook her head as she pulled into a parking spot at the courthouse. Plenty of room: the sunny street was empty on an early Saturday morning.

* * * * *

Detective George Files swung his long legs off the desk in his small office in the sheriff's annex by the courthouse. The tired brown eyes surveyed Alice. "Alice. We have to quit meeting this way."

"I agree. Horrible. All those people sitting peacefully on the grass in the park, listening to music, watching fireworks, thinking about barbecue. Meanwhile, in Founders' Grove, a young man gets murdered."

"Welcome to my world. I'm sorry you had to find him." He considered her for a moment. "Don't you have some role in this shindig?"

"The mayor asked me to head the Rules Committee. You have to have rules for the competition."

"Not including homicide, right?"

She managed a grin. "As chair of the Rules Committee I will swear to you that the rules don't contemplate murder."

He sighed. "What do you know about digital thermometers?"

"Well. I've got one. No, two." She thought about M.A.'s necklace last night. "Probably most, if not all, of the barbecue competitors have one. Temperature's critical, especially for brisket. You know the old ones that used to leave that big unsightly hole? Made you think, *That's a muscle?* Well, the new ones are so sharp they don't mess up the meat."

"Yeah. Well, they may not leave a big hole, but they're big enough to drain a lot of blood out of a kidney."

She shut her eyes. "Is that what happened to John Pine?"

"We don't know. He's got a puncture wound for sure. About the size of an ice pick. Or a digital thermometer." He looked up at her. "You never had any military training, did you, Alice? Special ops?"

Stunned, she shook her head. "No," she said. "What did pathology say?"

"Penetration wound to the right kidney, deep enough to cause instant shock, bleeding. He may not have even been able to speak."

"Why are you telling me this? You don't usually share."

"Did you have anything against John Pine?"

"No. He's pretty mouthy, but to me he was just a kid trying to make a living. I've read his columns but I met him for the first time yesterday at the mayor's press conference."

Files said, "Well, since you were unlucky enough to find the body, I need to hear everything you heard or saw. Also, I thought you could tell me who out there would have a digital thermometer—if that's what the killer used, which we're waiting to learn. And I want to hear everything you know about how John Pine spent the day yesterday."

She told Files about the confrontation between the judges and Pine at city hall. She recounted what she remembered about Tan's confrontation with Pine at the banh mi truck.

"I heard about that one."

"But surely Tan wouldn't have killed John Pine!"

"Hey, it's not your job to defend Tan. However, he's got a pretty solid alibi. Witnesses say he left right after that altercation. We've got statements from witnesses watching him all the way to his car. And he did show up at his restaurant after that at the time you'd expect for someone driving from Coffee Creek to Austin. Okay, what else, Alice?"

"I talked to Pine right after he and Tan faced off. I asked whether he might consider a less confrontational interview technique. He didn't say yes. In fact, he told me he was writing an exposé on drug use in Austin kitchens. He was coy about whether our chefs might be involved."

She thought for a moment. "But he didn't seem at all worried. He told me to remind M.A. he planned to take her up on her invitation."

"What invitation?"

Alice told Files about John Pine's visit to M.A.'s rig. "He'd promised to come back this morning around nine thirty so she could explain her brisket technique to him."

She watched Files type notes on a screen. She said, "A little smack talk, a little trash talk. You don't think that means any of those people at the competition would do something like this?"

"Come on, Alice. You've only mentioned a couple of incidents so far. I've already heard way worse from a bunch of people about what Pine said to this contestant, that judge, this council member, that innocent bystander. Guy had a mouth on him. Just as one example, Judge Sandoval's already told me about Pine getting into it with a football player named Travis Poole."

"Poole. Sounds vaguely familiar," Alice said.

"He played high school football at Westlake. Apparently he and John Pine graduated in the same class. Later he played at Texas A&M, and then he tried out for the pros, but didn't get drafted. Yesterday Pine went after him, too. According to the judge, Pine said something like, 'Couldn't make it in the pros, could you, Travis? So now you're gonna make it large on a barbecue farm team?'"

"Nice," Alice said. "Insulting Travis Poole *and* Coffee Creek. 'Farm team,' for goodness sake. So what did Poole do?"

Files lifted an eyebrow. "According to the judge, Poole kind of leaned over him—Poole's pretty big—and said, 'You say that again and I'll bust your chops, you little pussy.'"

"Ah. But no blows?"

"Oh, no. The judge says Poole just kind of—leaned over him, you know? Then Poole laughed and said, 'You never change, Pine. How about you show us *your* brisket?' Then Poole walked back to his rig. I've talked to Poole. His story tallies with the judge's."

"I assume Poole's got an alibi."

Files nodded.

She sat, thinking of the young man who'd promised to come see M.A. this morning. "So you don't know who sneaked up behind Pine in the dark and stabbed him in his *kidney*? You'd have to know what you were doing, wouldn't you?"

"The military teaches that technique in special ops—how to kill someone quickly, quietly, cause massive bleeding and instant shock."

"Oh." No, she sure didn't recall that from her law-school curriculum. Before her flashed John Pine's body, blood-soaked from the small of his back down—and he couldn't even call for help? The acrid sting of vomit rose in her throat. She grabbed her water bottle, managed to get the cap loose.

"Yeah," said Files, watching her. "Poor guy. Anyway, you think most of the contestants would have a digital thermometer?"

Alice nodded. "I'd put money on it."

He went on. "Of course there are different brands, different sizes and shapes. So I've got someone asking about that now. Whether anyone's lost a red one."

"Red?" She sat up straight. "Does that mean you found a red one somewhere?" She watched Files as she recalled the scuffling feet she'd heard in Founders' Grove.

Files nodded.

"Well, I know M.A. Ellison has one, but she was sitting at her rig with a friend."

"The whole time?" Files asked.

"Come on, you know M.A.! You can't be serious." Alice rolled her eyes. "Okay, M.A. and I left her rig about eight thirty. We walked past the pork people. She said she needed to be back at the grills about nine. But she wanted to go say hey to the piano players before they quit."

"So you separated from her—when?"

Alice wasn't quite sure.

"Okay, what next?"

"I went to the food trucks. I stood in line, had my talk with Pine. On my way back with the tacos I ran into the mayor. She was looking for Pine, too. But right then she had to go make her announcement about the fireworks. I started back across the park, got under the trees. Then the fireworks began. Then I fell over him."

She took a breath. "You know the rest. When I got back, M.A. was sitting in her lawn chair with her buddy. I'm sure she had no idea about John Pine when I told them what—what I'd seen."

Files looked noncommittal.

"Come on," Alice said, "she'd promised him an interview for this morning!"

"Just routine, Alice, just routine."

Chapter Eleven

The Moment of Truth

Alice drove from the courthouse back toward the park and jumped down from her truck. She'd dressed in jeans and boots for the judging and final ceremony. Normally she'd be enjoying the swagger her boots gave her. No wonder people wore cowboy boots, she thought. They let you stand a little taller, feel a little fiercer, dance a little better (at least your toes were protected during a two-step). Besides, her Goodson Kells were elegant. Since Friday was boot day, Alice often even wore hers to court.

But this Saturday morning, boot joy couldn't overcome the heavy sense of dread that increased with each step she took. She didn't like the way Files had focused on M.A. She didn't like that he seemed exceedingly interested in M.A.'s thermometer. She didn't like the memory of a young man's blood, black on the ground. She headed across the lawn toward the wide grassy area of the park and spied Caswell and Davie.

Zoom! A covey of drones (a drama of drones? a dizziness of drones?) soared through rings, dived under bars, twisted into aerobatic loops.

"We're just warming up, Alice!" said Caswell. "Davie's group competes next. He's the youngest. Ready, buddy?"

"Battery's charged, camera's set. Ready, Dad."

Davie was a head shorter than any other child in the group. All had white squares with black numbers tied around their necks.

"Time trial, Alice. They have to perform five specific tricks in thirty seconds."

Davie's turn. He put on his goggles. He'd told Alice they were called "FPV. That's for 'first-person view.'" He ran to the starting line, placed the drone, positioned his feet carefully behind the line, waited for the whistle.

She watched, riveted, and found herself yelling, "Go, Davie!"

Caswell smiled, lifted his phone to video Davie. But his eyes, unblinking, love and longing visible, followed Davie's every move.

Alice felt tears, furtively wiped them away. Jordie had watched John and Ann with the same intensity. She took a deep breath. Lord, parenthood. Make yourself totally emotionally vulnerable. Forever.

Tweet! The small racing drone lifted, rose, back loop, straightaway, left loop, right loop, back toward Davie, under the wire across the course, figure eight, land! Two more contestants to go.

His face glowing, Davie ran back to his dad, who was holding his phone. "Did you get it?" Davie demanded.

"Yep." They watched the video.

Then Davie watched the next two contestants, a boy and a girl. The boy's drone hit the wire. The girl landed a split second late. Davie took second place and stood proudly next to the winner, who loomed a foot taller. The organizers draped medals on the first-, second-, and third-place contestants, leaning over a bit farther to congratulate Davie. Parents snapped photos. Davie ran back to Caswell and Alice.

"Caswell Black Jr." Caswell, Alice, and Davie turned to see Annette in jeans and boots, dark hair glossy, her eyes fixed on Caswell.

"Hi, Annette," Caswell answered cheerfully. "It's Caswell Bond now."

"Bond?" But her eyes had dropped to Davie.

"You have a son!" She glanced back up. "You have a son! He reminds me of you, but smaller of course." She squatted down on her haunches in front of Davie, dropping her bag on the ground, and held out her hand. Alice thought, Surely Annette's never done that for anyone. Squatted in her boots?

Davie looked down at her hand and gave it a tentative shake. Looking up, he backed away from Annette's intense gaze.

Her voice soft, she said, "Davie, I'm your Great-Aunt Annette. I'm so glad to meet you. I see you won one of the prizes. Does your drone have a name?"

"Yes," said Davie. He paused, then leaned forward an inch and said softly, "Superbird."

"I love it. That sounds like a lucky name."

Davie nodded. "So far it's working. But don't tell anyone the name."

"I won't."

Alice was watching, astounded. Annette's voice as she spoke to Davie contained none of the artificiality Alice had heard over and over at library board meetings. Now she remembered hearing that Annette chaired the children's committee at the library, and reportedly read to children, a notion Alice had always rejected, since she hated to hear children being read to in the sort of saccharine voice she associated with Annette. But maybe Alice was wrong?

Davie was studying Annette, who appeared to be memorizing his face. Then Davie looked up at his father. "She knew you when you were little, Dad?"

Caswell nodded.

"Oh yes," Annette said to Davie. "I was so sad when your dad left the ranch. Without telling me." Her eyes traveled up to Caswell, then back to Davie. "I missed him very much."

Davie looked at her, questioning.

She answered as if he had spoken aloud. "No, I had no children of my own. So I missed my nephew Caswell—your dad—very much." Then she asked, "Have you gotten to go out to your grandmother's ranch yet?"

Davie nodded. "There's lots of room out there."

"For your drone?"

Again he nodded, adding the rare wide-eyed smile that caught Alice's heart.

"Obviously you couldn't stay out at your place since the old house is falling down," Annette went on.

He hasn't told her! Alice thought. Clay must have told her he'd seen Val with M.A. But he hasn't told her about the purchase of the Tindall ranch. Why not?

In the silence, Annette retrieved her bag and stood up. "I'm sorry your Great-Uncle Clay missed seeing this," she said. "He's probably already in the judges' tent."

Her face rearranged into the automatic too-sweet smile. Alice wondered if sometimes she herself presented such a smile, especially when she didn't mean it. Why, Annette? she asked herself. Must we women always look so helpful? So beneficent? But Alice suspected her own face sometimes might look—yes. Insincerely saccharine. The opposite of what she felt. Hmm.

"Good to see you, Annette," said Caswell.

Deft, thought Alice. Annette held his eyes, nodded briefly and turned toward the judges' tent. But not without a farewell handshake with Davie.

Alice bought Davie a snow cone at the food trucks; she and Caswell each picked up a cold beer. They walked back toward M.A.'s rig. "Everything okay last night?" she asked Caswell.

"I think so. Davie and I slept pretty well, considering. Of course I heard the tops of the Weber grills clanging every time M.A. added more charcoal. And she and Mom are getting tense about when to take the briskets off." He watched Davie walking up ahead, almost to M.A.'s grills, one hand holding the snow cone, the other his drone. "Any word on what happened to the reporter?"

"Stabbed in the right kidney, maybe with a digital thermometer," Alice said.

Caswell's mouth fell open. "You're kidding."

At that moment M.A. yelled, "Where the hell's my thermometer?"

They scrambled toward her. Val bent over, peered under the table, under the lawn chairs, under the car. Pink-faced, hair in an uproar, M.A. pawed through the box of tools. "Not here! You saw me put it on the table there, didn't you?" Alice nodded. M.A. grabbed the sleeping bags from the back of the Caddy, shook them out. "Where is it?" she stormed. "Hey, Harvey!"

Harvey yelled back from his rig. "What, M.A.?"

"Did you grab my thermometer?"

"Hell, no. But you are certainly welcome to borrow mine." He passed over a blue digital shaped like M.A.'s.

She subsided. "Thanks. Thanks, pal. We've arrived at the moment of truth over here." She handed the thermometer to Val, who delicately inserted it into the first brisket and inspected it judiciously. "One eighty-five," Val reported. "Lemme check the other two."

"Okay," muttered M.A. "This one, we ought to get it out and let it sit, let it stew in its juices." She unfurled a tablecloth, flapped it, spread it on the floor in the back of the Caddy. "My staging area."

She and Val were taste-testing small bits of each brisket, arguing over which brisket to use for their turn-in box. The box had to contain seven perfect slices, plus the ends of the brisket. Taste testing was key, but a beautiful sequence of slices was also necessary, to show the blackened, intensely flavored crust, then the unctuous slices inside, cut against the grain, of course, with the inside slices proudly sporting the red line showing the brisket had been smoked, not (horrors!) baked. Taste, tenderness, texture: they were rolling the dice in choosing the brisket. But different judges might have different opinions. And one brisket might be tenderer, one might be more delicious.

Alice stood frozen, watching the two women make their decision. How many red digital thermometers could there be at this competition? When did M.A.'s thermometer disappear? She remembered M.A. putting it on the folding table last night. Since then, how many people had marched past, or even through, M.A.'s setup?

Val and M.A. were muttering, voices intertwined, over their turn-in box. It had to look inviting, delicious, and the essence of brisket.

Alice left them debating, afraid to interrupt their careful preparation for final judging. A cold feeling in her stomach: didn't she have to call George Files, to report a missing thermometer? A missing *red* thermometer? Reluctantly, very reluctantly, she pulled her phone from her pocket. Then she thought, I've got to tell M.A. first.

She called M.A. over. "Listen, the police found a red thermometer. We need to tell them yours is gone."

M.A.'s face froze. "A red thermometer? Like *mine*?"

"I don't know. But don't worry," Alice said. "Just get your brisket ready."

With Val and M.A. still debating final arrangement, Alice called Files. "But please," she told him, "they had to borrow a thermometer just now to check their briskets. They're in the middle of getting ready for final presentation. Please don't bug them until after the brisket gets judged!"

She felt some confidence that he respected brisket enough to wait.

Chapter Twelve

Smoked 'Em

In the judges' tent, a buzz of voices rose—as the five judges, the contest officials tasked with monitoring contestants' turn-in boxes, and the city council members repeated: "John Pine?" "On the news?" "Who?" "How'd the little jerk get himself killed at our first competition?"

Word was out, Alice realized.

Soon contestants and spectators would be milling around outside. Contestants for each barbecue category would be ushered in, group by group, to watch the judges' critical appraisal of their carefully prepared and officially ticketed turn-in boxes of sausage, ribs, pork butt, then finally the queen of barbecue—brisket. Alice thought of Achilles' feast on the shores of Troy for the dead Patroclus, the funeral meats, the "well-fed swine," the "huge ox," the goat, the silent sheep. No sheep or goat here, though. And who was here to mourn Pine, slaughtered like Patroclus?

A bustle at the tent door. Clay and Annette smiled their way in, Clay crisp in chinos, Annette holding his arm. Always making an entrance, Alice thought, uncharitably. Annette began working the crowd, yoo-hooed at a couple of friends. Jane Ann Olson, fellow Rules Committee member, whispered in Alice's ear, "I heard last night Clay's gonna run for the open director slot on the Coffee Creek Electric Co-op board. Annette loves it, don't you think?"

Clay headed straight for Alice. "Any issues?"

Hadn't he heard? "If you mean on the rules, no, not so far as I know."

Behind Alice the mayor was talking to Councilman Hinojosa. "I've got to say something about John Pine at some point. Maybe after the judging at city hall?"

Clay's brow furrowed. He turned to Alice. "Why the heck does she need to say anything about John Pine? That little jerk?"

"He got killed last night."

"John Pine? Killed?"

"Yes, just as the fireworks started."

Clay's color drained away. His face was white, lips the color of chalk. She was afraid he'd faint. "Where?"

Odd question.

"Right by the playground, under the trees," Alice said.

"Are you sure?"

"Yes. You didn't know? It was on the news."

"We didn't turn it on. They're—you—you're sure that's who it was?"

She nodded. "Unfortunately, I found his body."

His eyes widened. "*You* did?"

Annette appeared next to him. "What's wrong, darling?"

"Nothing, nothing. Just . . . John Pine got killed last night."

"You mean the food writer?" asked Annette. "What happened?"

Clay looked back at Alice. "Who would kill him? Who would kill John Pine? Maybe one of the contestants?"

"No idea," Alice said. "He talked too much, but . . ."

"How—how was he killed?" Clay asked.

"Stabbed in the back," Alice said. "In the kidney."

"Oh, how horrible!" Annette exclaimed. "Who would do such a thing?" She looked up at Clay. "Of course I heard he said really tacky things to some people. But still!"

Tackiness didn't usually constitute grounds for murder, Alice thought.

Clay nodded several times, face serious, eyes fixed on the middle distance. Then he turned to Alice and shook his head. "That's terrible, Alice. Terrible. Very sorry to hear it."

He stood silent. Annette glanced up at him. Alice looked at her phone. Nearly noon.

Time to begin. The line of sausage contestants waited anxiously outside. Councilman Hinojosa walked to the tent door and rang his iron triangle again. The line of contestants began shuffling into the tent, seating themselves in flimsy folding chairs. Outside, the waiting crowd whooped and hollered, cheering on their buddies. The mayor demanded silence for the judging and assured contestants they would be booted immediately if they tried to call attention to any entry. The five judges marched up to the high-top rectangular table lent by the Beer Barn and slid onto their barstools. The contest officials, sober-faced, delivered to the table the first numbered plastic-foam turn-in box, with its carefully arranged sausage slices. Each judge would score each entry for taste, texture, tenderness, smell, and appearance before moving to the next entry.

Here we go, Alice thought. So far, so good, except for one dead body.

Alice and most of the Rules Committee crowded silently around their small corner table, watching the process. She looked around but didn't see Clay.

Sausage tasting began.

Alice surveyed the judges. A lifted eyebrow here, an expression of interest there. But the rules imposed silence on the judges. They could not talk, could not lobby for any entry. Robicheaux, wearing his chef's jacket, and Tan, in his hip tie-on cap, perched side by side, with occasional eye contact, more cordial than Alice expected. As at wine tastings, each judge had a sequence, a methodology. As far as she could tell, Judge Sandoval's procedure was, first, to peer critically at the sausage piece, then to sniff it, then to take an initial bite, followed by acceptance or rejection; if acceptance, a second bite was followed by contemplative chewing, with narrowed eyes and a thoughtful stare toward the top of the tent. Alice had seen that thoughtful stare in court and began trying to guess how he was scoring each entry.

The five judges finished all ten sausage entries. Time for a short break. Tan and Robicheaux chatted with each other, heads tilted. Alice had always thought that world peace could be achieved if combatants would sit down together at a barbecue, although she hadn't puzzled out what to do about sacred cows and pork prohibitions.

Outside the tent the crowd talked, watched, wandered. At twelve thirty, the sausage contestants filed out and ten pork rib teams began lining up and shuffling into the chairs at the rear of the tent. Once again the judges fell to. Alice salivated, watching each judge choose a glossy brown rib as each of the turn-in boxes was passed around. The judges reached swift opinions on ribs, marking the score sheets with decisive confidence.

One o'clock. Ten pork butt teams entered the tent. One team member emitted an ill-advised "Yee-haw!"

"Who was that?" barked the mayor. She pointed and a constable escorted the blushing whooper out of the tent.

After pork butt the judges got off their stools and took a ten-minute break for one cold beer each. "Folks, bear with us," said the mayor. "These judges have still got twenty brisket entries ahead of 'em."

Alice watched the Houston Hotties, Seguin Slow Burn, M.A.'s Coffee Creek Revival, and other teams march in, looking like proud but anxious parents. When the contest officials called out "Coffee Creek Revival," M.A. walked up in her "Chief Cook" T-shirt and presented her team's turn-in box. Per the Coffee Creek rules, sauce was forbidden. No garnish; nothing but perfect brisket in each turn-in box. Big John at Shade Tree had told Alice, "Proper brisket eaters abjure sauce," and Judge Sandoval had threatened to disqualify sauced entries. Surveying each other, the judges wiped their mouths, climbed back onto the barstools, and set to work.

At two fifteen Mayor Wilson stalked over to the judges' table, looking over her reading glasses at the judges. They looked back, shirts disheveled, mouths greasy, eyes glazed.

"Are you ready?"

They nodded.

She turned to the scoring table in the corner, where a serious-faced young woman was entering the last of the brisket score sheets into a laptop.

"Are you ready?"

The woman nodded, hit a button, and the printer whirred. She brought the tally to the mayor.

The mayor led everyone outdoors to the makeshift dais by the judges' tent. Councilman Hinojosa stood at a table topped with ribbons. Clutching her handheld mike, the mayor thanked the judges, thanked Rotary, thanked the contest officials, thanked the city and park employees, even thanked the Rules Committee, and thanked everyone for coming. Then she thanked all the contestants for participating in the First Annual Coffee Creek Barbecue Competition. "I predict it won't be the last!" The crowd roared.

"Now, for sausage!" called the mayor. She adjusted her purple glasses, bent her head to the tally list, and announced the winners. The teams came forward, waved their hats, waved their ribbons, slapped each other on the back, and were corralled into place by Councilman

Hinojosa.

"Pork ribs!" More winners.

"Pork butt!" She announced a tie for first. Whoops of delight from the crowd as both sets of first-place contestants crowded onto the dais.

Finally, "Brisket!" The crowd cheered, then breathless silence fell. The mayor paused, letting the drama build.

White curls gleaming in the sun, the mayor announced: "Third place: the Bandera Brisketvagen." Harvey and his three teammates surged forward, doffing their gimme caps, smiling proudly.

"Second place: the Seguin Slow Burn!" Whoops, cheers. The Seguin Slow Burn, a portly quartet in jeans, suspenders, and cowboy hats, wanted to thank everyone, but the mayor refused to hand over the mike.

The mayor surveyed the crowd, enjoying the suspense. "Okay. Ladies and gentlemen, our judges have awarded first place for brisket to"—and here she paused—"wait for it"—she paused another second —"the Coffee Creek Revival! Yes, we're talking about those three little kettle grills!" The crowd cheered.

M.A. started forward, waving and grinning. Holy cow, thought Alice, wondering if Val would join her in front of all these people.

"Bring your team!" ordered the mayor. "We've got to have pictures."

M.A. grabbed Val and headed up to the dais. Caswell followed, pulling a shy Davie by the hand. Davie's other hand clutched his drone to his chest. They lined up with the second- and third-place teams. Cameras flashed.

"Judge Sandoval, you're the chief judge. On behalf of the judges do you want to say anything?" The mayor handed him the microphone.

"Well, Your Honor," he said, "in this outstanding—I mean outstanding—competition, we congratulate every team. We must say that for first-place sausage, texture and taste combined brilliantly. For first-place ribs, succulence matched crunch and taste. For first-place pork butt, unctuousness reigned. And for first-place brisket"—here he nodded at M.A.—"for first-place brisket, the queen of meats"—he shook his head, an admiring smile on his face—"for first-place brisket, the combination of dark crunch, tender insides, and a mysterious but addictive rub raised the bar very high. We judges"— he looked around at Tan and Robicheaux, both nodding judiciously, and at the other two judges—"as I say, we judges are honored, I say, *deeply* honored to have participated in this stellar competition. We congratulate the winners."

Big cheers. The crowd milled around the winners, taking selfies proudly with their favorites. M.A.'s former students mobbed her, cheering and demanding to have their pictures taken with their high school biology teacher. Alice watched as Val, Davie, and Caswell quietly moved to the side, letting M.A. bask in the happy faces of the friends crowding around her.

A hint of too-sweet fragrance: Annette Black materialized next to Alice. Alice followed her gaze as Annette looked from M.A., surrounded by students, to Val, Caswell, and Davie standing in a knot nearby: three generations, close together. Val placed her hands gently on Davie's shoulders, smiled down at the top of his head. Annette's shoulders tensed. She clenched her hands at her breast. Like when you're holding the racket, set at the net to receive a volley, Alice thought, watching this reunion with interest.

Val, still gazing fondly down at Davie, felt the eyes on her. She looked up, straight at Annette, and she too tensed, erasing her face of emotion.

Annette walked forward. "Darling Valentine!"

Val stuck out her hand, fending off the proffered embrace. "Hello, Annette." No smile, just an unblinking examination.

"So good to see you, Valentine! It's been so long!"

"Forty years." Still Val scrutinized Annette. What was she looking for? Alice wondered. "And I go by Val now. You're well, Annette?"

"We're just fine. Just fine . . . Val. You know Clay's president of Cowman's Bank? In fact, he had to miss the judging because he had to run back to the bank for a meeting. And he's planning to retire now that the bank's being bought. I think he might run for the electric co-op board. He's so knowledgeable, everyone wants him on every committee in town."

Val nodded, eyes wide, encouraging Annette to talk. Val doesn't want Annette near her boys, Alice guessed.

Annette asked, "What brought you back? Clay says you're staying with M.A.? Did you come just for the barbecue competition?"

Val said, "M.A. persuaded me to join her."

"But Val—I mean Val, are you back? Have you come back for good?" Annette pressed. "Clay told me just before the judging that you've bought the Tindall place. I didn't even know it was for sale. Does that mean you'll be living here?" She looked around. "And Caswell? And your grandson? Are you all coming back, then?" The mix of hope and dread in Annette's voice shook Alice.

"No. Caswell was looking for an investment property."

"But won't you want to go out and at least spend the night at the Tindall place now that you've closed?"

"We just thought it was a great chance to invest in land," Caswell said. He and Davie had moved closer to his mother. "We're happy living where we are."

"Where are you living now?"

Val smiled. "I'm staying with M.A. at the moment." She glanced toward M.A. "And we'd better go get packed up!"

"But we'll come down sometimes, won't we, Dad?" Davie piped up hopefully.

Caswell smiled at him but didn't answer.

M.A. strode up. "Well! How about it?" She waved her hand toward the tent, the judges, the onlookers. "Smoked 'em, we did. Hee! And now I need my team to help me get the grills packed up. Good to see you, Annette."

Alice watched as Val and M.A. turned and headed across the park toward the Weber grills. Caswell followed, holding Davie's hand. Davie turned back to wave at Annette.

Her face was stark.

Chapter Thirteen

"Knock Me a Kiss"

At five that afternoon Kinsear was back at Alice's. He whistled when Alice emerged in jeans, boots, and the jacket embroidered with yellow roses. "Rodeo-festive this whole weekend," she said.

"We could head for the Beer Barn right now, or we could stay here and I could admire you a little longer," said Kinsear. "I could admire you with enthusiasm."

"The Pianorama starts in thirty minutes," said Alice.

But after he slid the jacket back down her arms, she knew they'd be late.

* * * * *

Tonight in the parking lot the Beer Barn's portable lighted sign read: "I would give all my fame for a pot of ale and safety. Henry V, Act III Scene 2."

"I completely agree," Kinsear said, nodding toward the sign as he held the door for Alice.

Inside, the air smelled of hops, hamburgers, and barbecue. The Beer Barons had saved a small table for Alice and Kinsear close to the stage. Already warming up were six piano players perched at six large keyboards. Alice smiled to herself, noting how vividly individual the six were. They each looked different and favored different styles of boogie, but right now they were joking with each other and drawing energy from the crowd. As she and Kinsear slipped into their seats, Doc Mason from Driftwood—oldest of the piano players—grabbed the microphone: "We're starting off with a tribute to Louis Jordan —'Ain't Nobody Here but Us Chickens!'" And he played and sang, mugging for the crowd, while the other five piano players had fun with variations on the thumping left-hand pattern.

Alice noticed that her own face, of its own accord, was smiling. She whispered to Kinsear, "Why is it boogie-woogie makes everyone grin?"

"That's the simple truth." Kinsear surveyed the crowd. The happy atmosphere expanded as the piano players tossed back and forth variations on "Saturday Night Fish Fry."

Doc Mason intoned, "Now, the 'Blue Light Boogie.' Time to grab your honey and show us you can slow dance, but a little bit fast." People started dancing around the tables and down by the stage. Kinsear pulled Alice out of her chair, grabbed her waist, joined the dancers. Then came "Choo Choo Ch'Boogie." One of the piano players leaned into his mike. "Time for some ro-mance, Doc. Louis Jordan style! Here comes 'Knock Me a Kiss.'" Kinsear sang along on that one, acted out a little bit, too.

Floyd Domino, cowboy hat pulled low, announced a switch. "Now you're going to hear from an almost forgotten keyboard hero, Freddie Slack! Let's start with one we played last night. See how it sounds with six players, not just two. It's 'Down the Road a Piece.'" The left hand started, gripped, built, and just when Alice thought she couldn't wait a second longer, the right hand pounded into life.

"I love this one so much," she told Kinsear.

"Just wait," he said. "Here comes the magic trick."

And it came . . . a rippling right-hand run, a slalom down the keyboard, the sequences of keys overlapping, harmonizing, surging together with the rock-steady left hand. "Oh, yeah," said Alice, mesmerized.

Domino nodded to the player next to him, who picked up the lead, started a reprise. As the set wound down Domino announced, "Now for one I'll bet you've never heard. This is Freddie Slack's theme song, 'Strange Cargo.'"

The odd left-hand rhythm caught the crowd, hushed the crowd. The right hand's haunting theme played once, got more complex, began to create dreams, memories, ambitions. When it ended, the room was quiet, then rapturous. "Again! Encore!"

They played it again, took a break.

* * * * *

"Ms. Greer! We want to thank you!"

Alice turned from the bar where she and Kinsear were waiting for their Negra Modelos and found two lean seventysomethings, a six-foot man, a five-foot woman, beaming at her. The man stuck out his hand. "Wayne Tindall! And this is—"

"Louise Tindall," piped up his wife, soft white hair, twinkly eyes. "We just want to say thank you! We didn't get to meet you at the closing, you know."

"It's not that common for a lawyer to get thanked by the folks on the other side." Alice grinned at them, then introduced Ben Kinsear.

"We're just so happy about selling our ranch. It was fast, no one knew about it, and now we're off on our trip around the world. This is our farewell party!" Louise pointed at a rowdy group at a table close to the Beer Barn stage.

"Around the world?"

"Yep," said Wayne. "Tomorrow we fly to London. Then we take that Chunnel to Paris."

"Paris!" echoed Louise. "The Louvre! The Eiffel Tower! Then down to Monte Carlo so Wayne can see the casino, walk in there like James Bond—"

"Holding tight to my wallet, though," Wayne added. "Then we're flying to Hong Kong. I haven't been there since R&R in sixty-eight."

"And Bali. And then Australia, and New Zealand!" said Louise. "We got two of those round-the-world tickets."

"Are you ever coming back?"

"Oh, probably!" Louise said, grinning at Wayne. "But we're delighted to be off the ranch. It was getting to be too much. And we're thrilled that little Caswell Jr. has it now, after all these years. We knew him when he was a baby."

"You did?"

"Oh yes," said Louise. "His parents were the sweetest people, the best neighbors. We always watched after each other's animals, you know." Her voice broke and she stopped.

Wayne spoke. "The little boy loved our creek, Quartz Creek. I saw him one day hanging onto their side of our gate, just looking at the water. I could see him from up at the house, you know. I walked down and said, 'Come in, neighbor!' I think he was maybe four. We walked down along the creek. He squatted down, picked up a white quartz pebble, looked up at me. I told him the name—you can find some real pretty white quartz pebbles along the creek bottom where the pink granite's showing. You know, that pink granite magma uplift underlies the whole ranch."

Alice nodded.

"I told him, maybe you'll study rocks! Maybe you'll be a geologist when you grow up! And I told him to pick out some creek pebbles. 'You can take those home to show your mama,' I said. And about then we heard his mama calling for him, so I walked him up out of the creek to the gate and I opened it and he ran back up the hill to his place." He shook his head. "Such a shame, what happened to his dad."

"I can't understand that Clay Black," said Louise. "He had to know that auger was dangerous."

That caught Alice's interest big-time. "The post-hole digger? How would Clay know that?"

"A worker trying to string fence for a ranch another mile down the road nearly lost his leg on that thing. The ranch owner wanted to get rid of it. I don't know if Clay bought it or the rancher just gave it to him, but I know Clay had it sitting in his barn," Wayne said.

"But would Clay have known about the injured worker?"

"Oh, I think everyone in the area knew about it," Louise said.

"Were you there the day Caswell—," Alice started.

"No. No, we were taking my mother back to Houston, to the hospital. If we'd even known he was going to try to use that beast, we'd have said something. Wayne would have offered to help Caswell. Caswell wasn't really himself yet. Still weak where he'd been hit. He should never have tried to use that machine by himself." Louise shuddered. "It just broke my heart."

"That's one reason we're so glad his son reappeared and bought our place," Wayne said. "It's like some sort of closure. That little boy always loved the creek. Maybe it'll—I don't know, wash away some of the blood." He looked bemused. "Can't believe I said that."

"You said it just right, darling." Louise tiptoed and kissed him. "Let's go dance." She turned back, wise eyes examining Alice. "Thanks again. We appreciate how you seemed to make everything go fast and smooth. Maybe that boy and his mother will have some peace now."

Peace? Alice thought. Val's face, Val's watchful eyes, rose before her. What would peace look like, to Val?

"Safe travels," Alice said.

At their table by the stage, between sets, Alice told Kinsear the rest of the story about Caswell's father. He winced. "God almighty, Alice, an auger like that, by *himself*?" He shook his head ruefully. "When we first got the Fredericksburg ranch I swaggered down to the rent-all and had them load one of those suckers in my truck. My new welcome-home-to-Texas truck. I motored off in my boots and jeans, in my too-new straw hat, trying to look like I knew what to do with it. Alice, I got that thing out on the ground and looked at it hard. Basically it was an outboard motor with this vicious pointed steel screw sort of thing about three feet long, maybe longer. Two big handles stuck out on each side of the motor on top. I started it up and"—here he looked up blankly, shook his head—"I was holding both handles and aiming for my proposed post hole location. I lowered the handles, to engage the clutch. That sucker bucked and bounced up into the air and started bounding around, me trying to control it, no hope of getting it to bite into the ground. When you let go of the handles, it's supposed to quit augering. I'm not really sure how I managed to turn it off. Actually I think I flung it down on the ground and crept up on the motor and turned it off. Finally wrestled it back into the truck bed.

"Then I drove it back to the rent-all. They just looked at me, maybe a very small twinkle in their eyes, as if to say, How'd you like Mr. Auger, big boy?"

"You're bigger than Caswell, and he's supposedly the same size as his dad," Alice said, imagining Kinsear, with his longer legs and greater height and strength, struggling to manhandle the auger. "One person said maybe it hit a rock and bounced up and got Caswell Sr. in the leg."

Kinsear looked at his beer, shook his head. "I've wondered sometimes what that's like, to bleed out, how long you stay conscious, what you're thinking."

The piano players were back, joined by a fiddler and a singer in a cowboy hat. Whose turn to start? Ah, the singer, who launched into "Texas Blues," Bob Wills style. Kinsear turned to her. "Alice. Let's dance. I need some dancing and I plan to hold you tight."

So he did, and they kept dancing, tangled up in the throng by the stage, through "Texas Blues" and "Pinetop's Boogie Woogie" until the extremely rapid end of the "Bob Wills Boogie." Flying fingers, flying violin bow, flying booted feet. The crowd burst into applause. Kinsear and Alice, sweaty, panting, clapped with them, looked at each other.

Then more dancing, more piano, and Kinsear whispered to Alice, "Can we go home?"

By which he meant her house. So they did. They opened the French doors. Orion was up in the sky. "The mighty hunter, back from New York," Kinsear said. "Don't I remind you a little of Orion?"

"Oh yes," Alice giggled. Then she said, "I'm really glad you came back," and kissed Kinsear, right in front of Orion, Sirius, Arcturus, and other onlookers, who didn't even blink.

Chapter   Fourteen

Dark Smoke

A Sunday morning drive with Kinsear. With Caswell and Val and Davie en route to Colorado after the barbecue competition, Alice had promised to check on the Tindall place. She'd stowed the house keys and the gate combination in her purse.

On the hills rippled the dried grasses of fall—the bronze of bushy bluestem holding high its white cottony seedheads, Canada wild rye bending with heavy curves of seeds, King Ranch bluestem with three-pronged seedheads like turkey tracks. In the ditches, splotches of bright yellow cosmos rose above white cushions of blackfoot daisies. Relaxed, Alice ran her hand around the back of Kinsear's neck, regretting his bucket seats. She'd like to lean a little closer, but seat belts, so unromantic, prevented such an incursion.

Ahead to the north a thin plume of dark smoke wavered in the pale blue sky, rose higher. "Someone's burn pile?" said Kinsear.

"There shouldn't be any," Alice said. "Llano County's got a burn ban on right now. Okay, we should be almost to the gravel road where we turn."

The road carried the old Land Cruiser around a bend and up a rise.

"Goddammit, you asshole!" yelled Kinsear, running the Land Cruiser almost into the ditch after dodging a black Chevy pickup that roared over the hill, right down the centerline.

"Yikes!" said Alice, releasing her tense grip on the dashboard and armrest. "He almost hit us!" She looked over her shoulder at the disappearing truck.

"Taking his half out of the middle. What an idiot," Kinsear muttered.

"There on the left, that's the road to the Tindalls' gate."

"Dust's still rising. I'll bet that guy just turned off this road."

They turned left on the gravel road that bisected the Bond and Black ranches. Alice, as was her habit, was mentally matching satellite view and survey and topo maps to the actual landscape. She pointed to the mailbox at a driveway leading left: "That's the half of the family ranch that Val owns, where Caswell's dad died." She pointed right, up the facing driveway leading into Clay Black's half of the ranch, with its gate and high fence: "That's Clay's drive. You can see his house up there at the top of his driveway." She peered uphill but could see no vehicles at his place.

"Almost there," said Alice. "This road tees into the Tindall gate."

The Tindalls' green ranch gate stood ajar. Its heavy chain, severed, lay in the gravel, the real estate broker's lock still attached.

"Took a big bolt cutter to do that," Kinsear said.

Alice stared up the long ridge to the west, at the fast-rising smoke plume. "Ben! There's where the smoke's coming from! Hurry!"

Kinsear drove in and veered right as the driveway curved and zig-zagged up a rugged hill crowned with live oaks. From the hilltop thick black smoke poured into the sky. At the top Kinsear skidded to a stop. The Tindall ranch house faced them, inside the usual "yard fence" that kept out livestock. The gate into the gravel parking area stood open. Through the window of the garage attached to the house Alice saw orange flames. The garage door was closed but tongues of fire licked its edges, moving higher and higher toward the roof of the house. Alice frantically called 911, repeated the address, told the dispatcher the ranch gate was open and the fire looked bad. "How close are you?"

"About four miles," said the dispatcher. Yikes, Alice thought.

Kinsear, already through the gate, grabbed a hose from the flowerbed by the front door and aimed water at the roof. Alice felt a rumble, then a deafening bang. The garage window blew out, shards of glass narrowly missing Kinsear. A wall of flame erupted from the roof. Sparks caught the dry grass. Kinsear backed away, spraying the yard and the gravel parking area.

"Get back! The propane tank!" yelled Alice, waving toward the Tindalls' propane supply, sitting just outside the yard fence. If it went—

Still spraying, Kinsear backed away, trying to soak the parking area, trying to stop fire from creeping across to the propane tank, from escaping the yard and lighting up the dry cedar, then the surrounding pastures with their tall brown fall grass. "Get the car out of the way!" he shouted.

Alice backed the Land Cruiser further down the drive. "Please don't get too close, Ben!" she yelled. She knew the house had a rainwater collection system—Caswell was tickled about that—and also a well. How long could the precious tank of water last?

It took an endless five minutes of Kinsear furiously spraying the house before the first Llano County VFD truck careened up the ranch drive, followed by the volunteer fire chief's SUV. Flames still billowed from the roof. Rafters collapsed, crackling. The chief climbed out, watched the firemen assessing, assigning tasks, bending a hard stream of water. "Something in the garage blew up right after we got here," Alice warned.

The chief walked up to the fence, called to the firemen. They regrouped further back, still directing their hoses at the burning house. The chief looked inquiringly at Alice and Kinsear.

"Alice Greer, from Coffee Creek," said Alice.

"Ben Kinsear," said Ben. "Fredericksburg."

"You're not the owners?"

"I represent the buyers," Alice said. She handed him a card. "They just closed on Friday and had to leave again for Colorado. We came up to check on the place. We saw the smoke and then saw the gate chain was cut. Something blew up in the garage after we got here."

"You know anything about what's in the garage? Welding equipment, gas containers?"

She tried to remember the inventory, shook her head. "Nothing I can think of. I think the water heater's electric. The propane tank's for the kitchen. Mrs. Tindall liked cooking with gas." She stopped, thinking of the black Chevy in a tearing hurry, roaring over the hill at them. "We might need the sheriff."

"He's on the way."

Above the house the dark smoke faded, replaced by gray. The steady play of water on the roof and garage slowly subdued the flames, but already blackened shingles reached across most of the roof. As she watched, part of the roof collapsed. The firemen had crept out to assure themselves that the valve to the propane tank was properly cut off. They stood by the driveway gate, spraying steadily, waiting for the fire to give up, die out. The country air reeked with the heavy smell of dirty smoke, burnt Formica, burnt wallboard. Inside they heard a wrenching sound, then a *thunk* inside what Alice assumed was the kitchen. "Counter's coming down," said a fireman.

A Llano County Sheriff's Office SUV crunched up the dirt road. The fire chief nodded his head toward Alice and Kinsear. The sheriff, six feet tall, two hundred twenty pounds, walked slowly over. Alice and Kinsear each shook his hand, provided cards, explained again why they'd driven up on Sunday morning to check out the house.

The sheriff showed some interest in the black Chevy. No, they didn't get the license. But: "I think there might've been a Coffee Creek High decal on the rear window," Kinsear said. "I just got a glimpse in the rearview mirror. Looked like a paw print, maroon and gold."

"I saw that too," Alice said.

"Hmmph," said the sheriff. "Anything else? Was there a brush guard?"

"No brush guard. But the tailgate was missing."

"Only hundreds of trucks around here like that."

Kinsear nodded. Carrying a long load you might take off your tailgate. Then you might keep it off until you needed it again. A tailgate could be hard to put back on by yourself; you might have to wait until a buddy came to help.

"No gas can in the back of the truck, then?"

"Not that I could see."

"Who was in the truck?"

"Just the driver. An older male, sunglasses, ball cap," Kinsear said.

"Ever seen him before?"

Kinsear shook his head.

Alice squinted her eyes, trying to retrieve the fleeting image of the man's jutting jaw and frown. "There was something familiar," she said, "but—I can't say."

The sheriff had his notebook out. "Your clients have home insurance?"

Alice nodded. "I believe so."

"You said they're gone. When did they leave?"

"They were leaving this morning from Coffee Creek, driving back to Colorado."

"We'll need to talk to them."

"They were staying in Coffee Creek with Ms. M.A. Ellison." She gave him contact information for M.A. and Caswell. "I think they were leaving pretty early."

"And they didn't come out here to stay in their new ranch house, because—?" He nodded toward the front windows. "I see some furniture in there."

A fair question. Alice had once slept with Jordie right on the floor in their empty new house. So eager to spend the night in their own new place, they'd decided they could do without a mattress. So they bedded down right on the hard floor, with only the picnic blanket from her car, but (as she pushed back the memory) that was in another country, and besides, the man was dead.

Instead she said, "The new owners didn't stay, because Dr. Bond needed to get his son back to Colorado in time for school tomorrow. On furniture, the sellers only agreed to leave a couple of porch rockers and the kitchen table and chairs. That's it. They supposedly moved everything else out by last Wednesday." The Tindalls' broker had told Caswell's broker that Mrs. Tindall would certainly have all the furniture out by then so she could do a thorough cleaning, being "house proud," as her broker said.

The sheriff naturally entertained the possibility that a burning house meant any new owner was after insurance money. Insurers wouldn't pay if an owner committed or procured arson. It seemed pretty bold, though, to burn your new house down just two days after closing. As for Caswell, he'd told Alice he'd roamed around the ranch on Thursday, before closing, but so far as Alice knew he hadn't been back since.

A white US Post Office van bounced up the drive and parked behind the sheriff. Alice knew that the post office, trying to balance its budget, now handled Sunday deliveries. The driver emerged, in his blue post-office shirt and shorts. "Sheriff," said the driver. "Ma'am," he said to Alice. He nodded at Kinsear, then focused on the firefighters. "Just glad to see the guys are putting it out. I called it in about half an hour ago."

"Then you saw it before we did," Alice said.

"Yeah. I was driving down the highway and the smoke just didn't look like a brush fire or grass fire. Too dark. So I came on down here past the Blacks' place and saw the gate open and the chain on the ground."

"You see anyone?" said the sheriff.

"Let me think. Out on the highway earlier I saw some of the neighbors go by on their way to church, back toward town." He tilted his head, nodded north. "I don't think I saw anyone else." He squinted up at the diminishing plume of smoke. "I've got to finish these deliveries. Call me if you need me." He left.

"Sheriff?" a burly fireman called from outside the burnt-out garage door. "You need to see this."

The sheriff stalked over, talked to the fireman, peered into the garage. He came back. "There was a big ol' gas can in there. Metal, two gallons. Pretty rusty and there's a hole in the top. That's prob'ly what you heard blow up. We really need to talk to your client."

Alice found Caswell's number. "Caswell? Where are you?" She listened. "Between Santa Anna and Abilene?" So Caswell, Val and Davie were already over three hours north of Coffee Creek. "Listen, the Tindall house caught fire."

"What?" said Caswell.

"I'm handing the phone to the sheriff."

She did so. The sheriff walked off with her phone, where she couldn't hear.

He came back. "I'll be asking the Tindalls about that gas can."

Alice nodded. "If you can get them before they leave the country, on their trip around the world."

"Sheriff?" Same burly firefighter. He gestured, pointed downhill to the north of the house, to Alice's right.

The sheriff followed him.

"I think I know what they're looking at," Kinsear said quietly. "There's a patch of burnt grass on the far side of the gravel parking area, just inside the fence. If I had to guess—thinking about the dark smoke we saw, driving up, and the blast of dark smoke after the explosion, right?"

Alice nodded.

"Gasoline and kerosene both burn dark. But you'd have to be nuts to light a fire with just gasoline. I'm betting someone left that big gasoline can in the garage, then started a fire leading across the gravel parking area into the garage, using kerosene or at least something that would give that person enough lead time to make it back to his truck."

So it'll be important to know who left that gas can and how much gas was in it, Alice thought. An old rusty can like that—she imagined it standing in the Tindalls' barn, or old well house. A little leftover fuel from some project, waiting for a rainy day. But the firefighters hadn't mentioned finding a kerosene can anywhere on the premises.

Alice and Kinsear walked around the fenced parking area to the far side, staying clear of the firemen. Alice gazed across and down the hilltop toward a line of trees along the creek that ran the length of the Tindall place. Then she turned her head north, staring down at the smaller hill across the Tindall fence line. Clay Black's ranch house, and bunkhouse, and barn. "Look, Ben," she said, pointing. "Clay Black was right. Look how the Tindall ranch house overlooks his place."

Alice had imagined how she'd hate having someone overlook her place: she'd feel the uphill neighbor had a more brilliant view of the stars at night, an unfairly larger share of the landscape. She'd feel short-changed, because the neighbors' view was bigger than hers: it included *her* property. But it was worse than she'd imagined. She turned to Kinsear. "You'd know every time you went outside, ran after the donkeys, sniffed a rose, that the neighbors could see you."

"No more nighttime revels in the yard." He squeezed her hand.

So, yes, she understood why Clay Black wished he'd bought the Tindall ranch. But surely not enough to set it on fire. Right?

* * * * *

They drove back, mostly silent, both thinking about what they'd seen. Kinsear headed to the airport to catch his flight to New York. "I'll probably be up there another week, Alice. Maybe we can finish up sooner. I hope so."

That night Alice took a long shower to get the smoke out of her hair. Not a great end to the week. She hoped next week would be better.

Chapter Fifteen

Saddle Up,
Kiddo

Monday morning: Red Griffin on the phone. "Alice? Talk me down. I'm so angry!" Voice trembling with fury.

"What in the world?" said Alice. She'd almost never heard her best friend this mad. Red combined the sharp brain of a CPA (which she was) with the blonde looks and big smile of a former high school rodeo queen (which she also was). After she'd left her high-powered Houston firm for Coffee Creek, to set up a rescue ranch for abused horses, she'd talked Alice into moving her law practice from Austin to Coffee Creek. Red's favorite color was red—for clothes, for cars. But she usually wasn't *seeing* red.

"Alice, that damn electric co-op—totally incompetent! My power is out for the third time in two weeks! It's been out all morning! I can't run water because the pump won't work! I can't water the horses, I can't fill the troughs, I can't do bills on the computer, I can't do anything! Well, that's not quite true. The gate works on solar power so at least I can get off my property. I'm tempted to drive to the co-op office and have a hissy fit in front of God and everybody. They're so inefficient! And so disorganized! And they don't give a damn about their customers!"

"Are you having the same problem every time?"

"Yes! They promised me a year ago they'd be upgrading the lines from the highway to my place. But they haven't. I asked if it was in the long-range plan. They said yes, but not on their list yet. I hate to keep berating the poor lineman. I drove out once and confronted him and he 'ma'amed' me over and over, apologized, practically cried. He said he wished he could replace the transformer and upgrade the lines but the co-op is telling the line guys just to put Band-Aids on everything. My neighbors are furious too. They're on the same line. One man said he lost all the meat in his freezer this last go-round."

She paused. "That neighbor told me I should run for the co-op board." She paused again. "So did two of the cowboys I do taxes for." Red, adored by local cowboys, had started helping them with their taxes and, after urging from Alice, set up a limited liability corporation for her niche accounting practice: tax returns for rodeo competitors. She also served on the board of the nonprofit Coffee Creek Riders. "There's a little upheaval going on. Wally Phifer—you know he's been general manager forever—he announced in July he's going to retire by the end of the year. And you remember that the chairman of the co-op board died a couple of weeks ago? So now his board seat is actually coming up for a special election."

"Maybe you *should* run, Red!" Alice said, interested. Visions of Red on campaign posters, cowgirl hat tilted, CPA skills highlighted, popped into Alice's head. "What's your slogan?"

"Responsible government! Transparency, reliability, and accountability! But come on, Alice, I don't have time for that."

"Yes, you do. You'd read over the financials and know just what's needed, with your steel-trap CPA brain." Alice was quite taken with the idea.

"Actually," Red confessed, "the lineman said the same thing. He said I should run for the open slot. He said he'd also heard that Clay Black might run for it, and that Clay Black is tight as a tick with Wally. He says the co-op keeps some accounts at Cowman's Bank. But he says Clay hasn't filed yet."

Alice pulled up the co-op website on the computer. "Listen, Red, you've only got a few hours to make up your mind. Filing deadline is today at five p.m."

Silence on the phone. She could almost hear Red thinking, calculating.

"Poster," Alice said. "Your picture. Boots. Red: Reliability, transparency, accountability! But you need to get over there with your filing fee."

"There's another item of interest, Alice. I had to finish my annual CPA classes last week. I ate lunch with a woman from Coffee Creek who works in accounting over at the county offices. Her husband's a repair supervisor at the co-op. She said he's been asking her why the co-op's always dipping into reserves and not making capital repairs."

"Poor management?" asked Alice.

"Maybe. I'd like to know the answer myself."

"Well, saddle up, kiddo. This might be fun."

* * * * *

Red held an impromptu campaign planning meeting that Monday night at the Beer Barn, with enthusiastic attendance of some of the Coffee Creek Riders. The word was that Clay Black had filed shortly before Red did, and that a local barrel racer, Ginny Lou Hamer, had filed at the very last minute.

On Tuesday morning, climbing into her truck, Alice noticed that her truck's inspection sticker would expire in two days. Damn, she thought. Better take it to the garage today. Then, roaring down the creek road toward Coffee Creek, Alice spied a new campaign sign at the intersection just north of town: "CLAY BLACK FOR CO-OP BOARD: EXPERIENCED LEADERSHIP!" This race could be serious. Alice wondered if Red knew the property owners. Maybe they'd let Red put up a sign too.

Red on Alice's cell phone. "Alice? Alice, have you looked at Facebook today?"

"No. What?"

"Someone posted an ad saying 'Airhead cowgirl or commonsense banker? Your choice is clear!'"

"Airhead?" Alice bristled. "You've managed a major law firm, started your own business — make that businesses. Who posted that ad?"

"A group called Coffee Creek Common Sense."

"What's that?"

"No idea."

Alice hung up, caught Silla on her cell phone, and explained the problem. "Can you find out who the hell this is?" She had great confidence in Silla's investigative talent.

"Sounds like a trip to the Camellia Diner. I'll be back."

Alice knew that every morning a few of Silla's courthouse buddies met for coffee at the diner, requisitioning the corner booth.

Thirty minutes later Silla popped her head around Alice's door, red ponytail bobbing. "There's a new LLC called Coffee Creek Common Sense. An Austin lawyer, Gary Thorn, filed the registration online. No other names appear. The word from the corner booth is that this new LLC could be a front for Clay Black. But there's no evidence, really, except somebody checked back in the records and found Gary Thorn also registered Clay Black's LLC for his hunt club at his ranch."

She grinned. "Do not ask me who did the checking."

"Aha." Alice thought for a minute. "Silla, if you wanted to counter this kind of trash, how would you do it?"

"Red's horse buddies—the Coffee Creek Riders. I'll do a post and comment on the ad and they'll all, I mean all, support Red. I'll start calling. Also Red should get her own ads up right away. Does she have a campaign organization yet?"

"Reclaim Your Co-op—Red for Responsible Government! Red put in a rush order for some signs at the print shop."

"Kind of clunky," Silla sniffed. But in her well-connected way Silla managed to schedule a meet-and-greet for Red late that same day at the historic Roscoe House in Coffee Creek, then persuaded the *Coffee Creek Caller* to send a photographer to take pictures of the Coffee Creek Riders waving signs for Red.

Alice sighed. Better go get the truck taken care of.

* * * * *

An hour before lunch Alice parked her tan Toyota truck and walked into the Coffee Creek Central Garage, a downtown fixture. She trusted the owner, Leo Koziar, a tall, long-limbed man, his face elongated as in an El Greco painting, but always smiling. Leo offered customers his smile and a firm handshake while keeping an eagle eye on his mechanics and his bottom line. Inside the echoing garage Alice waited at the cashier's window behind a burly T-shirted man sporting a Garrison Distillery cap.

"Now I just need this truck to pass inspection, Russell," the burly man drawled to the cashier. "This ol' gal's twenty years old." He and the cashier squinted out the open doors at a battered red Ford F-150.

"Didn't you have that one back when you played center for Coffee Creek?" Russell joked.

"No, but one just like it. This'n's my haulin' buddy."

"Okay. We should be through with the inspection in half an hour."

"Well, don't just go looking for problems, okay?"

Russell smiled. The truck owner shambled over to the office wall and stared at some photos—Alice thought they were football team pictures. Then he wandered back outside.

Her turn. She said, "Russell, my Toyota's parked out there. I'm due for inspection. And could you change the oil?"

"Sure. Can you wait for about forty-five minutes?"

Alice nodded and chose a beat-up chair—the cleanest looking—from the row outside the cashier's window. Refugees from an old dinette set, she thought. She pulled out her phone and began scrolling through emails.

"That your truck out there?" The big guy was back, thumbing toward the parking lot. "Tan Toyota?" He sat down beside her, trying to fit his frame into the too-small chair.

"Yes," Alice nodded.

Silence. "Are those bullet holes in the back?"

Surprised, she turned, surveyed the square face, a couple of days' beard, blue eyes looking right at her. "Yes."

"How'd you get those?"

Should she tell the long story about her driving, dodging, twisting, turning, hiding under the overpass from the gunman on the helicopter?

"I was driving my client to a groundwater conservation district meeting. Someone didn't want us to get there."

"What happened to the someone?"

"He . . . um . . . didn't make it."

Unblinking, he continued looking at her, and nodded slowly. "Are you that Alice Greer?"

She nodded back. He stuck out a large, large hand. "Sounds like you are a—a *person* to ride the river with." She appreciated his modification of the old saying, which went, *a man to ride the river with.* "I'm Eddie LaFarge. Glad to meet you."

"I see you've kept your truck a long time too."

"Yep. Nothing wrong with that truck that a facelift and complete transmission overhaul wouldn't fix. I've got another means of transportation, a' course. But a guy my size—a truck feels about right."

Now she was curious. "What's the other means of transportation?" She was guessing a giant SUV, an Armada, an Invasion, a Flotilla.

122

"Porsche. I like to do a little racing."

Heavens. "Where can you do that?"

"Oh, there are places. I've got a short road course out on my ranch."

She raised her eyebrows.

"Sounds like you've occasionally had to do some fancy driving yourself," he said.

She laughed, then grimaced a bit, thinking of the helicopter incident.

"Seriously, you want to come out some time and try the Porsche? Or if you don't want to do that, I could coach you on some defensive driving in that truck of yours." He nodded his head toward the parking lot. "These roads out here can be dangerous." He looked at her again. "For a practicing lawyer."

"What do you do for a living, Mr. LaFarge?" His name was familiar, and his face, but she didn't remember actually meeting him.

"I'm retired. I played a little football."

Ah. The penny dropped. He'd played for—who? Some pro team back in the day—a linebacker? No. Center. Her dad had taught Alice to respect centers deeply. "They control the key, Alice." And hadn't her dad mentioned LaFarge with approval?

LaFarge went on. "Last few years I've had a place out north of here. Maybe you've heard of the winery? Raptor Cellars?"

"That rings a bell. What wines are you making?"

"The first ones came out just this fall. This may sound weird . . . . I'm trying to use local grapes for more old-world-style wines." He gazed at her, appraisingly. "You think that's odd, given that we're in the middle of the Hill Country?"

She shrugged. "Old world—like what?"

"This fall, my first Viognier. And sitting in barrels waiting for another year, a Sangiovese and a Mourvèdre. I mess around some with the barrels. You know, different types of oak."

Alice actually had no idea. "Why would that make any difference?"

At that moment the employee called from his window, "Hey, Mr. LaFarge! Your truck passed. It's ready to go."

He stood, dug in his jeans for a card, handed it to Alice. "I'm inviting you out to a wine tasting. Tomorrow at four. Bring a friend if you
want." Pause. "I mean it about the driving, too. George Files told me
about your little helicopter stunt. You ought to work on your driving.
Lemme know."

LaFarge sauntered out to the beat-up Ford F-150. The cashier
called to Alice. "Ms. Greer? Yours is almost ready." She walked up to
the window to pay. He said, "That Eddie is one great fellow. You know
he played high school football here?"

Alice shook her head no.

He nodded toward the wall. "Check out the pictures. Of course
Mr. Leo's up there with him. They won regionals, back then."

Oh. Now that was interesting. She scanned the players, the front
row kneeling in white uniforms, each resting one hand on a helmet
on the ground. Then in the back row she saw what had to be Eddie
LaFarge and Leo, heads a little tilted like they'd just made a joke and
been told to hush. "Wildcats Class of '77," the caption said. Her
eyes moved to a black-and-white photo hanging to the right, labeled
"Wildcats Class of '64." Wasn't that about Clay Black's vintage? Alice
squinted at the caption. Damn, she needed reading glasses. Did it
say—yes, it said "Clay Black." She found him in the second row, staring straight into the lens, next to someone who looked like Leo's twin.

And at that moment Leo himself came around the corner. "Aw,
you're lookin' at the glory days." He stood next to her, grinning.
"That's the year we won state. Field was covered with ice that day."

Leo's sunny smile was irresistible. Alice smiled back. "I was talking
to your customer Eddie LaFarge."

"Yup, there he is. Good man. We were buddies." Leo pointed
at the picture on the left. "There we both are. I had hair back then.
Okay, we got your truck all set, changed the oil. But with those bullet holes—you ever think about getting another vehicle, Ms. Greer?
Something new and zippy?"

"Not yet. That truck's running fine, thanks to you!"

"Yeah, and I guess those bullet holes are badges of courage, sort of.
I read that in high school."

Alice returned to the cashier's window to sign the charge slip. Out of the corner of her eye she saw another man round the corner from the office, heading for Leo. He looked almost like Leo's twin—tall, long limbed, long faced—but older, balder, sparer. No smile: instead, deep frown lines grooved between his eyes and framed his mouth. He ignored Alice. Something nagged at her brain.

Leo stepped in front of him. "I told you not to be coming around here," she heard Leo say as he walked the man back around the corner.

"Who's that?" Alice asked the cashier. He grunted softly. "Mr. Leo's older brother, Mikey." He shut his mouth tight, handed Alice the receipt, then whispered, barely moving his lips, "He used to work here. Mr. Leo's tried to help him. But not lately." Alice took the receipt and walked over to the team pictures again. The man in the second row next to Clay looked like Leo, but he had no smile, and the frown lines were already visible. Caption: "Mike Koziar."

Her truck stood ready in the center of the parking lot. Alice climbed up, started the engine, glanced forward. Someone had parked a black pickup in the corner next to the building. The back window sported a maroon decal—a Coffee Creek Wildcats paw print. This truck had a tailgate, though. And how many locals had Wildcats decals? She looked around Leo's parking lot and spotted two more.

Chapter Sixteen

Not a Great Morning So Far

That same Tuesday afternoon at four, Red stood on the courthouse steps in her tailored red suit, holding a microphone in one hand and her red reading glasses in the other. She smiled as a curious crowd gathered, then looked around, face somber, and spoke into the mike.

"Friends, I've reviewed the Coffee Creek Electric Co-op's financial statements for the last ten years. I've looked at the publicly available audit. I've talked to linemen at the co-op. I've talked to employees. I'm a numbers person. What I see concerns me. The co-op's financial controls need improvement. The co-op's reserve account should be larger and should have systematic capital projects queued up. The co-op's done no real planning for growth. I believe new blood"—here she waved her red reading glasses—"new blood is required to keep a sharp eye"— she placed the glasses on her nose—"a very sharp eye on co-op money. That's your money, my friends, our money. It's been too cavalierly treated. So I hereby offer my time and energy to reclaiming the co-op for its owners. The owners of any business owe that business a responsibility, and since we're a member-owned co-op"—she removed the glasses and leaned forward—"that means you, me, and all of us. It's time to step up. I'm willing to do it, but I need your help. I'm asking for your vote."

A heckler at the back yelled, "What do you know about running a business?"

"Plenty," Red shot back. "I've been a certified CPA for twenty-five years. I've managed a Houston law firm for eighteen, then started Red's Rescue Ranch here, as well as my CPA firm. I've served as treasurer of Rotary and Coffee Creek Presbyterian Church and I volunteer every year at the Peoples' Tax Clinic."

A tall cowgirl carrying a "Red!" sign had squeezed through the crowd to confront the heckler.

"Hey, Harry, didn't you file bankruptcy last year? What kind of business management is that?"

Harry scowled. Then, with a reporter and cameraman heading his way, he melted back into the crowd. The next day Red smiled at everyone from the cover of the weekly *Coffee Creek Caller.*

* * * * *

Wednesday morning, 7:00 a.m.: Red called Alice at home. "Alice, damn it. Can't we do something about this—this crap on social media? One day they're calling me an airhead, the next day they're calling me an ambitious upstart."

"Huh," Alice said. "Hold on, Red. Let me see what you're talking about."

She put down her coffee and pulled up Facebook. She looked at Red's page. "I see the airhead comment," she said. "But Red, you don't want to pour gasoline on the flames. People who know you aren't going to believe this stuff."

"What about the ones who don't know me? I need their votes!"

"Hey, remember those seminars you used to arrange for your lawyers, to learn how to handle press?" Alice asked. "You don't respond to merely tacky language. You do have to respond in your cool, collected way to misinformation, any supposedly factual information that's wrong and damaging. Is anyone lying about your qualifications or work history? I don't see it."

"I know, I know. But not responding—it's easier said than done, Alice. It makes me so damn mad!"

"I know. Look, aren't you scheduled to talk about your positions at Rotary next Monday? You versus Clay Black?"

"Yep."

"Let's get some video from that and post it. Free ads. And you can practice your speech on me and Jane Ann. How about that?"

* * * * *

Wednesday morning, 8:00 a.m.: when Alice walked into the office, Silla stood before her like a sentinel. "Your new ranch client's changed his mind. He's not coming in to talk conservation easement."

No? Alice felt the small-town lawyer's wave of disappointment, then anxiety. "Why not?"

"Why, I don't know. But there's a phone message from him saying he's not comfortable because he understands you're anti-realtor."

"Anti-realtor?" What did that mean?

Alice got coffee, stewed about the situation, finally called the ranch client. "I'd be very disappointed not to work with you, though I'll understand if you've decided to use someone else. But what did your message mean, that you hear I'm 'anti-realtor'?"

"Oh, a good friend of mine told me this morning that on that Tindall ranch sale you refused to let the Tindalls use a broker."

Alice sat stunned. "That's not the case. The Tindalls did have a broker, a woman from Llano. In fact, each party had a broker."

"But there was no listing."

True, Alice thought.

She said, "The ranch wasn't listed because the sellers hadn't put it up for sale. They took the buyers' offer for a private sale. Both brokers were paid at the closing, which Jane Ann Olson handled."

Silence. "I see."

"I'm puzzled that someone would call that anti-realtor. Both brokers did a great job." That was true; the sellers' broker realized that Caswell's offer was not only well above market but would let her clients sell the place as-is with no inspections, no staging expense, and no strangers traipsing through their home. No one buttonholing the Tindalls at the grocery store, no broker calling to say, "I've got a broker whose clients just got into town; can I show the house this morning at ten?"

"Well, someone just got it wrong," said the rancher. "Glad you called."

Alice waited for a second.

"I'll give you a call about rescheduling," said the rancher.

Well, that was something. Maybe he would call back. She'd sure like to know the "friend" who invented this story.

* * * * *

Wednesday morning, 9:00 a.m.: "Alice." The mayor's penetrating voice boomed from the speakerphone. "I've got a project and I've got a problem."

"Yes, Mayor?"

"You heard the bad press the city got over the last road bid."

"I did." The *Coffee Creek Caller* had listed in exhaustive detail the delays and problems—bumps, dips, wavy striping—of the city's major road-surfacing project, as well as the contractor's bankruptcy and disappearance.

"You remember I told you the city's legal counsel's been after me for months to revamp all our contract forms. He says some hard-ass lawyer needs to take a hard look at these good ol' boy contracts the city's getting stuck with."

"And he can't do it?" asked Alice.

"He's the one who suggested you. He's got too much on his plate right now."

This isn't exactly in my wheelhouse, Alice thought, but it would sure help build connections in Coffee Creek. Besides, she felt great confidence in her contracts. She wanted this assignment. "Like I said before, I'd welcome the chance to do it."

"Well, I liked your work on the Rules Committee and Judge Sandoval says nice things about your legal work. You can write a contract?"

"Yes, Mayor. That's part of what I do. Various kinds: trust agreements, conservation easements, real estate contracts, and anything to do with wills."

"I suppose an opponent might say city contracts for goods and services aren't exactly the same. Anyway. I've been wanting to tell the council we need to hire you to review our contract forms. But—"

But what? thought Alice.

The mayor's voice changed. "Like I said, I've also got a problem. I'm hitting resistance from a couple of council members, Lane Spencer and his buddy who always votes with him. Lane thinks you're too close to the Beer Barons."

"Why is that an issue? They have no contracts with the city!" said Alice, stung.

"No, and Lane is trying to get a contract for his own pet project, which may be the root of the problem. He doesn't want you anywhere near; you'll ask too many questions. Anyway, right now I just can't afford opposition to this contracts project. I've either got to hire someone else or put it on hold."

Alice held her breath.

Slowly the mayor said, "I can put it on hold for a while. I want a good job done."

"Got it," Alice said. That meant it was Alice's job to figure a way through this thicket. The mayor hung up.

She knew Lane Spencer hated her. But who else?

* * * * *

Wednesday morning, 10:00 a.m. As Alice hung up the phone, Silla stood frowning at Alice's office door.

"What?"

"While you were on the phone I took a call from that VP at Cowman's Bank. The one who wanted you to revise his will."

"And?"

"He doesn't want you to revise it now. Says he doesn't appreciate his lawyer taking a political position. I said, 'What political position?' And he said you were interfering in the co-op election. He said he'd heard you were supporting Red Griffin."

"But he knows we've already finished the work—we sent him the revised will. Did you mention that?"

"Yes. He muttered something and slammed the phone down."

Alice didn't like this. First, the rancher who nearly pulled his business, calling her "anti-realtor." Next, the mayor's call. Now, a bank VP, pulling his will file. Admittedly he was at Cowman's, where Clay Black might be badmouthing her, but she hated to lose a client who was in a position to make referrals. Panicky feeling in her stomach: would her Coffee Creek practice fail? Immediately she envisioned her bank statement showing zero, having to borrow money from her 401(k) to pay Silla. At least she'd already paid the kids' fall tuition. Only one more semester to pay for John, three more for Ann. Surely she could make it. Right?

"Don't worry, Alice. We'll be fine." Silla spun on her heels and marched off, ponytail swinging. She brought back a mug of coffee. "You could work on that talk you're giving next month on the impact of the tax bill on conservation easements. Or you could finish up the letter to the mediator for your will contest case. The mediation's coming up."

Alice shook her head, managed a smile. "Thanks, Silla. Okay."

Maybe this was how Red was feeling. Fingers pointing, social media denigrating her brain and intentions, all for trying to do the right thing. Which Alice was trying to do as well. She thought it was much more irritating to be criticized for doing the right thing than if she'd actually done the wrong thing. Which—had she? Surely not.

Not a great morning so far.

Chapter Seventeen

What's Wrong with This Picture?

Alice sighed and reviewed the case law on will contests, her least favorite litigation. Silla opened her office door once again. Alice tensed for more bad news.

Silla ushered in a young man who thanked her and stepped inside. Anxious. African American. Very short hair. Well dressed, in an unimpeachable navy suit, red tie, blue shirt. He clutched a small attaché case. She recognized him from church. She'd never actually talked with him. Yes, Silla had said a couple from church had called to make an appointment to discuss their wills. But not today. So—why was he here?

"Come in!"

He smiled, took a breath, shifted the attaché case to his left hand, shook her right hand. Oh, good, no "finger shake," so bone-crushing; he gave her an acceptable palm-to-palm handshake, gaining immediate credibility. But what did he want?

"Alice Greer," she said.

"I'm . . . I'm Scott Whitaker," he stammered. "My wife, Jean, made a wills appointment but this is different. Do you have time to talk for a moment?"

She waved at the chair by the tea table, took the other chair.

"I need to ask you something in confidence. Can it be confidential?"

"Well, of course client communications are confidential. But you aren't here about your wills, right?"

"Right. It's about my work."

"If it's about your work, not your wills, I'd need to check conflicts." She scrutinized his face. "Sounds like you think this is serious."

He took a breath. "You don't represent the Coffee Creek Electric Co-op, do you? I did check. Or Ross CPA, that's Linda Ross's firm? They do the co-op's audits."

"Correct, I don't."

"Well, I need some help. I don't know what to do."

She studied him. "Would you like coffee?" She stepped out, asked Silla for coffee.

When they were settled with their mugs, Alice said, "Tell me."

"I've worked three years for Ross CPA. I started with Ms. Ross right after I got out of A&M and passed my CPA exams."

"And your wife works too."

"Yes. Jean works at the urgent care clinic. She's a PA, a physician's assistant. She loves her job and she loves Coffee Creek. We're saving to buy a house here."

"And—?"

He read her mind. "Yes. One little boy, eighteen months old. Happy as a clam. So, yeah, I need my job."

"What's the problem?"

"The problem." He looked down at his hands, grimaced. "Ms. Ross assigned me to the co-op audit. I'd just started on the capital reserve account, and I began to question several payments. A couple of invoices seemed sketchy. The co-op had paid a bill for a board retreat out of the reserve account. It included skeet shooting and golf. That didn't seem like a capital expenditure. Then there were several payments to a bank marked 'loan payment' on the check register, but I couldn't find any loan number associated with those payments. I looked back at last year's audit, looked at the list of loans. The co-op does bank this capital reserve account at Cowman's, but I could not find a loan number. I've got those notes somewhere." He took a breath. "Anyway, when I called the co-op bookkeeper she said she'd look into it and call me back. But she didn't. I was about to phone her again when Ms. Ross stopped by my desk and told me not to worry about the retreat expenses; they had been discussing capital funding, but the golf and skeet charges would be moved to another account. And she also said not to worry about the loan payments to Cowman's, because based on what she'd been told they sounded appropriate. Then she said I could just wind up my look at the capital reserve account; she'd take it over and finish it up. Then she switched me to the co-op O&M account, that's operations and maintenance expenses, and told me to tackle that."

"I'm not a CPA. What's wrong with this picture?"

"Well, you know capital reserve accounts are restricted in what they can be used for. Capital accounts are for long-term capital investment projects only. So if those payments weren't for long-term capital expenditures—and I couldn't confirm that they were—then I can't approve that part of the audit."

"Maybe your boss got the explanation?"

"She apparently did. Someone called and I overheard her saying, 'Oh, I see.' She came over to tell me not to worry, saying the new bookkeeper at the co-op was just sloppy. But that means the co-op called her and told her I'd raised these questions, instead of calling me back. It felt funny."

"You're still working for her, though?"

"Yes. I finished the co-op's O&M account and then she moved me over to the hospital account, which is her other big one."

"So, you aren't in trouble."

"No, I guess not. She's trusting me with the hospital account. But look, a CPA has professional obligations under the state rules. If I see something wrong, I can't just let it slide. People depend on these audits!"

"Tell me what you mean."

"The co-op takes out loans, and the lender depends on the audited financials. The audits are used to set rates, too. So to you they may not look like much but to me they're a big deal. I want to know if I should say something."

Yikes, Alice thought. Maybe he'd get marginalized and then laid off for some trumped-up reason; maybe neither his boss nor her client, the co-op, would thank him for discovering fraud. Would he even get a decent reference from Ross CPA? If he thought he might have an obligation to report to the state board of accountancy, he'd better be sure he'd collected enough data to support the claim. That would be tough now that she'd moved him off that account. Maybe he should start looking for another job. An African American in Coffee Creek; how easy was that? And really, how serious was the co-op issue? It sounded like Ms. Ross had gotten an explanation that satisfied her. That would mean he'd need to be awfully sure he was right, wouldn't it?

Alice was about to say, "She'll be the one signing the audit, not you," when Whitaker went on: "Of course I just thought Ms. Ross was right, the new bookkeeper was sloppy, maybe everyone at our firm but me knew about that bank loan. But then. My wife walks most mornings with her best friend, whose husband works for the co-op.

He repairs lines, replaces transformers, that kind of thing. My wife's friend's been telling Jean how frustrated he is, and Jean knows I've been worried about work, so this got her attention. For instance, her friend says her husband can't understand why the co-op doesn't replace the lines and poles out on Rocky Creek Road."

Red's road, thought Alice.

"She says he's tired of making excuses," Whitaker went on. "He comes home, says he's been out there again on the old lift on the co-op repair truck trying for the umpteenth time to fix a line that should've been replaced ten years ago, all the while wondering if the lift is going to keep him safe one more time, not dump him and break his neck, and meanwhile people stop by in their pickups and yell out the window, 'What do we have to do to get decent service out here?' He says he looks at the co-op budget and can't figure out what the reserves are getting spent on. It's sure not capital projects, he says. And since I'd only gotten started on the capital account, I don't know how to evaluate what I hear he says."

And just what am I supposed to do about this? Alice wondered. Am I supposed to second-guess his CPA boss?

"What would you ask me to do? Do you want me to look at the information you've got and see whether you're obligated to report to the state board?"

"I don't know. I'm just worried, I guess. I mean, maybe everything's okay."

"You don't have knowledge of a crime."

"That's true, I don't."

"Your boss, your supervising CPA, seems satisfied. The co-op's correcting part of the board retreat invoice, the golf and skeet shooting part. If the co-op refused to correct it, presumably some board member could be persuaded to provide an excuse like 'Oh yeah, we discussed the upcoming capital budget the whole time we were on the golf course.'"

"True."

"You told her your worries about the loan payments and she said those were appropriate, although you yourself couldn't find the loan number. And now you're off that assignment and may not be able, may not have a chance, to tie down those payments to a specific loan. Besides, isn't she still working on it? It's not final yet?"

"Right."

"And—you know and I know that if you keep pushing to tie down payments on an account you're no longer auditing, you may find nothing that confirms your suspicions, and the pushing may leave you just where you are. Worried and uncertain. And maybe out of a job."

"So, you're saying, maybe I should find a different job?"

"For your own peace of mind, you might consider it. And I'll make a couple of calls for you, see if anyone wants a very conscientious, very careful accountant."

He grinned. "An overwrought over-worrier?" He sobered. "I'm still concerned I may have an obligation to the state board."

"But you're not ready to hire me to look at that, right?"

Whitaker nodded. "Not right now." They shook hands and he left. He'd be in the next week with his wife to work on their wills.

But she couldn't stop thinking about his predicament. She vividly remembered a document discovery crisis at the Houston firm where she'd spent the summer as a law clerk, and where she'd met Red. One night she stayed late on an emergency project requiring her to rush through boxes of documents the firm's big client had just produced in a bitter lawsuit. Since the client had been ordered to produce them the next day, her job was to segregate and tag for production any non-privileged documents that fell within the opponent's document request. About midnight the litigation associate she worked with—he was coming up for partner soon, she knew—came in and began thumbing through her stack, then staring at her with horror. "These undercut one of our claims!" he said.

"But they're still relevant and non-privileged, right?"

"I dunno. I—I'm gonna have to talk to Rex." Rex, a high-powered litigation partner, ran the case.

"But don't you think we have to produce them?" In her head Alice heard the bow-tied civil procedure professor at her law school pontificating to the class about ethical duties in document discovery.

"You mean under the rules?"

"Of course."

"Rex says sometimes the discovery rules don't have to be obeyed. He calls them the '*suggestions* of civil procedure.'"

Astonished, Alice stared at him. "Do you agree with him?"

And at that moment she'd decided she'd never work for this firm, and, if she was ever on the other side of a case from Rex, she'd send a litigation-hold letter right away and be damned sure he produced every document she asked for. But did she blame this young associate for not charging off to report his boss's potential ethical violation to the state bar? You had to think about the impact on your client, which made it even more important to be dead sure there was no basis, no privilege that provided a justification. Very uncomfortable.

Similarly, handling audited financial statements for the co-op appeared to be uncomfortable. What would Red think about that?

Red would call balls and strikes with certainty, that's what.

Then she wondered whether and when Red would have a chance to look at the actual co-op books.

* * * * *

Alice slogged away for another couple of hours on her least favorite case. She represented the estate in a will contest set for trial in November. The parties had agreed to a mediation date. Alice found will contests depressing. Usually the plaintiffs claimed that the testator couldn't have meant to leave them so little—meaning the testator must have lost mental capacity, or alternatively, another nefarious heir had used "undue influence" to con the testator into changing the will. Alice had not grown up rich. She never assumed the world owed her a large pile of unearned wealth. She recognized (and thought it might be a character flaw) that she didn't have a truly open mind to cases where aggrieved heirs challenged a will. In this case Alice was defending the estate—i.e., the will. When she'd deposed the plaintiffs, they had displayed shocking outbursts of what she viewed as tacky behavior. Mediation required her to assess all the personalities and come up with an outside-the-box creative solution. Alice knew she was in danger of becoming too emotionally involved. She needed some distance.

At two, Alice handed Silla the draft letter to the mediator. What a horrible day. Maybe a little outing would cheer her up. Eddie LaFarge's invitation—wine tasting at four on Wednesday afternoon—sounded tempting. She called Red.

"Can't, Alice. I'm speaking to the Coffee Creek Women's Association."

But Miranda, her banker buddy, accepted with alacrity. "Roland's out of town, I've funded the restaurant loan, I'm bored, and that winery's out north, about fifteen miles up McElrath Road, isn't it?" she said. "I love to drive that road. How about I pick you up at your place at three? We can prowl around the winery for a minute, before the wine tasting."

Oh lord, driving with Miranda in that Jag, thought Alice, hanging up the phone. Try to be zen. Miranda hasn't had a major accident yet. So far as you know.

Chapter   Eighteen

I'm Still Alive!

The county's idea of paving McElrath Road involved merely applying a thin layer of asphalt to an old Comanche trail, later a wagon trail. No banking; no road crown. Just asphalt soaring up and down the hills and around sudden curves. Alice held her breath as Miranda, tall, blonde, and elegant, narrowed her sharp blue eyes and took the curves at an almost-safe speed. Friends accused Alice of speeding but—surely she didn't drive like Miranda? Finally the road straightened. "Ten more minutes," Miranda said.

Alice tightened her seat belt. "Tell me about your restaurant loan," Alice said.

"Since when are you interested in the restaurant business?"

"I just wondered how much it costs to start a restaurant."

"Depends whether we're talking about a food truck in Coffee Creek or a new space in downtown Austin. But it always, always costs more than the chef thinks it will. And when you've got backers with egos, wanting a name chef and rave reviews, we're talking a couple of million, at least. Funny thing to invest in, when so many restaurants fail." She glanced at Alice. "Of course I won't tell you details, but my loan was for a new owner of an existing Driftwood spot, so for significantly less. Still, those owners have stars in their eyes."

Alice held her breath as Miranda braked hard, then sped out of a sharp left curve.

"Hey," Alice said. "You know Clay Black's retiring from Cowman's Bank, right?"

"Doesn't everybody? He loves to talk about how he got the perfect buyout offer for the bank. Then he likes to hint about his parachute. Platinum."

"When's the deal supposed to close?"

"Year-end. Why?"

"Are there any contingencies?" Alice asked. "Anything that would keep the buyer from closing?"

Miranda nodded. "I heard he needs to keep deposits and reserves where they are. I mean, if Cowman's lost a couple of big depositors, the buyer could walk." She glanced at Alice, belted tightly in the passenger seat, clutching her armrest. "Come on, Alice, I'm a wonderful driver.

Why are you asking about Cowman's? Thinking about this co-op election?"

"Yes," Alice said. "Doesn't the co-op keep some big accounts there?"

"Oh yeah. It started while Clay was on the board. That's when the general manager, ol' Wally Phifer, moved the reserve accounts to Cowman's. Of course, Wally's gonna retire, isn't he? I heard he's bought himself a really nice place out in the Pecos Wilderness near Santa Fe. The next general manager might want to move those co-op accounts. Of course if Clay wins the open board seat, he'll try to make sure the board doesn't move them."

"But if the bank sale doesn't close, Clay would still be president of Cowman's, wouldn't he?"

Miranda pursed her lips. "Maybe his shareholders would let him go without that nice parachute. I know a couple of major shareholders who are a bit restive with Clay. They're ready to recoup their investment in Cowman's and put it somewhere else. So they want this bank sale to close and maybe get out of the banking business for a while."

They were about to top a hill when Alice pointed: "There!" On their right a sign read "Raptor Cellars." Miranda drove through the winery entrance and into the gravel parking area. She and Alice climbed out of the car, drawn immediately to the broad view before them. To the southeast, on the horizon, blue hills marched away. On the slopes below the parking area stood row after row of trellised vines, grape leaves turning red and purple in the fall sunshine.

They turned to look at the winery. "Interesting," said Miranda.

Homegrown, Alice thought, intrigued. Someone had planned a tall metal structure partly walled with blocks of limestone—old seabed put to new use—and partly walled with glass.

She and Miranda pushed open the tall entry doors into a high space, cool, orderly. Light poured in from clerestory windows. Tables for four or five; a long polished wooden bar; floor-to-ceiling windows looking out on the terrace, which faced north. Eddie was waiting, a little incongruous to her in this winery setting, with his big shoulders, his outsized presence. She couldn't help thinking, Large football player. Tackles people.

She introduced Miranda. "You're with Madrone Bank?" Eddie asked. "I hear the service is pretty good there."

"It is," Miranda said.

"Not to forget the fresh-baked chocolate chip cookies," Alice pointed out.

"Tell me about this place," Miranda said. "What led you to start a winery?"

"Well, after I retired from football, I stayed out in the Bay Area. I had an automobile dealership, which was enjoyable. But when I started visiting the new wineries—Sonoma, Napa, Santa Cruz—they caught my imagination. I became a winery groupie, volunteered to help harvest, help label, you name it. My friends with wineries really let me learn; they generously shared their knowledge. I even took some wine-making courses down at UC Davis. One fall, a friend invited me to watch her make the big decision on when to pick grapes, and then let me follow through that entire vintage: when to stop fermentation, when to barrel, what kind of barrels to use, how long to age—I got hooked. And though I love California, I was starting to miss the Hill Country here. I'd bought this property way back when I got my first big signing bonus. So I thought—how about going home and trying to make wine on my hills? And when I got here, I lucked out. Everything I know about making old-world wines in these limestone hills I learned from the folks over at Hawk's Shadow Winery, north of Dripping Springs. My Viognier wants to taste like theirs someday."

A small wine-tasting group had coalesced around them. Miranda knew and greeted several of them. "Okay, we're all here," Eddie said. "Let's taste some wines."

Two hours sped by. Alice learned more than she'd ever known about French oak, American oak, Hungarian oak. She tasted the subtle differences that different oaks could impart to the same vintage. She took notes. New worlds opened before her. She couldn't wait now to taste the Sangiovese that was sitting quietly in its barrels in the cellar. She fell passionately in love with the all-Mourvèdre vintage that Eddie let them taste, pulling it straight out of the barrel. "It's not ready," he said. "But it's going to be so interesting. Don't you think?"

She did think. Kinsear would love this place, she thought. She'd have to bring him back here.

Miranda, Alice, and the rest of the wine tasters bought their take-home bottles at the long wooden bar. While they were loading their cars, Eddie walked over to Alice. "Let me show you something." He took her out to the terrace. "See down there?" An asphalt track with some sharp right and left turns ran between the vineyards below, up and around a rise, and then back. "If you'll come back tomorrow morning at eight I'll show you a couple of evasive driving techniques you ought to know. That's first light, and I'll be busy later on. Deal?"

She looked into the humorous blue eyes. "You won't get me killed?"

"Nope. I'm hoping you'll actually live longer. Eight o'clock?"

To her own astonishment, she agreed. "My truck, right?"

"Yep, your very own dangerous vehicle."

* * * * *

In Thursday's predawn darkness Alice filled the truck with gas and replaced the gas cap, giving it an extra one-eighth turn, wondering if the poor old truck would survive Evasive Driving 101. And would she?

She still found it interesting, rolling back up McElrath Road, that Eddie LaFarge had taken such interest in her driving skills.

He stood ready in the parking lot of Raptor Cellars. "Hi, Alice. Thought you might not show up. Here, put this on." Good lord, a padded vest. He laughed at her alarmed face. "Just, sometimes the seat belts pull on you too hard. This too." He handed her a helmet and put on his own. "Okay, let's go. You drive. We're heading down to the track."

Self-conscious in the outfit, very aware of Eddie in the passenger seat, Alice put the truck in gear and started downhill toward the track. Eddie's property was bigger than she'd thought. "How many acres, roughly, do you have?"

"About five hundred. Half of it's in grapes and olive trees"—he waved at the unmistakable gray-green of olives creeping down a slope Alice hadn't seen from the winery—"and the other half has my house, a couple of guesthouses, and this track."

Alice had driven halfway down the straightaway part of the track. "Okay, stop here," said Eddie.

He produced a map of the track. "Now we're not after any race car stunts, Alice, not in your truck. We're just going to learn three basic techniques. But first, let's talk about curves."

He pointed a pencil at one of the right-hand curves. "Suppose you're taking that curve. This point right here on the inside of your turn"—he made an X—"is the apex of the curve. Your perfect line or geometric line makes the turn wider by using the left lane too." He penciled an arc onto the map, through the curve. "So you'd take the turn by moving to the left, then turning toward your apex, then with minimal steering and braking coming out on the far side of the turn."

Alice felt her brain seizing up, the way it felt in high school physics when the teacher explained the inexplicable. She pointed at the map: "What if someone's in the left lane?"

Eddie laughed. "Well, in that case you adjust your plan. There may come a day when you need that left lane. But Alice—this apex concept will grow on you. You'll get it."

She drew her brows together and gave him a skeptical look.

"I sense doubt," Eddie said. "But you'll see. Okay. Let's get rolling, but backward. First, we're going to see how fast and straight you can back your truck."

Damn fast, thought Alice. Funny about the backing stuff. She loved backing down a long driveway, sometimes speeding. And she loved her tennis backhand. Huh, I'll knock his socks off with my backing. But why practice this?

"Why?" she asked.

"Backing fast can be essential to evading a bad situation. Plus you need it for the first and second techniques. First is the K-turn, for quick turning around on a road. Second is the J-turn, and you need to do it starting in reverse. Third's a secret but you'll like it. Okay. Start forward and when I say 'Stop!' you brake and put the truck in reverse and go straight back as fast as you can. Look over your shoulder when you do it."

She raced the engine and took off.

"Stop!"

She screeched to a stop, put the truck in reverse, started backing, sped up . . . wait! A curve back there. She overcorrected and the truck was in the grass.

"Not bad. Let's try that again. Stay focused on where you want the truck to go."

Forward, then— *"Stop!"*

Backward now, faster, keep staring out the rear window—

"Okay—you can stop."

She did.

He nodded at her. "Not bad, Alice! Not bad at all. Okay, let's try the K-turn. Simple. Start driving. Get it up at least to fifty. When I yell 'Blockade!' you imagine a blockade ahead. Always stop where you easily see the tires on what's ahead of you. You want to make the shortest possible turn and head the other way. So you brake, turn your wheels left to the edge of the road, reverse while backing a bit right, then roar straight back down the road. Easy-peasy. But don't go off the road surface."

Right, she thought.

"Blockade!"

She braked, eased, turning left, braked hard, got the truck in reverse, then started forward.

"Faster!"

She accelerated.

"When you get back in forward gear, jump on it, Alice! Also, you ran off the road. Keep it short. Aggressive and short."

Again. Again.

"Okay, drink some water."

Alice sank back in her seat, took the offered water bottle, found she'd emptied it. He handed her another.

"Now the J-turn, Alice. You'll like this. You're stopped, then you accelerate straight backward, always looking out the rear window, then you come off the gas fast, jerk the wheel a hundred and eighty degrees left, then shift into neutral and back into drive and hit the accelerator. So, you start out fast in reverse, spin the truck, and wind up facing and driving forward in the same direction. Remember *The Rockford Files?*"

She nodded.

"So you'll remember the Rockford spin, maybe?"

She shook her head no.

"Oh, well. That's basically what this is. I wouldn't let you do it in a big SUV or a taller truck because of the risk of rollover, but you've got this ancient, titchy little Toyota. I think we'll be okay."

That wasn't too encouraging.

"Ready?"

She nodded.

"*Go!*"

She roared backward, looking over her shoulder.

"*Off the gas. Spin the wheel.*"

She lifted her foot and spun the steering wheel, still looking backward, and the truck began spinning left.

"*Neutral. Now forward.*"

She moved the shift, started to accelerate, realized she was heading way off into the grass. She braked and sat, panting. She wiped her sweaty hands on her pants.

"Not bad. Not good, but not bad. Let's try it again."

Two more tries and she finally had the Rockford spin, though shaky and inelegant.

"How do you feel?" he asked.

"Well . . . kind of cool. But surely to goodness I won't need this."

"Never?"

She thought about the black pickup racing down the road the day of the Tindall house fire. That was a two-lane blacktop. If she'd needed to escape, would either of these turns have worked? Maybe not. But what if she'd wanted to turn around and chase that black pickup, get the license plate? Hmm. Not her style, but still possible. "I can't use either of these on a divided highway, though."

"That's true, Alice. But you do a lot of driving on winding little two-lane blacktops. Or even one-lane, right? And out here in the Hill Country we've got a lot of tight curves, correct?"

"I'll give you that."

"Okay," said Eddie. "Up ahead you've got a tight right, then a tight left. Identify the apex. Use the entire track and take the turns, trying for the least braking and steering."

She went too fast on the first, braked too hard, tires squealing, and braked too soon on the left turn.

Dispassionate voice from Eddie. "Turn around and let's do that again in the other direction."

She did.

"That's better. Okay. More water?"

Lord, she thought. Her hands and arms trembled with tension.

Eddie looked over at her. "Yeah, it's a lot. All right, Alice, time for the third trick. It's called the 'Scandinavian flick.' It's advanced but I think you need it. It could help you take those tight curves a little faster. Sound good?"

"If you say so." She took a deep breath, surprised at how tired she felt.

He chuckled. "Drive us back over the rise and down and then you'll see a sharp right turn and a straightaway. Notice how slow you have to take the turn."

After a few minutes she stopped, turned the truck around, and looked at him. "I didn't want to take it at more than forty-seven or forty-eight miles an hour."

He made her go back through the curve and turn around. He showed her the map again, pointing at the turn with the pencil. "This time, on the right-hand turn, move left of the centerline here—if we had a centerline, which we don't—and then just ahead of the curve point the car a bit left, tapping your brakes a bit, and then turn sharply into the curve. Let's do it in slo-mo. You won't really feel the weight transfer but when you speed up, the rear will shift around to the left and help you get the truck pointed into the curve faster."

Slo-mo felt odd. "Now you know where to make your moves, right?" said Eddie. "Ready to try it?"

Back to the starting point. As they approached the right-hand turn, he said, "Ready? get left of center. Ease off your brakes so you know you can make the turn."

She complied. "Now, slight turn left, feathering your brakes, and quick turn right!" She felt the truck fishtail slightly, then point straight into the turn.

She let the truck slow and stop. Her heart was pounding.

"But you felt good about it, right?" he said, watching her face.

Alice smiled up through the windshield at the sun. "I'm still alive!"

He laughed. Then sobered. "Alice, remember this if you ever have to take a turn fast. You might be able to lose whoever's chasing you. Or get wherever you're needing to go. Okay, we're done."

Back in the winery Alice trotted gratefully into the restroom to pee, then looked at her face in the mirror. Flushed. No lipstick. Older and wiser? Learned a new trick or two? Gonna feel good heading back down McElrath Road? She bought six bottles of Viognier and put her name on the list for the first Mourvèdre. "Thank you, Eddie." She realized he actually took her seriously. He'd heard about the helicopter incident, and maybe about the rammer truck on US 290. "Can I come back?" she asked.

"Anytime. Your old Toyota's learned a couple of tricks, I believe."

So have I, she thought. So have I. Then she thought of something. "Can I buy you a glass of wine? I want to ask you a question."

He laughed. "It's only nine. So I believe I'll just have a glass of this breakfast Viognier that's open here. What about you?"

She shook her head no.

"Okay, what's the question?"

"I know you and Leo were high school buddies."

"Right. Good man, ol' Leo."

"What about his older brother, Mikey?"

He looked away, knitted his brows, swiveled on the stool. The blue eyes looked sharply at her. "What about him?"

"Well, that day we were getting inspected, I heard that Mikey doesn't work at the garage anymore. Then Mikey came in, and Leo wasn't happy to see him."

"That's because he's made trouble for Leo all his life. Mikey's never been an ideal big brother. Or employee. Leo's the little bro, but he's the one who always took care of their parents, made an honest living, tried to pick up the pieces behind Mikey." He stared at Alice. "In fact, you don't want to know Mikey and you sure don't want him taking an interest in you. He did some hard time back in the day and it wasn't for shoplifting. I know Mikey's bright enough but he's got a temper on him, I guess what these days we call 'anger-management issues.' Leo's given him many chances, too many, really, including keeping him on at the garage for years, but now ol' Mikey's pretty much run his string with Leo."

"What about Mikey and Clay Black? Mikey and Clay were in the same high school class, right?"

"Yeah. Ten years ahead of me and Leo. They had no time for us, thank goodness."

"Were—are they close? Are they buddies?"

"I think they still talk to each other. Since I moved back I don't recall seeing Clay hanging out in public with Mikey much. I mean, Clay's a big frog now, he wouldn't hang out with Mikey. Though come to think of it, I saw both of them at that barbecue competition." Alice remembered Clay, down the street by the food trucks, talking to a tall man. Mikey? "But I guess that's high school football in a small town, you don't forget who you suited up with," Eddie went on. "Why are you asking?"

"Leo seemed quite upset that Mikey came to the garage."

"Look, Leo's bailed Mikey out many a time. He also knows people in town don't trust Mikey, or are scared of him, or both. People know he's a mean'un, so Leo doesn't want him in the garage, putting people off. Now you asked about Clay: I used to think Clay egged Mikey on with some of his bad stunts. Like at one football game, Leo and I were down on the sidelines watching and I heard Clay tell Mikey to take out a guy on the other team—short little running back, short but fast. Mikey got thrown out of the game for what he did to that guy."

Silence. Alice wasn't sure how much more to say. She wasn't positive Mikey had done anything . . . but there was that paw print decal.

Eddie turned to her. "Are you asking whether he'd do some mischief if Clay Black asked him?"

"Exactly."

"Yeah. I'm afraid he would. Don't get in his way." He looked hard at her. "Seriously."

"Right." Reluctantly she stood, looking at the open bottle of Viognier on the counter, bottled sunshine. But the workday had just begun.

Eddie carried her box of wine out to the truck—the battered old tan Toyota, now an evasive vehicle. Alice patted its hood. "Thanks, Eddie. I'll get a little medal for the truck."

He waved and watched her turn out onto McElrath Road, then headed back into his winery.

Alice, driving south toward Coffee Creek, now evaluated the road's twists and turns differently. She was considering trying the Scandinavian flick on the next uphill right turn when she spied a Coffee County Sheriff's vehicle poised in a driveway at the top of the hill. She took a deep breath and maintained a sedate speed on the way into town, considering the problem of Clay Black and his old buddy Mikey. Mikey who got kicked out of a high school football game, Mikey whose own brother had forbidden him access to his business, Mikey who might have been speeding away from a burning ranch house. But how could she nail that down? Go talk to Mikey? Uh-uh, not without more evidence. How, then?

Chapter Nineteen

Road Trip

lice was back in the office by nine thirty Thursday morning, tired but still exhilarated from the driving lesson. Silla greeted her. "Hey, that mediation letter looks good," Silla said. "I'd settle if I were on the other side."

Good, Alice thought. "Can you get all the exhibits ready for the mediator?"

"Done," Silla said, producing three notebooks—one for Alice, one for her clients, one for the mediator. Silla looked out the window. "Well, look, here's the candidate. Red herself."

Red had stopped by to borrow the full-length mirror behind Alice's office door. She stood before her reflection, dabbing concealer on the dark circles beneath her eyes.

"Ain't livin' long like this, Alice. I don't know if I can last another two weeks. I'm speaking to any group that asks and inviting myself to some that haven't. Have I met some decent people? Yes. But I'm so tired." She squinted into the mirror. "Look at these lines around my eyes! That's from reading all the crap I'm getting on social media."

Waving the tube of concealer, Red turned to Alice and declared, "If ever again I tell you I want to run for anything, dogcatcher, whatever, just shoot me. I am so ready for this to end. Okay, I'm off." And she vanished out the door.

Hmm, Alice thought. Maybe Red needed a little distance too?

Kinsear would still be in New York this weekend.

So when Caswell Bond called later Thursday morning and said that his mother wanted to discuss putting the Tindall ranch in a wildlife-management program and also wanted to talk about a top-secret new project with her buddy M.A., Alice thought: Road trip to Colorado?

She reached Red on her cell. "Couldn't you take one short weekend away from the campaign? Can someone watch your horses? Fly up early tomorrow, get back late Sunday night?"

"Alice, the election's just two weeks away!"

"Well, what's scheduled this weekend?"

Silence. "I'm looking at the schedule. Nothing until Monday, but that's my Rotary campaign speech, and it's not even written."

"You could write it and practice it on the plane to me, your captive audience," Alice said. "And what if Silla and Jana work on getting you some more speaking events next week?"

"Hmm. Okay," Red said. "Maybe I need this. I'm too wired. If I don't get out of town I'll go nuts. Jana can watch the horses. I'll call her; she's holding down the fort all day." Jana, an eighteen-year-old horse whisperer, had persuaded Red to hire her, had made herself indispensable, and now lived in Red's bunkhouse. "But listen," Red added, "I absolutely have to be back Sunday night." And she hung up.

Next, Alice called Val in Estes Park.

"Val? It's Alice Greer. Is it snowing up there yet?"

"No! The aspen are golden. It's gorgeous, for another few days. Can you come up?"

"Yes!" said Alice. "Caswell mentioned you're interested in the possibility that Granite Hawk could put part of the Tindall ranch into the county's wildlife-management program. We could talk about it."

"Sure," said Val. "And also our new project! And please bring some maps when you come. Caswell has to have maps."

* * * * *

On Friday at 5:30 a.m. the Austin airport was already crammed with travelers. Alice and Red fought their way down to their gate, stowed their carry-ons, and sank into the scantily padded plastic buckets that passed these days for airline seats.

"Remember, I get to plan our signature hike." Red had led hikes at the YMCA of the Rockies one college summer and still grew rapturous talking about the mountains. Alice sighed, knowing she'd be panting up the trails after Red, who'd predictably call over her shoulder, "It's just around the corner!" But Alice herself loved nothing more than reaching the tundra—moss, boulders, and fairy-sized wildflowers under the so-close sky. Fairy primrose, tiny blue forget-me-not, pink moss campion, sky pilot. Maybe not in October; instead of flowers, just streams of aspen along the valleys, glowing gold against the cerulean sky.

In their rental car they headed up US 36 to Estes Park and dropped their bags at a rental condo. Red walked down to her favorite outdoor

157

store. Alice took the ranch survey, the wildlife-management application, and a topo map and headed for Val's. On the way through Estes Park she caught sight of a black pickup with a maroon paw print on the rear window, parked at the Donut Haus. Another Coffee Creek tourist? She headed west out of town on Riverside, watching for the left turn up the slopes toward Val's place—"It'll say 'No Outlet,'" Val had warned.

As always she caught her breath when the front range of the Rockies came into view: half the horizon lined with jutting dark granite masses, already patched with snow, crowned by the iconic mass of Longs Peak. Up ahead she saw the turnoff to Val's road.

Val's cabin sat on a sunny slope with the front range looming to the west. Ponderosa pines with lofty green tops, red-gold bark glowing in the afternoon sun, lined the steep uphill drive. Alice parked and slipped out of the driver's seat. She sidled over to one ponderosa, covertly scratching and then leaning close to sniff the bark, loving the vanilla fragrance. She walked on up the drive to Val's cabin, charcoal-colored with red window frames and red window boxes. The cabin had grown like topsy: here a lean-to, there an add-on, in front a long covered porch.

In the porch swing, feet gently pushing back and forth, sat a capable-looking young woman patting a baby. Three months or so, Alice guessed. The baby peeked at Alice, then buried her head in her mother's neck. The young woman shook her head, eyes twinkling at Alice. "This is Anna. I'm seriously doubting she's planning to take a nap. I'm Bonnie, Caswell's wife." Bonnie stood up, cradling the baby with a muscular arm, and shook Alice's hand.

Alice admired the baby, repressing her urge to grab it and nuzzle its nape. She told Bonnie how much she'd enjoyed meeting Caswell and Davie. "He's a remarkable kid."

Bonnie smiled. "That he is. If he's still alive at the end of the day, I think I'm doing okay as a mother. The things he wants to do!"

"Was his dad like that?"

"Val says so. As a kid Caswell reportedly explored every corner of this town, climbed every trail up every mountain, fished every creek, measured the temperature in Lake Estes all winter . . ."

Alice raised her eyebrows.

"Yep, he dreamed up new science projects every day. That was just one." Bonnie sighed. "Val says she had to race out in a paddleboat once to rescue him before he froze in Lake Estes. I'm waiting to see if Anna's like her dad." But maybe she's like her mother, Alice thought —bright-eyed, ready for whatever came. Alice guessed that Bonnie was a Colorado girl.

"You're from here, right?"

Bonnie nodded. "Yep. Raised right here, over off Devil's Gulch Road."

Devil's Gulch led north from Estes Park, in a wide valley dominated by a ranch that evoked the early days, when cattle herds first wintered in the deep snow. Yes, Alice thought, if you grew up in that landscape, you could handle nearly anything—certainly snow, cold, silence, winter.

Bonnie disappeared inside with the baby, then reappeared and perched on the swing. "Val'll be ready in a second. Let's sit out here for a bit. This may be the last warm afternoon of the fall."

Alice pulled over a metal porch chair and sat. Bonnie might think it was warm; she herself was glad of her down vest.

"I've got a question," Bonnie said.

"Sure," Alice said.

"How safe is Coffee Creek?"

Surprised, Alice sat straight up. "Safe?"

"Well, we bought the Tindall place and right away someone torched the house. And your barbecue competition ended in a murder that's still not solved, right? That poor food writer?"

Alice nodded. In a phone call yesterday, George Files had told her in disgusted tones that one entire group of suspects—all the people insulted one way or another by Pine—had alibis.

"Really, Coffee Creek's usually pretty safe," Alice said. "But it sounds like you're linking those two events. Does something make you think they're related?"

Bonnie's eyes bored into Alice's. "I'm asking you to convince me they're not. Can you?" She waited a moment, then said, "Look, Alice. Caswell's talking about moving Val down to Coffee Creek, at least half the year. This cold just wears her out—especially when we get the winds blowing down off the mountains. And her new head chef's managing the mountain restaurant just fine. Val could spend the summers up here—she still loves the hiking—and then spend, say, five months in Coffee Creek, maybe part of the time up at the ranch but mostly in Coffee Creek with those long-lost friends. And she's got an idea for an enterprise in Coffee Creek with her friend M.A."

The new project, thought Alice.

"But I don't want to let anyone in our family—from Val to Caswell and our kids—stay down there if it's not safe for them to go back yet."

"Yet?"

"Yet. Don't you know the history?"

"I've heard some about Caswell's dad's death."

"Well, I only know bits." Her shoulders rose; she sighed and stood on the rough porch planks. "It's really Val who should tell you."

On cue, Val appeared at the door. She smiled a welcome, the quiet voice thanking Alice for coming. "Let's go in where we can spread the maps out. It's getting chilly out here."

Inside, Alice saw warm wood, bright Indian rugs, a vast wooden trestle table with mismatched chairs, and two old Aladdin lamps standing tall on the mantel. A little blue smoke waved around the fireplace, where someone had just lit the kindling, sparking and sputtering beneath a tepee of short piñon logs.

"I made coffee," Val said, offering Alice a mug. "I want my brain awake for this! Tell me about this wildlife program you're talking about."

Alice unfolded her survey across the long table and overlaid the topographic map. Val bent over, tracing the elevation lines and the ranch boundary with her fingers. Alice had asked the surveyor to add in the two halves of the Black ranch, which bordered the Tindall ranch on the north. Val pointed at the high point on the Tindall ranch, with its circle of ever tighter elevation lines and the inked outline of the house and barn. "I guess there's no more house there, unless we rebuild." Her finger traced down the curve of elevation lines, onto Clay Black's property. "Clay wouldn't have liked us having a house there anyway. The hill overlooks his property."

"How do you know he wouldn't have liked it?"

"He always gloated that his half of the Black ranch overlooked ours." She paused. "He used to tease us, used to say he knew whether we were in the house or out . . ." Her mouth tightened. "Kind of voyeurish, you know. Once he sang me that Christmas carol, 'I know if you've been naughty or nice,' and told me to be sure to draw the curtains."

"Surely he couldn't see into your house," said Alice, astonished.

"Only with binoculars, I imagine." Val went silent.

Behind her, Bonnie stood staring at Alice, as if to say, *See what I mean?* Then she disappeared into the kitchen.

Alice focused on Val's face. Maybe she'd talk. "Is there anything about Clay I should know, Val? Or about Annette? Or about both of them, Clay and Annette?"

But Val's face closed. "No, I don't think so. Tell me about the wild-life management. I'm definitely in for native grasses and birds, and turkey and quail. Do we have to have cows?"

"You could manage for native grasses, turkey and quail, native songbirds. The creek with its trees could be turkey shelter, turkey habitat. You could reseed the big pastures, try to replace some of the invasives."

"I could get rid of the cows?"

"If you want."

"I don't have to high-fence for a deer lease like Clay?"

"Nope. You'd probably want to high-fence if you decided to pursue a wildlife-management plan for hunting, but you don't have to include hunting in your plan."

Alice walked her through the draft application. "Here's what the consultant suggests. You'll need to build wildlife shelters and renew them every year. I do it with Christmas trees and all the cedar we chop, and the limbs that we trim or that fall. Also, you'll need alternative water sources. You could put out some water troughs with floats for the birds, with a stack of rocks at the end, and some chicken wire and sticks over part of the trough so the birds and lizards and small animals can drink. You could connect those troughs via hose to the well house." Val nodded. "And you see the schedule for planting native grass seed? You'll need some help for that, given the amount of acreage involved. Do you know anyone who could do that? Someone out close to the ranch?"

Val shook her head. "I could check with M.A. She knows people up there. The ones I knew are mostly dead, I expect."

"Lloyd Neighbors?"

Val lifted her head. "I remember him. He knew my husband."

"Okay if I check with him?"

"Yes. But look, Alice." Val stood up. "Let's go out on the porch." She walked Alice outside and over to the porch railing, looking out at the sunlight spilling on the aspen down below. "I've never told my son the whole story about Clay, about how he haunted me while my husband was in Vietnam. When my husband finally got back I thought Clay would surely stop. But he just kept looking at me that way. You know what I mean? You know that dirty feeling, the 'Is it somehow my fault he won't let me alone' feeling?"

Alice nodded. Yes, she knew.

Val took a deep breath. "After—after the day of the auger accident I got desperate and moved into town with my parents. Clay followed me there one day. He said he'd leave Annette, couldn't live without me, etcetera. Horrible. I couldn't bear it. I swore my parents to secrecy, took little Caswell and left Texas, changed our names." She took another breath, then looked up at Alice.

"Val, what really happened that day, the day your husband died?"

"I never talk about it. I buried him and I buried what I saw."

"I wish you'd tell me," Alice said.

Long pause. Val scanned the horizon, peered over her shoulder at the closed cabin door, shivered in the growing chill. "Okay. It was late afternoon. My husband was down by the gate looking at the auger, checking how many fence posts he needed to replace. A section of fence was loose and we were expecting a truck trailer full of cows. I left little Caswell playing in the yard by the house with his new toy truck and drove over to the Tindalls' house—I'd promised Louise I'd feed her dogs while she took her mom to Houston. I stopped at our gate. I reminded my husband he'd promised to wait till I got back before he cranked up the auger. He nodded. Last words he spoke to me: 'Don't worry, honey.'"

Val looked off toward the mountains, then went on. "I never got to say goodbye. When I got back, he was lying there curled up in all that blood. Little Caswell had heard him call out and had run down to him and was standing in the bloody dirt, crying." Her mouth tightened. "I threw away those bloody little shoes."

"No one saw what happened?"

"I knelt down by my husband, calling his name. I grabbed his wrist, felt for a pulse. Nothing. I stood up to run for the telephone— you know, the desperate hope an ambulance could save him. I saw a little flash of something, up the hill across the road. It was Clay, just disappearing around the corner of their house."

He was watching, Alice thought. He knew. "Does he know you saw him?" Alice asked.

"I don't think so. For my son's sake, I've always hoped not. Back then they were both working in Llano—Clay at a bank, and Annette at the hospital. Clay told us later that he'd come home early and didn't hear anything, didn't see anything. When Annette drove home that day she saw us loading Caswell's body into the ambulance. But I didn't know what little Caswell saw. If he'd seen, if he knew Clay had just stood there, I was scared to death for him. I needed him to forget it. He would never be safe, knowing that. Do you understand? And he wasn't safe if Clay knew *I'd* seen, either. So I knew we had to go."

Alice nodded.

Val went on. "We buried my husband just down the road from the ranch, at the old Turkey Ridge Pioneer Cemetery. I've never been back to his grave since we left Texas. But for years now my son has been bound and determined to get the Tindall ranch. He's got his reasons, whatever they are. Maybe he's looking for some sort of peace. So I'll sign whatever you give me, Alice, but I doubt you'll see me out there. If I do come down to Texas I'll spend my time in Coffee Creek, not the ranch. Especially with the Tindall house gone. That takes the pressure off."

"What pressure?" Caswell Bond had opened the cabin door and now stepped out onto the porch, followed by Davie. "Hi, Alice! Great that you could come up here! Davie, show what we caught."

Davie held up two small trout. "Wow," Alice said.

"Mom's cooking them for supper," said Davie, proudly carrying his catch back to the kitchen. Alice, Caswell, and Val followed him back inside.

Caswell stood looking at the maps spread out on the table. "Did you guys figure out the wildlife management? I'm happy with whatever you do, but keep the creek clear."

"Clear?" asked Alice.

"I mean, exclude the area where the creek enters the property from the wildlife-management plan." He pointed to the hilly end of the map on its western edge. "Keep this part of the creek out of the plan. The rest, downstream, can be bird habitat or whatever." The bright brown eyes looked back at Alice's questioning face. "I just want a completely private area up there where the stream comes onto the property from the big hills to the west. My—my own refuge."

Alice frowned. "Is it okay to plant native grasses? Have birdhouses? I'd hate for you to completely exclude it from the plan and maybe lose part of your ag exemption."

"Maybe grass and birdhouses," he said, shrugging. Okay, he was the client.

"Take a look at the draft application and let me know." Alice looked at the cuckoo clock on the wall. "I should go," she said. "Val, remember Red and I are taking you out to a girls' dinner tonight."

Val smiled and nodded. Bonnie returned, holding the wide-awake baby.

"And also," Alice said, "Red and I are hiking tomorrow."

Caswell's face brightened. "Where?"

"Still deciding. Want to join us?"

Val and Bonnie said no. "Davie and I have a date at the old Estes Park movie house," Val said.

But Caswell asked, "What time and what trailhead? I'll just meet you there!"

"We'll decide at dinner. Val will have the details." Then Alice gathered up the survey, topo map, and tax application and said goodbye.

Bonnie followed her to the door. "I don't feel any better," she said softly. "So, Alice, you aren't off the hook. I'm worried about my family's safety."

Chapter   Twenty

Good Luck!

Halfway down the porch steps Alice stopped, heart-struck: the valley lay before her, gold with glowing aspen. Beautiful. Time for dinner, firelight, and wine. She felt a sudden wave of longing for dinner with Kinsear across the table, the humorous eyebrows, the attentive eyes, the hand reaching across the table to hold hers. The passionate attention to the menu, the scrutiny of the wine list, the decisive ordering, the contemplative tasting. She would ask him about books, the treasures he'd found, or sold. But then he'd say, "Enough of that. I've missed you, Alice!" And the rest of the evening, the rest of the night, would wrap her in warmth and joy.

But tonight was girls' night.

* * * * *

As they left the condo to pick up Val, Red stared at her phone, then placed a call. Alice heard her say, "He didn't give a name?" Then, "Okay. Thanks." She turned to Alice. "That's weird. Jana says some guy from the state called yesterday while I was out, wanted to know where I was and when I'd be back. She told him I was heading up to Estes Park, back Sunday. But when she asked did he need me to call back and could she take a message with his name, he just hung up."

Alice knew that Red had a state contract to board, rehabilitate, and finally sell the abused horses the state rescued.

"Don't you always deal with the same folks at the state?" Alice asked.

"Yep. Jana knows them too. That's why this is weird. I think Jana started thinking she shouldn't have told this caller where I am."

Maybe a reporter? Alice mused. But now they'd reached Val's driveway. Val was already descending the front porch steps, ready for dinner at the Twin Owls restaurant, near Devil's Gulch. That was Val's choice: "I don't want to eat at my place, make our staff nervous," she'd said. "And I like the elk steaks over at Twin Owls."

The waitress seated them in the tall wood-paneled dining room, pine rafters crisscrossing far above. "It's sweet of you two to take me out," Val said. "Let me buy the champagne. I'm so excited about this cooking project M.A.'s dreamed up. So let me tell you about it."

She leaned forward, her still beautiful face, creased from mountain sun, glowing in the candlelight, hair streaked with silver, hands speckled with brown age spots, so capable, so deft. "M.A. and I want to buy that Tea Garden house, over across the courthouse square from you, Alice. It's got a bona fide commercial kitchen, a little dated. An apartment upstairs where I can stay. And that gorgeous porch. Imagine if we screen the side porch and serve drinks and appetizers out there . . . then afterwards in they'd come, our delighted guests, and we'd serve them in the lovely dining room. We'd only be open three nights a week at first. We'd feature some local wines. Do you know some people, Alice?"

Alice nodded. Eddie LaFarge, for sure.

"Okay, here's our brainstorm," Val said. "We'll take local kids— they have to be sixteen — and run a cooking school, restaurant school. The kids'll learn how to serve, how to be knowledgeable about food. And, most important, they will each have learned to cook every dish we offer."

"You're not worried about someone stealing your secret recipes?" Alice said, thinking of nondisclosure.

"Honey, I'm not. These recipes will be part of the curriculum. If they want to try these somewhere else later, they can modify the recipes, make them their own. I want them to learn creativity! Don't you think this could be a way forward for kids who are interested in a culinary career?"

Red nodded. "Kids that age—sure, they try to be cool, but they're so anxious, so eager to learn. Each semester I take on a couple of high school interns at the rescue ranch. At first they're taken aback by the sheer amount of hard work involved. Mucking stables, rubbing down the horses, all that. Then they start bragging about it, start being proud about it. I've only had one or two that didn't, what would you say, appreciate the opportunity."

"What will you put on the menu?" Alice's stomach was growling.

Val nodded. "I've thought a good bit about this. We'll make our own breads, using flours from the new miller out on 290 who buys locally raised grain. Of course we'll feature local meat and vegetables. But the recipes will vary. Maybe our own short ribs, our own osso buco, but also vegetarian plates, homemade tortellini, with sage and brown butter. The wonderful Roman classic cacio e pepe spaghetti, with pecorino cheese. A miniature chicken-fried steak, with tiny potatoes. Smoked trout like you've never had it, so fresh, so cool, with homemade crackers nearly paper thin. Bean salad, but also like you've never had it. I call it glorified picnic, glorified potluck."

"I'm already salivating," Alice said. The waitress was back with champagne, moisture beaded on the dark bottle. She popped the cork and poured. Alice watched Val's face in the yellow candlelight. Val picked up her glass.

"Here's to you, Alice, and to you, Red. Just being with you makes me feel I'll be welcome back in Coffee Creek. You can't really know everything this means to me. Someday, I may just tell you. Meanwhile, I lift a glass to you two . . . and I hereby dub you honorary Mountain Women." Val grinned and lifted her glass to each of them.

While they were working their way through elk steak, Alice heard scuffling at the table just behind them, and glanced over her shoulder as a man scooted his chair under the table. She couldn't see his face plainly; it was shaded by a gimme cap. Not a smiling face, though. Deep frown lines. He disappeared behind his open menu. Maybe he'd been stood up, and why not, Alice thought, wearing your gimme cap in this restaurant and looking so angry? Who'd want to sit across from you? Alice turned back to her own plate.

Red, face alight with interest, was quizzing Val about Val's own favorite climbs. "I hear you've climbed them all, Val. All the Front Range and the Never Summer Range and many fourteeners."

Val laughed. "I'm a rock junkie. I love working up those couloirs, panting my way up those ridges, coming over the last rocks and—surprise! There's the world from the mountaintop! Those summits. All different, all forbidding, but when you're there, you feel like you've conquered the world. And when you look west and see the gray clouds coming fast, the heavy gray clouds with a little buzz, it's time to beat feet to timberline." Val sat straight, a rangy figure, with the confidence of a mountaineer. "But Red. You know all that. You worked out here, right? At the Y camp? Took flatlanders from Kansas right up those mountains?"

"Yup. For two summers. And we want to hike tomorrow. Maybe Thatchtop or South Arapaho, or maybe taking the back way down Audubon. What do you think?" Red signaled the passing waitress for the check.

Val looked thoughtfully at Alice.

"Oh, I can probably make it," Alice said. "I'm used to tagging along behind the mountain goat over there." She nodded at Red.

"Well, no question you could have fabulous views with rivers of golden aspen if you choose Audubon, in the Indian Peaks," Val said. "You're thinking stroll up the front of Audubon and pick your way gingerly down the back?"

Red nodded.

"Wish I could go with you!" Val said. "But listen, after the floods last year we had some rockslides and a couple of trails were damaged. I'm thinking you might have to cross one of those on the back side of Audubon. But you should be okay. Just be careful—you don't want to start a rock river."

"A what?" Alice hadn't heard of a "rock river."

"Oh, you know those long streams of rock, up close to summits? Like on Ypsilon, those flat plates of rock that skitter around underfoot and are such a pain to cross?"

Alice nodded.

"I've only experienced a rock river once. My hiking buddy was crossing a rockslide way above me and she accidentally dislodged a couple of rocks. She was yelling, 'Rock! Rock!' I heard the rumble, looked up, and the whole shebang was moving down the mountain toward me. Lord. I had to step lively to get out of the way. So be cautious. And if I remember right, the rocks on the backside of Audubon are very sharp-edged. Broken basalt. I'd take some gloves." She turned to Red. "I've still got a couple of projects for this lawyer so don't get her incapacitated tomorrow, okay?"

Red smiled.

Val leaned back in her chair and looked around. "You know, it's quite restful, having dinner where I'm not worrying about whether the staff's too forward, whether the silverware is impeccably clean, and whether the cauliflower is tender enough."

"But you're going to start up another one in Coffee Creek!"

"Glutton for punishment. And M.A. and I will have some laughs." She stopped. "Oh, and Alice? Davie and Caswell and I will be back in Coffee Creek next week, on Wednesday morning. So Caswell can see the Tea Garden house."

Time to go. Val agreed to tell Caswell to meet them at the trailhead at six thirty. Red signed the check. As they stood to leave, Alice stole another curious glance at their neighbor. He was invisible behind the menu. Studying desserts? No, thought Alice, you've already paid. The leather folder lay on the table, ticket sticking out of the top.

* * * * *

Climbing out of the rental car at the Audubon trailhead the next morning at ten thousand feet, breath visible in the chill air, with a headlamp for the predawn darkness, Alice felt the delighted dread that altitude inspired in her. The first long pull through the forest, the puffing, the constant query—how far? Watching the side of the path for the bright red of squirrel candy. Listening for birdcall, for squirrels fussing. Reaching timberline, with its views. Always hoping to see (but so far no such luck), high up, a bear shambling across the moraine above timberline, sleepy, ready to hibernate. Or an arctic hare, usually invisible in its mottled gray-brown camouflage, now turning white to be invisible in the coming snow.

Alice snapped shut the adjusting tabs on her hiking sticks and stuffed a small bag of trail mix into her pocket. Backpack, water, sticks, lunches, hats, gloves, sunscreen, first aid bag. She looked up to see Caswell, in fleece, hiking boots, and his perennial cargo shorts. "You parked down at the Blue Lake trailhead and walked?" she asked.

"Yep. Assuming we keep to the plan and go up from here and then back down to the Blue Lake trailhead, at least you won't have to walk back here. I'll drive you."

Red trotted back from the trailhead toilet, lifted her head, yodeled.

"I didn't know you could do that!" Alice exclaimed.

"You know I can't sing. I can sure as hell yodel, though. Hi, Caswell. Are we all ready? Let's go!"

Up the side of the moraine the trail zigzagged through pine and aspen. Suddenly they were out of the trees and working their way up and onto a vast bare ridge crisscrossed by trails that mimicked the Ute trails of past centuries. Off to the east the rim of the sun hurled light across the plains and onto the faces of the mountains. Red was leading, setting a steady pace, with Caswell in the rear. They all stopped to breathe, their faces glowing pink in the light.

"Okay, Alice," said Red. "That first pull is always hard. Now it's just up and around until we get to the boulder field below the peak."

Alice nodded. No talking. She couldn't breathe.

"And drink your water!" ordered Red. Alice obeyed. They trudged silently up, around the mountain's huge shoulder, watching the length of the Front Range come into view. Two hikers far ahead looked small as ants.

Little humans, thought Alice, little humans, with only feet, no vehicles, little humans, crossing these mountains for centuries, knowing these trails like the backs of their collective hands. Trudge, trudge. Red was now way ahead of her, Caswell still bringing up the rear. Alice took a deep breath and settled into the work of rounding the mountain and making it to the long pull up the boulders to the summit.

She hated the boulder climbing, the uncertainty of where to put a boot—would this rock betray her? But suddenly they'd finished the worst part. The steep rock climb flattened out. Ahead, Red bounced along. "I'm looking for a lunch spot!" she called down. Alice sighed, swigged more water, and started up again. She and Caswell found Red seated in front of an enormous boulder. "No wind if you sit down here by me," she said. "Look at this view!"

Enormous. Far to the south, the Gore Range. Off to the west, the pink and gray of the Never Summers. North, the Medicine Bow Mountains in Wyoming. East? Nebraska, Kansas, the Platte, Mississippi, and Missouri Rivers. The other two hikers waved at them. Kids, college students probably, dangling their legs off the summit's abrupt drop to the south, sharing lunches, looking like this hike was a walk in the park. Caswell, head down, was examining the crystals embedded in a granite boulder. Alice flopped down by Red and dug her lunch out of the backpack. And her wool cap. It was cold. Where was her chocolate bar? Maybe she'd start with that.

Too soon, Red ordered them up. They shook out their stiff legs, rearranged their packs, picked up their hiking sticks, and cautiously approached the back side of the summit. The lake shimmered, far below. The two students were packing up. "You guys going down that way?" asked one. "Hey, that's cool. We haven't taken that route before. Good luck!"

Looks like we're gonna need it, Alice said to herself.

Chapter Twenty-One

Unleashed Rock River

"Okay, the guidebook says stay close to the cliff, going down," Red said, "but because of the slides after the rain last year, which wiped out part of our trail down, there's a spot where we'll have to cross the rocks to get back to another trail that comes off that mountain over there. It'll get us back to the lake." She pointed west to a lumpy hump. Alice could see the faint trail that zigzagged down its side into the valley between the two mountains. "We're aiming for that trail. And I'm putting on my gloves and you should too."

Alice and Caswell dutifully pulled on gloves and the trio started down, one step at a time, staying close to the cliff. A narrow, wet path, glistening with mica, separated the cliff from the vast rockslide to their right. Ice from an early snow sparkled between the rocks. Alice stowed one of her sticks and kept her left hand on the cliff face, with one stick in her right hand for balance. Down, down, down. Twice Alice slid and had to grab the waist-high slabs of dark basalt that edged the rockslide, sharp-edged as axes, and was glad for her gloves. Below her, Red pointed at a cairn, halfway across the rockslide off to their right. "We have to head that way!" she called up to Alice.

Red waited for Alice and Caswell at the point where a sketchy path, small patches of dirt amid a sea of broken slabs and shards of mountain, left the cliff and headed horizontally across the rockslide. Caswell stared up at the cliff, running his fingers over fractures and veins in the rock. Red squinted into her camera and bent over, trying to catch light on the iridescent basalt, black against patches of snow. "Okay, I'm going," Alice said. She readjusted her sticks and started gingerly across. Slowly does it, she said to herself. Watch your feet, Alice. She wanted to get across this death trap.

She glanced back. Red was still squatting down, taking pictures. Caswell was loading rock samples into his backpack. Well, I'm still going, Alice told herself. I'm slow on these rocks, they're faster, and I don't want them waiting for me.

When she was nearly across she looked behind to see Red moving gracefully along the rockslide path, halfway across. Caswell had just taken his first steps off the cliff path and onto the rockslide. Some movement in her peripheral vision? Alice gazed up at the top of the slide. She saw silhouetted against the sky, very small at this distance, a man in a red stocking cap, standing with hiking sticks. As she watched, he suddenly stomped fiercely on the rocks at the midpoint of the slide, then moved a few steps lower, kicking harder. A few rocks slid, then a few more.

What the hell's he doing? she thought.

"Hey!" she yelled uphill, waving. "Stop!" The man continued kicking down into the mass of rocks. "Stop it!" she shouted.

Caswell, already a few yards onto the path through the slide, stared over at her and then uphill. The entire rock mass was starting to move. He leaped backward onto the cliffside path and clambered for protection behind an outcrop of solid cliff face.

"Red! Hurry!" Alice called to her friend, still just over halfway across the slide. Alice herself leaped the last two steps and jumped away from the rockslide onto solid ground. She turned to watch Red. "Come on!" A steady deep rumble, a sliding noise, rocks grinding across each other, faster and faster. *"Red!"*

Now rocks were bouncing in the air, crashing off each other, and Red frantically fended off one flying rock after another with her sticks, trying to keep her balance. She still had ten feet to go. Alice dashed back down toward Red, grabbed her and hauled her bodily over the last few feet of the rockslide path, then jumped to safety, tugging Red up by her parka. Shaking, hearts thumping, they turned to watch the show.

Tons of knife-sharp rock roared past them. Finally the noise began to subside; the rocks slowed. The cascade slowly ground to a halt. The path across the slide—gone. The cairn—vanished. Alice looked up at the top of the ridge. No one was there. The mountainside bore a new scar. Far on the other side of the rockslide, Caswell waved. Now he had no rockslide path—only rocks. He started across again, carefully balancing, using his sticks like a lobster with feelers to see whether rocks would stay put or betray him. Without the path, Caswell's trek across the rockslide became an arduous balancing act.

Red's ankle was bruised. One of her sticks was bent into an L; the other was gone forever. Otherwise, she claimed, she was fine. Alice had pulled some muscles hauling Red out of the slide. But she too was fine.

Meaning: alive.

"Who the hell was that?" asked Caswell, stepping across the last yard and onto the path with them.

"Red stocking cap. That's all I know," Alice said.

"He had to know exactly what he was doing," said Caswell. "Although for me, as a geologist—I confess it was pretty interesting. I've never seen that happen." The bright brown eyes sparkled. Then he looked worried. "But maybe don't tell Bonnie?"

"Well, I'm sure as hell going to tell the rangers or whoever's working the park entrance," Red said.

"Right. A man—we think it was a man—who we can't describe except for a red cap, which he's probably tossed in a trash can somewhere." Alice brushed her hair back and looked back up at the mountain's new tattoo, wondering how many tons of basalt had crashed past her.

The three trudged silently down the faint path between Audubon and the next mountain, until they met the path that led down from Paiute Pass to Blue Lake. Alice caught herself repeatedly squinting up at the ridgetops above them, watching for a red cap.

"I've always loved this path," Red said when they stopped for water. She pointed down long switchbacks with stunning views, down the stream of snowmelt that fed Blue Lake and the waterfall at its end. Across the lake the whaleback ridge of moraine rose at its far end into Apache and Navajo Peaks. "But I'll never think of it again in quite the same way."

The air smelled fresh; the path was well maintained. But someone had tried to smash them to bits with the terror of an unleashed rock river. Wait, Alice thought. That someone wasn't after me, at least not in particular. "I wonder if he was after you, Red. Or maybe Caswell."

Red nodded, speculation on her face as she looked at Caswell. "Yeah. You'd just started out on the crossing. Could've been me, could've been you. I imagine it's hard to control your timing perfectly on a rock river."

So, who? Why?

Finally, they were in the shelter of trees, below timberline; finally, they climbed past the last waterfall; finally, they finished the interminable last stretch and at long last through the trees could see parked cars glinting at the trailhead where Caswell had parked. He drove them back to their rental car at the Audubon trailhead, where they'd begun their odyssey. Looking out his driver's-side window, he said, sober-faced, "Glad we all made it."

Red and Alice stowed their packs and sticks in the trunk and flopped into the car. "Safe!" said Red, rubbing the fierce bruises on her shin and ankle. "You were awfully lucky," Alice said, starting the car. Then she saw a truck pulling out on the other side of the parking lot. "Holy cow."

"What?" said Red.

A black truck exited the parking lot, a maroon paw print on the back window. Tires squealed as it turned onto the park drive.

"Is that the guy?" Red asked, frantically buckling her seat belt. "Try to get his license number!"

But the black truck had vanished. They couldn't catch it, didn't see a glimpse of it anywhere on the drive back to the highway. They found no one at the entrance booth so couldn't report the deliberate effort to start a rock river. Nor did they see the truck after they turned onto the highway back to Estes Park. "I guess that truck could have hidden in any parking lot at any of these trailheads," Alice said. "Or could have hightailed it out of here and gone the other direction, into Ward."

"I didn't see a red cap," Red said. "Couldn't see the driver at all. Could you?"

"Nothing." Alice shook her head. "Well, sorry, Red. This was supposed to be a nice restorative road trip for you. I hadn't planned on a raging rock river."

Red fingered her ankle. "Maybe I'll wear boots instead of high heels for the rest of these campaign appearances. That'll work. Lord, Alice, why did I sign up for this gig? Do you really think that guy was trying to get *me*? Or Caswell?"

"I wonder if that's the same truck that Ben and I saw racing away from the Tindall house fire," Alice said. "Which would argue that Caswell was the target. But the man started the rocks moving when you were in midstream and Caswell was just starting. If it is the same truck, what's it doing up here in Colorado? And how did it know

179

where to find us?"

They drove slowly up to the condo, then simultaneously turned to each other.

"The phone call to Jana!" Red said. "Had to be."

"Then you must be the target," Alice said. "But if so, what about the Tindall fire? Maybe that's got nothing to do with it." She shook her head, baffled.

Chapter Twenty - Two

Squaring Off

Back in the office on Monday morning, Alice checked in with Silla, who glared grim-faced from the office kitchen.

"Everything okay?" Alice asked, sure that it was not.

"At the office, yes." Stony hard voice.

"What's up?"

"That wretched twit Ginny Lou Hamer! Look at this smarmy interview!" She thrust the latest *Coffee Creek Caller* at Alice.

Alice knew that Silla detested Hamer, who'd edged her out in the college rodeo barrel-racing championship. They still didn't speak.

"You don't think she's qualified? I don't think you have to be a CPA or a bank president to serve on the co-op board."

"She's not interested in serving anything but her own interests," Silla snorted. "I think she needs the money. You get a hundred bucks for every board meeting."

"Surely she's not running just for that?"

"Rodeoing costs money, Alice. It's expensive, keeping your horses. They eat all winter, you realize? And vet bills pile up whether you're racing or not. Then there are entry fees, gas to get from here to Amarillo and Estes Park and Laramie and Calgary, motel bills, and of course your outfits."

"Doesn't she have a day job?"

"She teaches gymnastics and works at a stable. But the gig economy's not enough to support a horse habit."

"I know you can't stand Ginny Lou, but a hundred dollars a meeting can't be why she's running for the co-op board. Maybe she's turned a new leaf."

That got a rise out of Silla. "Public service? Give me a break. Okay, here's another theory. You know her brother, Dwayne?"

Alice didn't.

Silla went on. "He's got his CPA, started a small accounting firm last year. I'll bet he's going to bid on doing the co-op audits."

"But, Silla, Ginny Lou couldn't vote on that. She'd have to recuse herself."

"She'd lobby the other members. She's got about the same sense of ethics as a polecat." Silla stomped back to her desk.

Alice herself worried that a three-way race might mean a runoff.

She called Red.

"I know all about Ginny Lou," Red said. "She's not getting the cowboy-cowgirl vote."

"Oh?"

"I won't say it's locked up, but she's caused some dissension among the cowboys. They, um, call her a two-timing etcetera. And they say she flirts with the judges. That irritates them."

"Okay," Alice said. "Will she be at this Rotary deal today?"

"She was invited. Don't worry, Alice, she's not a serious contender."

But what if she causes a runoff? Alice shook her head.

* * * * *

Today, Monday meant not only Rotary but also Red's campaign speech. For the umpteenth time in her three-plus years in Coffee Creek, Alice tugged on the bright red—geranium red, fire engine red—sweater Red had required her to wear to her first Rotary meeting in Coffee Creek.

The candidates were was squaring off for the open seat on the Coffee Creek Electric Co-op board. Each candidate had ten minutes to speak. Red had practiced her speech in front of Alice, Jane Ann Olson, and Silla. "You three are damn tough," she'd said.

At the entrance to the Rotary dining room Alice picked up her name tag from Jane Ann. Jane Ann cocked an eyebrow. "Ginny Lou's not coming," she told Alice.

"Why not?"

"She claims she's already scheduled to film a TV commercial to-day in San Angelo. Highly unlikely, I'd say."

"Red's already here, right?"

"Yup, and she looks ready," Jane Ann said, sotto voce. "But take a look at Clay Black." Head high, shoulders square, in blue suit and red tie, Clay was systematically glad-handing around the room.

Alice took her place in the buffet line behind Judge Bernie Sandoval. The judge looked avidly at the fried chicken, then down at his portly self. He shook his head morosely, sighed, and double-dipped on salad. "This diet's killing me, Alice. Sitting on the bench means too

183

much sitting."

"You could stand," Alice said, opting in solidarity with the probate judge for an all-sides plate—black-eyed peas, cornbread, green beans, corn salad. "But if you stand up behind the bench you'd look pretty terrifying to us lawyers. It would give you more leverage on the gavel, maybe? Not that you need any." Judge Sandoval ran a tight courtroom.

"So, Alice," he said, tilting his head down, examining his fruit cup, "who's gonna win this thing? Clay Black's got more name recognition, maybe?"

Alice didn't agree. "Lots of people ride around here, and have horses. They see Red's horse rescue work as pretty heroic. And Red's CPA practice has a sterling reputation. You can ask around, but I don't think the IRS has ever nixed any tax return she's done." Alice followed the judge to a ten-top table where her favorite clients, the three Beer Barons, had saved them places.

The clatter of forks and clamor of voices rose, then subsided into an expectant buzz. Jane Ann, program chair, rose and marched to the podium, beckoning the candidates to follow her. Red nodded at the crowd, resplendent today in scarlet boots and a matching suit ("My only Armani," she'd whispered to Alice). Clay Black, looking supremely confident, lifted his chin and smiled as Jane Ann began the introductions.

"Clay's president of Cowman's Bank, but scheduled to retire shortly given the impending sale of the bank. He served on the co-op board for two three-year terms and now, after a two-year break, he's running again. He and Annette live in Coffee Creek but also have a ranch in Llano County. They lease it to hunters."

She turned to Red. "Red Griffin started Red's Rescue Ranch; she's a certified public accountant with a growing practice here in Coffee Creek and around the county. Before coming to Coffee Creek she managed one of Houston's largest law firms for eighteen years." She turned to the candidates. "You each get ten minutes and I'll cut you off right smartly, so don't run over. After that we'll allow questions from the floor, just to check that someone out there was listening. So, don't be boring, you two." Crowd titters. "Then you each get one minute for final remarks. Red, as challenger, you start."

Red smiled as she surveyed the room. Then her face turned serious. "Thanks to all you Rotarians, with whom I've worked for many years as a volunteer, program chair, and then as your treasurer." Smart, Alice thought. Remind them that they think you're competent. "My friends, county co-ops were created to bring us low-cost power, locally owned and operated. Our co-op is member-owned. That's a two-way street: we members are responsible for the co-op. We should run it with the same care and attention to the bottom line that we give our own businesses and indeed our own family budgets. I know each of us plans ahead for the next car we'll be buying. We each budget for the new roof we expect to put on. Many of you have grown your own businesses; you've developed and revised your operating budgets and long-range plans. You've budgeted and planned for success. Don't you agree your success means you're meeting customer needs?" Alice saw some nods at various tables.

Red leaned into the microphone, scanned the room. "Our co-op is not meeting our needs. How many in this room have experienced a power outage this year?" Many hands went up. "How many have experienced more than two?" At least two-thirds of the hands stayed up. "How many of you have called the co-op about those outages?" Many hands. "Well, guess what. When I asked the co-op for records of calls about outages, the official records custodian said the co-op had no record of your calls. Yes, that's what she said: no records. The co-op does not keep track of whether you called or not! Or maybe the co-op does not want anyone to know how many of you had to call. For instance, how many of you along Rocky Creek Road have called about repeat outages?" Twenty hands went up.

"Now, have any of you been told the co-op has a long-term plan to upgrade your lines?" Red asked. Heads turned, eyes sweeping the audience. But no hands went up. "Guess what the co-op told me when I asked for the long-term plans and long-term capital budget?" Expectant silence. "The long-term plan has not changed in five years. The long-term capital budget is, quote, 'subject to income.' Wouldn't that lead you to conclude the co-op's not making enough money? Or needs to raise rates? But no! The state co-op survey shows that our co-op rates are higher than any co-op in central Texas . . . In fact, only two co-ops statewide have rates higher than ours! But the current board either doesn't know, or doesn't care, or knows but doesn't care to tell us—apparently the board thinks we owner-members should just ignore the situation."

She shook her head mournfully, gazing around the tables. "But we can't ignore this. We are *owner-members*. We're *responsible* for the co-op. With my CPA training, I'm ideally situated to monitor the budget. With my background, I'm deeply familiar with long-range plans and capital costs. I hereby pledge to you that I will ask staff to keep and maintain records of member complaints, co-op repairs, and capital repairs. We need records and data. We need exemplary audits. We all own this co-op; and *we will manage it*." Silence, then hearty applause. Red stood tall in her red boots, nodded at various tables, then sat.

Clay, with a tolerant smile, leaned over and said to the microphone: "Of course we have records. If not, I'm sure that oversight can be rectified. Of course we have a capital plan. I'm not sure what Ms.—Ms. Griffiths looked at, or what she asked for." Red tilted her head at Clay, then stared, eyebrows raised, at the audience, telegraphing her opinion about his mispronunciation of her name. Alice watched, anxiety rising. Clay went on. "Maybe managing a *Houston law firm*"—he drew out the syllables, knowing that his rural audience would be unimpressed by Red's Houston pedigree—"I say, maybe managing a *Houston law firm* gives some preparation for imposing fees on hardworking businesses, but not for a nuts-and-bolts utility. Running a horse rescue ranch does not prepare you for high-tech capital repairs in the utility business." He looked around. This last line did not get traction; most local businesses knew that a horse rescue ranch (or feed store, or CPA office, or bank, or grocery, or tire store) knew damn well what sort of utility service it needed and certainly knew what it was paying for.

Question time. "This one's for Red. What was your law firm's annual budget?" Pause.

"Fifty million," came the clear answer.

"Follow-up question: did you have capital expenses?"

"Of course. Computers, software, servers. Building expansion and interior build-out. High-tech courtroom equipment." Someone had tossed her a softball, and she'd done well.

For Clay: "Hasn't running Cowman's Bank helped you understand co-op needs and issues?" Oh, very softball, thought Alice.

"Certainly," Clay said, nodding at the questioner. "We've handled co-op accounts for years; we certainly understand co-op finances." Misstep?

Follow-up from another corner of the room. "Isn't that a conflict of interest? You being on the board and also running co-op accounts?"

Clay bristled. "I think it gives me a broader background to understand co-op finances and needs."

"You didn't answer about conflict of interest." Anonymous voice from the back. Alice craned, trying to see who had spoken.

"I defy anyone to show any impropriety."

For Red: "You've had no experience with power lines and transformers, have you?"

Alice tensed.

Red leaned forward. "Oh, yes I have! My line off Rocky Creek Road has had repeat outages that left me without a working pump to get water to my horses, and without lights to tend to sick horses at night. Indeed I've had experience with power lines and transformers! In fact, the co-op linemen have apologized to me time after time for the inconveniences to me and my neighbors. I've stood by the road while several of them have showed me how antiquated the transformers are and in what poor condition the lines are. They've told me they don't understand why they never get permission to replace outdated equipment along Rocky Creek Road."

"Who was that?" barked Clay.

Red stared at him, eyebrows raised. "I'm not naming names of these people and putting their jobs at risk. They're putting their own lives at risk every time they come out and climb into the bucket of the repair truck to go up and repair outdated equipment. They should be praised, not persecuted, for speaking truth." She turned and looked around the room. "And everyone here who's got power coming off Rocky Creek Road appreciates those linemen. And would like to get lines upgraded along Rocky Creek Road and all the other district roads where updates are long overdue!" Applause.

"Okay," interposed Jane Ann. "You each get one minute. Red, you go first. Clay, you get to wind up."

Yikes, Alice thought, wishing Red had the last word.

Red took a deep breath. "I'm running for responsible government. I'm running for transparency and fiscal responsibility. If you elect me, I'll work my tail off to get all of us the electric service we need"—she took another breath—"and have paid for all these years!"

Clay walked confidently to the mike. "Most of you know me. *I'm not a newcomer.*" He looked around, nodded once or twice. "I grew up here."

I guess that's aimed at Red, Alice thought.

Clay surveyed the room. "You folks know I'm uniquely positioned, with my bank background, to preserve co-op assets and to monitor co-op finances. Here in Coffee Creek I've helped you build businesses for decades. At the co-op I served for six years. Now, after a two-year break, I'm again standing for election. I'm proud of what we did during my earlier term and believe there's still much to be done. I appreciate Ms.—ah—Griffus's comments here but I feel confident our fine co-op staff members maintain all the required records. I urge you to let experience be your guide. I humbly ask you to elect me again to the board so that we can continue our pursuit of excellence."

Alice sat back in her chair. He'd glossed over the issues Red addressed. Chairs scraped the floor. Clay's supporters were shoving back their chairs, coming forward to slap him on the back, shake his hand. Alice saw her old foe Jeff Treacher, two VPs of Cowman's Bank, the tire store manager, and others she didn't know. The three Beer Barons elbowed each other and headed for Red. Two city council members and the mayor were working the room but appeared to be heading in Red's directions. Councilman Hinojosa was asking Red questions; she was answering; both looked serious. Well, we'll see, Alice thought. It's a long shot. The co-op had already mailed out ballots to the members. Alice suddenly wondered about the counting process.

Tyler Junkin joined Alice outside as she walked to her truck. "Hey, I haven't forgotten you and your little visitor, Alice," he said. "But someone used some fancy encryption on it. I've got a call into this

Austin drone guy for some help."

"Thanks, Tyler." She felt her blood pressure rise again, just thinking of the hovering drone.

"Well, we'll see. And tell Red she made a good speech."

Chapter Twenty-Three

This Damn Murder

Alice was feeling mildly optimistic after Rotary, until she glanced out her office window to see a grim-faced M.A. trudging up the sidewalk toward her front door. What? She put down the Neighbors file and pulled open the front door before M.A. could knock.

"You in the middle of something? I should have called first," M.A. said. No smile.

"No, no. Come sit. Want some coffee?"

M.A. didn't answer. She sank into a chair at the tea table under the east window, shoulders slumped, head sagging. Alice had never seen her like this, even when they'd dug up a murder victim on her place. On that day she'd stood erect, vigilant, guarding the process with her shotgun.

"M.A. Tell me what's wrong."

"It's this damn murder! The poor John Pine boy!" M.A. burst out. "Nobody knows who did it!"

Alice nodded.

"But everyone knows it was my digital thermometer. That sure made the news. Found under the oak leaves in Founders' Grove. And of course since it was mine I had to go talk to George Files and identify that thermometer. With its—its evidence tag. And be finger-printed. I had to tell him I sure didn't see who took it. But you know what folks are saying, Alice? They're saying I'm one of the people without an alibi."

Alice's heart sank. "But can't the police determine you were out in the crowd or back at your rig when he was killed?"

M.A. shook her head. "Apparently I'm not off the hook. Even though I told George Files all the people I remembered seeing or talking to after you and I split up, you know, when I went over to see the piano players."

"But really, M.A., who's saying you don't have an alibi?" Alice did not think George Files would say any such thing.

"Oh, it's little murmurs and mutters at my church. I'm supposed to start teaching the communicants class in a week. I understand some people asked the pastor about that. He stuck by me, but it doesn't feel good. Then I always show up at the high school to help in the biology lab when the kids are looking at amoebas and parameciums. This morning when I was there, one bold character hollered, 'Watch out, don't let her get you with the thermometer!'"

M.A.'s face flushed; her eyes filled. Alice was horrified. M.A., her beloved paragon of tough Texas women!

"Normally you would just laugh this off, M.A.," Alice said. "Wouldn't you? You'd quell them with one of your looks!" She thought about all the years M.A. had taught high school biology. "But you're thinking about John Pine. You treated him like one of your students. You were going to improve him, the next morning, weren't you? Give him a little life lesson."

"I was! You got me on that. Didn't happen, though." She sat up. "But Alice, I'm a spinster. Remember that word?" Alice knew M.A. had never married after her college beau died in a head-on crash. "I live by myself. Speak my mind. Fix things when they break. Protect my property. Work for my political candidates. Teach Sunday School. No one has ever questioned my—my—integrity, I guess I'll say. Sure, they lump me in with the town 'characters,' but they respect me. Now some of 'em are laughing behind my back, talking and tittering in a fake-horrified way. Then of course there've been the Facebook comments. I don't look at Facebook much—just to keep up with my kids." Alice knew that "kids" meant her former students. "I can't stand it, Alice." Heavy sigh. "Me, the empress of the biology lab, Ms. Safety, always ragging on the kids to put away pipettes, be careful with the Bunsen burner, not poke themselves with the dissecting tools.

"And with all these amateurs and children and strangers around, what do I do at the barbecue competition? I show off. I show off! I'm smug, I'm proud I'm competing, and I leave that murderous thermometer out there on the table where someone can just pick it up and kill that poor boy!" She stared bleakly at Alice. "I'm mortified. And I am so sad about that boy."

Alice had never seen M.A. so off-kilter. She'd seen her tender, angry, sad, even consumed by an avenging fury, but never with her sense of self at risk. Not M.A.! M.A. bestrode the world like a female colossus, Western style, Alice thought, confident, acerbic, sure of her rights, of her opinions, of her identity. Alice had also never known anyone to have the temerity to vilify or accuse or even try to minimize M.A. Which led Alice to wonder whether public opprobrium, or cowardly anonymous attacks on social media, could in this day and age still transmute an older lady living independently into—a witch?

And M.A. had no motive to kill John Pine. He'd bad-mouthed a lot of people—but not her.

Alice reluctantly agreed there was only one solution to M.A.'s situation: solve the murder. Identify the person who actually thrust a six-inch-long needle into John Pine's kidney. Determine who stalked Pine beneath the thick shade of the live oaks, and who killed him, while joyful piano music rolled over the crowd, while fireworks began, while lovers kissed on blankets. As a start she would call George Files, try to learn how much longer M.A. had to hang in limbo.

"That's not all I'm worried about, Alice." M.A. sat up taller, looked a little more like herself. "I also don't want to spoil Val's plans. You know she's dead set on coming down to Coffee Creek to start this cooking school. She's planning to come back next week so we can decide whether to go ahead with an offer on the Tea Garden house."

"Right," Alice said.

M.A. gazed out the window, up at the sky. "That house could be perfect, commercial kitchen and all. We could teach those kids practical chemistry, practical biology! They'd learn about yeast, bread, gluten, roux, béchamel sauce. To graduate they'd each have to make one signature dish they could always take to a dinner. Think of the self-confidence they'd get!" Her face fell. "But the whole concept is on life support with this John Pine murder hanging over me. Just imagine what parents would say as they looked around the kitchen at the sharp objects—ice picks, skewers, thermometers. I mean, just imagine the questioning eyes."

M.A. sighed, her shoulders sagging. "I can't let this screw up Val's plans, Alice. For the first time in years—she's excited! She says she might stay in Coffee Creek half the year! And I'd have someone to—" M.A. cut off her own sentence.

M.A.'s feeling old and alone, Alice realized. She's aching for companionship, for more than an occasional gig at church or her old school. She's longing for a project.

"M.A., stop worrying. I'll check in with George Files. Can't guarantee he'll tell me anything but maybe he'll offer an update."

"Thanks, Alice." M.A. couldn't manage a smile.

Alice watched M.A. trudge back down the sidewalk as she called Files. Voicemail. She left a message.

She wondered how serious M.A.'s lack of alibi was. Should she call her buddy Tyler Junkin to check whether M.A. would be wise to hire a criminal defense lawyer? But surely Files didn't seriously consider M.A. a suspect. And probably others were still in the frame—contestants in particular. In the dark of night after the murder, Alice had wondered how she herself had escaped suspect status. She'd bet Files checked her alibi with the mayor, who'd seen her toting the tacos and tea, as she headed, hands full, for Founders' Grove. Still, Files had questioned her pretty sharply. After all, she'd watched M.A. and Val arrange their equipment. She'd seen visitors come by, greeting M.A. and Val. But she had no motive, no animus against Pine. And neither did M.A.

Projectus interruptus. Where was she?

"Lloyd Neighbors is here," said Silla from Alice's office doorway. "I put him and his documents in the conference room. The bank ladies are set to come over and witness his signature."

And there was something Alice wanted to learn from the Llano historian.

* * * * *

When Alice walked into the conference room, Lloyd Neighbors stood and smiled, crisp in ironed khaki shirt and trousers. His hat was on the table. He shook her hand, then hugged her. "Glad to see you. Everything looks good. I'm ready to sign."

"Do you have time for coffee first? It'll take the bank ladies a few minutes to walk over."

"Sounds good."

Alice and Neighbors went to her office and sat at the tea table. He lifted his eyebrows, waiting, as she thought about the question she wanted to ask. "Okay. Can you tell me again your recollections about Caswell Black's death? Any other details?"

"Caswell Black, hmm?"

"I can tell you now that his widow and his son bought the Tindall ranch. I couldn't mention it when you were last here."

He nodded, eyes fixed on her face. "I told you he'd been hurt in Vietnam?"

"Yes. A Purple Heart, you said."

"He got hit on the right side, both shoulder and leg. Took some time to recover. I don't think he'd gotten back his strength but he was so eager to come home—you can imagine. So there he was, back on the ranch. I'd seen him that once in town, remember? He was still a little unsteady, right leg wasn't right yet. And he could barely shake my hand with that right arm. I thought about that handshake a great deal later." He looked out the window.

"How come?"

"Well, it's the way those post-hole diggers work. They've got handles on each side, sticking out of each side of the motor like bicycle handles. You'd start up the motor with a pull rope, like an outboard motor, or the old lawnmowers. Yank it, you know. Then you'd squeeze the handles—they had a sort of lever underneath like a bicycle brake—and when you squeezed the handles the clutch would engage and the auger screw would start to spin."

Alice nodded.

"To stop it you'd let go of the handles, so the clutch would disengage and the motor wouldn't stop but the auger would stop spinning."

"So what do you think happened to Caswell?"

"Those older one-man motors back then—they were heavy, with a lot of torque. You could pretty easily get thrown sideways. The motor could fall on you, the auger could gash you. If you weren't strong, and if your leg slipped, you got thrown off balance. The way I figure it, I'm thinking maybe Caswell was leaning on the auger trying to get some purchase to get the auger screw started in that hard dry dirt out at the ranch, chock-full of rocks, and the auger hit a rock and bounced up at him and he couldn't control it, and it got him right in his thigh. That's where he bled from, I recall."

"Is that the same thing that happened to that worker at the ranch down the road, before the rancher sold his auger to Clay Black?"

He looked at her in surprise. "How'd you hear about that?"

"The Tindalls mentioned it to me. Just before they left on their round-the-world trip."

"I heard that worker got his leg torn up pretty bad, but the guys who were stringing fence got him to the hospital with a belt buckled tight around his leg. Now, madam lawyer, that's just the story. I never saw him myself." The brown eyes considered her. "Are you digging up ancient history?"

"No. I just couldn't help but wonder."

Silla stuck her head through the office doorway. "Witnesses are here."

Neighbors stood and took her hand. "Okay. Once again, it's a pleasure working with you. Thanks for watching out for me."

Alice smiled. "Anytime. I've really enjoyed it." Working with someone like Neighbors—well, it was why Alice practiced law.

They joined the party in the conference room. Alice stood, asking the requisite questions, getting the requisite answers before the bank ladies. Watching Neighbors sign, Alice thought of a wounded man trying to control an auger. As Alice walked him to the door, Neighbors said, "Oh, I wanted to tell you something. Don't know if you'll be interested, but I'll have an article sometime soon in the Austin paper. It's a little piece of history, about the silver rush in the 1880s in Llano County. Course the silver rush was a bust, but still intriguing. I've been digging into it some."

"I'll watch for it," Alice promised.

Chapter Twenty-Four

Something Too Sweet

S illa's freckled face at her door again. "Alice, call George Files back. He wants to talk to you."

Adrenaline charge. She called, waited for him to pick up.

"Alice," he said. "I got your message. Of course we're trying to confirm all the alibis we can, including M.A.'s."

"She's very upset. And you know she's got no motive!"

"Mmm," he said, voice neutral.

"And what about that 'drugs in the kitchens' exposé Pine was writing? I mean, with Tan writing a cookbook and Robicheaux opening a new restaurant, they can't afford to be labeled druggies. They've got a lot at stake," Alice insisted.

"I get it. We're looking into everything, Alice. Pine's cell phone had a couple of threatening voicemails, which you might expect given how abrasive he was. I can't tell you about that, okay? Different topic. Listen, my notes from talking to M.A. Ellison say your client Caswell and his boy left Ms. Ellison's rig the night of Pine's death, and took along a drone. She thought the little boy was trying to catch pictures of the fireworks."

"Right. At least they did leave with the drone."

"And I've got witnesses who say they saw both the boy and his dad out there. We've learned there were two other kids and grown-ups out that night with drones as well. Obviously we want to see the footage." He paused. "Maybe it'll help M.A."

Alice didn't remember seeing Davie or Caswell, but she'd been staring down at her cardboard tray of tea, trying not to spill.

And how long had Pine been dead before she tripped over him? She realized she'd never heard the exact time. Suddenly an image appeared before her: Pine standing in front of city hall, waving to catch the mayor's attention.

"Pine had one of those fitness watches, didn't he?" she said to Files. "One of those watches that tracks how many steps you've taken, how long you've run, how fast your heart rate is?"

Silence. "Yes."

"Does it tell when Pine died?"

"Come on, Alice, that's not public information." Files sounded gruff. "I'm going to look at all this drone footage. Will your folks get it to me?" He didn't say, *Or do I have to come get it?*

"Caswell and Davie are supposed to be here a week from Wednesday," Alice said, feeling frosty. "I'll ask them to bring the drone and whatever its contents are, or were."

"Then I'll look for them at noon on Wednesday at my office, okay? Thanks, Alice."

"Wait," she said. "Now look. We're talking about a nine-year-old boy and his dad. They aren't suspects or persons of interest or any of that, right?"

"No, they're not. I'm talking to the other two kids with drones and their parents too."

* * * * *

On Tuesday morning Alice finished marking up the Whitakers' draft wills. She handed them to Silla. The Whitakers were due at four to review this final version.

"Don't forget library board at noon, Alice. Brown bag," Silla said.

Alice grabbed her sack lunch—apple, string cheese—from the office fridge and headed to the Coffee Creek Library. She hoped Annette would be there. She had a question for her.

Alice slipped into her chair at the library board meeting. Annette, her perennially sweet smile now turned toward the head librarian, was asking in pointed tones how the library had spent the funds raised by Friends of the Library. "Some people are asking me why we don't have more copies of the Caldecott winners in the children's section. We need multiple copies for our young readers!"

The board chair took up the slack, deftly deflected Annette's question to the budget committee, raced through new and old business, and gaveled the meeting over. Alice sidled up to Annette, who turned the same sweet smile on her. How to broach the topic? Directly. "I had to get my truck inspected at Leo's garage last week," Alice said.

"I just love that Leo. He always reminds me to change my oil, and he always squeezes me right in."

Alice smiled. "Right. I was looking at the pictures of the football team he has on the wall—you know, the high school team."

"Oh, yes! Clay's up there!"

"I saw that. He's there and so is Mikey, Leo's brother, right in the same row."

Annette's smile disappeared. "I'm sorry about Mikey, but he's turned out to be a disappointment."

"How do you mean?"

"Well, he's just been a problem, you know? Leo's tried to help Mikey time and time again. And of course Clay's tried to be a friend to him, as much as one can."

"So does Clay still see him from time to time?"

Annette lifted an eyebrow. "I'm not sure what you mean. They are not close. I don't even know the last time Clay mentioned seeing Mikey."

"Oh," Alice said. "I just wondered because I think I saw them talking the night of the barbecue competition."

"Are you sure?" Annette furrowed her brow. "I don't recall Mikey being there at all. And Clay and I were together almost the entire time."

"This was out by the food trucks."

"Oh. Well, I'm sure Clay was just saying hello. He's always so polite to everyone. But he has mentioned he doesn't like to be around Mikey these days." Annette focused her attention across the room. "Excuse me, Alice. I must go mention something to the chair." And she swished off, leaving a cloud of something too sweet.

Well, Alice, that was worthless, she thought, driving back to the office. She had too many unanswered questions, like—had Mikey started the Tindall fire? Was he even in Estes Park when she and Red were there? Could it be Mikey who'd started the rock river? Seemed unlikely; he was Clay's age and it seemed improbable that he'd bound up Audubon on the off chance he could do harm. But if it was Mikey, did he mean to knock Red out of the co-op race? Or was Caswell in his crosshairs for some reason? Or both? And had Mikey called Jana about Red's whereabouts?

* * * * *

Promptly at four, Scott and Jean Whitaker arrived. Jean, tall and smiling, shook hands with the happy self-assurance, compounded of competence and goodwill, that Alice recognized in the best nurses and PAs. If she were my friend, Alice thought, I'd know she had my back.

The Whitakers nodded thoughtfully as Alice explained the changes she'd made, consulted with each other over the gifts section, and said the wills looked good.

"Let's get these puppies signed, Alice!" said Jean. "We've got a kid! So we've got to get our just-in-case guardian properly appointed." They agreed to stop by after work on Wednesday to sign.

Jean headed out the conference room door but Scott hung back. He whispered to Alice, "I've got some good news."

"Yes?"

"Your friends at the Beer Barn made me an offer. Beer Barn accountant!"

"Are you accepting?"

"Haven't completely made up my mind but I think so. It's an opportunity, with the new distillery and the mini-brewery. But there's more."

"What?"

He widened his eyes and said, "Ms. Ross still hasn't finalized the co-op audit. She's told the co-op she needs more time on the reserve accounts." He nodded. "I knew she was solid."

Well, well.

* * * * *

On Thursday morning Alice felt disgruntled, at loose ends. Her will contest mediation was scheduled for the following Tuesday. Once again she reviewed her prep notebook and exhibits. She called her clients to take their temperature on settlement strategies. She had an idea—a little off the wall, but still promising. Reluctantly, she worked on draft PowerPoint slides for an upcoming continuing legal education presentation, thinking she'd definitely hit the bottom of the task barrel. She sighed and stared at the phone, anxious for some client to call. The mayor had not called again about Alice reviewing city contracts. The rancher who'd been told she was "anti-realtor" had not called again. The Cowman's Bank VP had not called, and had not yet paid his bill.

If she'd never left her big-city firm in Austin she wouldn't be at loose ends like this.

Text from Kinsear in New York: "Made my flight, barely. Will call with proposition for weekend. Stay tuned." At noon he called from the Austin airport.

"Alice," he said. "I've got to drive to New Mexico. Like, tonight. Can you come?"

"Tonight? To Santa Fe?"

"Well, we certainly could wind up in Santa Fe. But first I need to meet your gun guys, Bang-Bang and Banana Clip, by lunchtime tomorrow in Las Vegas, New Mexico."

"Bang-Bang" meant Elliott Barker, an astronomer who was also expert in long guns; "Banana Clip" meant a former construction contractor named Clem Curtis, known for making custom guns and rebuilding antique firearms. The two had a ballistics lab in Santa Fe and a shooting range in Ribera. Barker and Clemson had identified the antique rifle used to kill her client's father in an inheritance case. Barker had served brilliantly as her testifying expert. Alice had loved working with them: quiet, funny, knowledgeable, reliable.

Kinsear went on: "I've got a potential project that includes them. Can you leave with me tonight? A little road trip, Alice. How does that sound?"

Sounds like a casita at La Posada, she thought, with dinner across the table from Kinsear's quizzical face, a piñon fire in the fireplace, and no interruptions.

"You're on."

She needed this. Never a bad idea to get out of town. And besides, a thought had emerged. Wasn't the Pecos Wilderness close to Las Vegas, New Mexico?

She raced home and packed.

Chapter Twenty-Five

Just Roll with It, Alice

At five on Thursday afternoon Alice parked in Fredericksburg behind Kinsear's bookstore, The Real Story. He loaded her bag into the Land Cruiser and they sped northwest out of town on US 87.

"What's the gun project?" she asked. "What have you inveigled my guys into?"

"Okay, here it is," Kinsear said. "There's a market out there for a book on ranch guns, on what people actually relied on, out on the frontier. And when I've been at some of those legendary South Texas ranches to talk to owners about their books"—Kinsear dealt in rare cowboy and frontier books—"I've seen some stunning long gun collections. I think it could be a good project. And I need a project."

I'm glad, thought Alice, glad to hear about a non–New York project. "And what's in Las Vegas, New Mexico?"

"Bang-Bang and Banana Clip tell me we absolutely must see an antique dealer's gun collection there, and the guy's not available on the weekend." He checked the route guidance on his phone. "So we've got to boogie."

They made it to Big Spring that night, then left before dawn, clutching wobbly cups of motel coffee. Kinsear took the dawn leg of the drive. When she'd finished her coffee, Alice said, "You should let me show you my new driving tricks! The K-turn, the J-turn. And the Scandinavian flick!"

"What the hell is that?" asked Kinsear, eyebrows soaring up.

"Oh, the driving tricks that Eddie LaFarge taught me out at his winery."

"Eddie *LaFarge*? The center?" He looked at her, disbelief on his face.

Alice told him about meeting LaFarge while waiting for her truck to be inspected. "He said I needed to learn some evasive driving techniques. He invited us to a wine tasting at his winery."

"Us?"

She told him about the trip with Miranda.

"Eddie LaFarge, greatest center in the last twenty years! You get to meet him and he has to tell you why he's famous!" Kinsear shook his head at the injustice. "Alice, will you take me out there so I can get my picture taken with him?"

"You're serious?" Alice laughed. Men and football. Heavens.

"Of course I'm serious!" Kinsear's fingers tapped the steering wheel. "Dare I hope he was, perhaps, a little bald? A little paunchy?"

"Nope," said Alice. "But he walks like his knees hurt."

"He needs to meet *me*, realize that I am your best beau. Right?"

"Of course," said Alice. As the West Texas miles sped by, flat and vast, she recounted the early-morning thrills at Eddie's track. "I haven't had a chance to try what I learned yet."

"Evasive driving. Good Lord, Alice. Let's hope you don't need it."

* * * * *

Right at eleven on Friday, Kinsear exited off the interstate into downtown Las Vegas, New Mexico. He parked the Land Cruiser on the curve next to the green lawns of the historic plaza.

Alice climbed gratefully out of the car, stretching her legs.

"So there's the famous Plaza Hotel," Kinsear said, nodding at the broad brick building across the street. "But we're meeting our guy in the office above the antique shop that's kitty-corner from the hotel. You want to come?"

Alice stood on the sidewalk, looking around. Downtown was attractive, with its ornate brick buildings and new storefronts—galleries, boot stores. A little breeze stirred the cool desert air, sparkly with mica dust. "No, I'm going to poke around," she said. "Text me when you're done."

Kinsear strode off and Alice walked across the street into the Plaza Hotel. Just thirty seconds, she told herself, admiring the carved wooden staircase in the lobby and the woodwork in the bar. She smiled "No thanks" to the hostess at the dining room, where early lunchers sat beneath red glass chandeliers, and vowed to return with Kinsear. But right now she was on a mission. She'd checked: the Pecos Wilderness was partly in San Miguel County. Back on the sidewalk in the sunshine, she checked directions on her phone and hurried down National Avenue toward the courthouse complex.

Inside, she smelled the familiar courthouse smell, compounded of disinfectant, paper, people. The security guards pointed her to the clerk's offices and property records. "Sure," said one of the women at the clerk's counter. "Most of it's online these days. Let me show you the drill."

Deed records. Miranda had mentioned a pricey cabin on the Pecos River belonging to the Coffee Creek Electric Co-op general manager, Wally Phifer. Could she find a deed to Wally Phifer? Wallace Phifer? Alice did. From the metes-and-bounds description in the deed, she couldn't tell exactly where the property was. She should be able to find the address from the tax assessor's records. Could there be anything else here? A mortgage?

Even better. A mortgage to Cowman's Bank, dated just three years ago, and a mortgage release, filed earlier this year. Note amount: $250,000. Pretty quick work, paying off a biggish mortgage and getting the mortgage release in just a couple of years. She scanned the three documents—deed, mortgage, and release—into her phone.

And now the phone felt dirty. What was she, a voyeur of other people's venality and greed? Come on, she thought, the transactions could mean potential theft from the co-op, if Wally paid back his loan from co-op reserves. But for you to investigate, when it's only potential? Couldn't the loan from Clay's bank to his buddy Wally be perfectly legitimate? But maybe the loan gave Clay leverage over Wally. She felt duty bound, for reasons she couldn't yet confirm, to pass these on to Red. Red could weigh their importance.

She pocketed the guilty phone, which beeped.

Text from Kinsear. "We're done. Where are you?"

She texted back. "Standing outside the courthouse, on National."

* * * * *

Followed by the gun boys in their truck, Alice and Kinsear headed west on Interstate 25 and exited at Ribera, the little town on the historic Pecos River crossing that sat just below the red slopes, crowned with green piñon, of Rowe Mesa. Alice and Kinsear had once explored the ancient adobe customs house buildings that still stood by the river, roofs fallen, flowers growing up from the foundations.

The parking lot at La Risa Cafe was full of Friday lunchtime pick-up trucks.

Alice jumped out and hugged Bang-Bang and Banana Clip. They matched in some ways—bright blue eyes, short gray hair, careful opinions—although their backgrounds differed: one an astronomer, one a builder. "What kind of mischief are you getting into with Kinsear?" she said. "If you become authors, are you going to raise your expert rates?"

Any meal at La Risa made Alice smile. She relished the hot corn tortillas, toasted chiles, and roasted salsa. She admired the adobe walls, draped with dramatic posters of beautiful señoritas and dashing vaqueros. She settled into her chair, scrutinizing the menu. Bang-Bang recommended chilaquiles, which Alice ordered. Kinsear dived into a platter of red and green enchiladas, topped by a sunny-side-up egg. Conversation stopped, except for satisfied sighs.

"You two want to come up to the shooting range and decorate our art object some more?" said Banana Clip. The "art object" was the steel frame of an old washing machine that they intended to transform, shot by shot, into a lacy creation. One rifle hole was Alice's. "I was up fishing on the Pecos yesterday and brought home some trout. We could fry 'em up."

"I promised Santa Fe," Kinsear said, nodding at Alice.

"Speaking of the Pecos," said Alice, "have you run into someone up there named Wally Phifer? He might have bought some property."

"Phifer," mused Bang-Bang. Barker had grown up hunting and fishing in the Pecos Wilderness outside Santa Fe. He turned to Banana Clip. "Isn't that the guy we saw learning to fly-fish last summer? Had a guide with him? In that hole down below Terrero."

"I remember," said Banana Clip. "Brand new fishing vest with shiny new tools dangling from every loop. Brand new waders. Expensive bamboo rod. Didn't he ask us what kind of flies to use?"

"Yep. That irritated the guide, of course. The guy hadn't caught anything, despite his fancy outfit. After watching him cast awhile, I doubt he caught anything after we left. Except his ear."

"Yeah, he did get his ear that one time," Banana Clip said.

"Have you seen him up there recently?" Alice asked.

Banana Clip nodded. "I actually saw him yesterday out on the deck of what I assume is his house. Pretty fancy, for the Pecos. Big peaked roof, big glass windows, enormous deck. I noticed because I was back fishing that same hole."

"Who's Phifer?" asked Kinsear.

"General manager of the electric co-op," Alice said, and busied herself with more chips and roasted salsa.

* * * * *

Alice and Kinsear left their friends and Ribera behind, traveling west on the interstate into Santa Fe. Yes, nodded a smiling clerk at the reception desk at La Posada, their casita was ready. Adobe walls; vigas lining the ceiling. Yes, small piñon logs stacked in a tepee in the fireplace. Yes, champagne in an ice bucket covered with condensed moisture.

Kinsear picked up the matches. "I'm going to light this fire," he said. And he did.

"Now I'm going to open this bottle of champagne." And he did.

Then he said, "Why don't you come here?"

She did.

There were no interruptions.

* * * * *

Later, holding hands, they walked toward the Plaza in chilly air, the night sky brilliant with stars, for dinner at Coyote Cafe. Kinsear told tales of hedge fund negotiations, Alice imagining the competing suits hurling demands back and forth.

Then he asked about her Colorado road trip with Red. Alice still hadn't told him about the rock river. As she described the bouncing plates of basalt careening down the mountain, his face grew solemn, his brow furrowed.

"Good God."

"But whoever-it-was wasn't after me," Alice said. "Obviously he was after Red. Or maybe Caswell, though he was barely on the cross path when the guy started stomping."

"But why? Because Red's running for co-op board?"

Alice shrugged. "Not sure why anyone would be after Caswell either."

She told him about the mystery pickup with the maroon paw print. "That truck reminded me of the one that nearly ran us off the road the day the Tindall house caught fire," she said. "But we never saw it again, and anyway we couldn't see the driver. So whoever was kicking those rocks on top of the rockslide may have been a complete stranger. The village sociopath." She paused. "Probably someone who knows mountains, though. We flatlanders wouldn't have a clue, right?"

* * * * *

Saturday morning dawned cool and blue. "Let's loll," Kinsear said. "Let's play today."

They drove off to Ten Thousand Waves for massages and hot soaks. Alice felt languid, spoiled, erotic. Later that afternoon they walked up a piñon-covered hill to tour the Indian Arts Research Center. They fell silent before the artistry of baskets, the bold statements of pottery.

Then back to the Plaza and over to revisit the O'Keeffe Museum. On the way, Kinsear told Alice the history and aftermath of the Pueblo Revolt of 1680.

"Humans," said Kinsear. "So murderous."

Alice stood thinking of John Pine, the pierced kidney pumping out blood.

"But with some redeeming qualities," said Kinsear, looking at an O'Keeffe flower painting larger than either of them, opening its wild beauty on the gallery wall.

Murder, Alice thought. The fly in the ointment, the flaw in our makeup.

Later, over a loud and spicy dinner at Cafe Pasqual's, she finally told Kinsear about the rancher who canceled his appointment, the banker who didn't want to pay for his will, and the councilman who, according to the mayor's phone call, still detested Alice.

Kinsear shook his head. "Don't chase 'em. You're good, the best in town, and they'll be sorry. Just roll with it, Alice."

"Easy for you to say, Mr. Golden Parachute."

"Hey, you knew small-town law would have its ups and downs. You're still glad you made the move, right? Keep the faith, Alice. You know you help people."

"Yes, and I'm still paying double tuition this fall."

"Me too," he said. "We're just working stiffs. Okay, let's get serious about dessert. I'm thinking flan. You?"

Chapter Twenty-Six

We Need a Turnaround Here

Monday morning, Silla caught Alice at the front door of the office. "Listen, I saw M.A. at church yesterday. She looks grim. Can't you do anything? It's not fair. We need a turnaround here."

Alice sighed. She hated the thought of M.A.'s misery. "I agree. But first, it's mediation prep day. The clients will be in this afternoon." She reviewed her mediation notebook again. The key facts. The likelihood her clients would win at trial. What her clients really might accept to resolve this fight—exactly the sort of family dispute everyone hated to live with.

When her clients got to the office, she reminded them that settlement in mediation could be outside the box. In one case, her client had suddenly agreed to accept a horse instead of money damages. The Chinese called it saving face—so important. In her experience, parties to a mediation wanted to come out with a satisfactory narrative, a solution that let them tell their story afterward. So what might really resolve this? Her clients came up with ideas, and she floated hers: something to address the hurt feelings on the other side. Her clients liked it.

During a break in the prep session she stepped outside to call George Files, and left a message that the Bond family would be here Wednesday morning, with drone footage.

He called back before she got back inside. "Tell them please bring in the drone and the video or whatever they have Wednesday at noon. The other two drone flyers are coming in tomorrow."

* * * * *

Tuesday morning: mediation day, and also co-op election day. Black suit for Alice. Sunday dress for her clients. Serious faces for all parties as they sat at the mediator's conference table and listened to him recite the risks each side faced if they couldn't settle, if mediation failed and instead a jury of strangers decided their case. Off the parties trooped to their respective huddle rooms. Eventually it emerged that the plaintiffs' hurt feelings over being left out of the will could be assuaged by a smallish sum of money, with the following addition: plaintiffs' names would be prominently included in the list of donors on the plaque to be affixed to the new stone bench her clients had ordered, which her clients would pay for, and which would be dedicated to the decedent and installed at his church. Moreover, plaintiffs would be invited to participate in the dedication.

Turning point, thought Alice. Both sides now had a narrative they could live with, that gave a nod to their sides of the story. We all want that, she thought. After the requisite time (in Alice's experience a successful mediation required "tincture of time"), with many back-and-forths between huddle rooms, the mediator gathered them together and listed the points of agreement, the lawyers used a laptop to bang out the settlement, and everyone signed. At six thirty, Alice climbed into her truck.

Cell phone call from Red. "You're coming, right? I'm here at the co-op already! They're counting ballots! I want you by my side!"

"On my way."

* * * * *

At seven Tuesday night Alice pulled into the parking lot of the Coffee Creek Electric Co-op. Ahead of her Clay and Annette Black were climbing out of a big white Ford pickup truck, the King Ranch model, with an Air Force Reserves decal on the rear window.

Alice had never visited the co-op building. She'd never attended the annual meeting. After Jordie died she'd just taken over paying the ranch's electric bills. So, walking into the lofty co-op meeting room, she looked around curiously at the rows of wooden chairs for attendees, and the dais with heavy chairs behind a long table for the board members. The flag stand in the corner held the flags of the United States and Texas. At a table between the dais and the rows of chairs, a harassed-looking woman and her assistant were tallying votes.

More people filed in, milling around and talking.

The assistant called, "Could you all keep your voices down? We're trying to count!"

Clay and Annette circled the room, smiling, confident. Clay looked the part of a small-town banker in his blue suit and red tie. He shook hands with everyone who caught his eye. Annette, hair perfect, greeted people with her small, restrained shrieks of joy, her air kisses. Alice spotted Red working her way forward from the back of the room, smiling, shaking hands, patting people on the shoulder. Red suit, cowgirl boots. She'd lipsticked her smile to match the suit, and sauntered along like the rodeo queen she'd once been. But her sharp eyes darted often to the table where the two women were still tallying votes.

Alice waved her own way back toward Red, surprised to see so many people here. And now, crowding into the room, marched a dozen people who had to be Red's Coffee Creek Riders. Booted, grinning, some in fancy chaps and sequined rodeo wear, they clustered around Red. So, not supporters of Ginny Lou Hamer, Alice assumed. She didn't see anyone in the room resembling Ginny Lou.

The assistant called for quiet. The co-op board members filed in and took their seats at the dais. The center chair was vacant. The current vice chair of the board, a pudgy sixtysomething with a red nose, banged his gavel on the dais.

"He's been chairing since the chair died," Red whispered.

"I declare this meeting open. Madam Bookkeeper," he said to the harassed-looking woman, "do we have a count?"

"Yes, sir. We make it one thousand five votes for Red Griffin, four hundred ninety-eight for Clay Black, and ninety-three for Ginny Lou Hamer."

Cheers erupted. Alice, watching Clay's face, saw it close, saw the eyes narrow, saw him struggle to control his lips, which he compressed.

"Will we need a runoff?" asked the vice chair.

"We will not."

"We thank our three candidates for running a fine race. I congratulate the winner and welcome Red Griffin to the board, beginning at our next meeting. Do I hear a motion to adjourn—," began the vice chair. The second and the vote to adjourn were drowned out in whoops and excited talk. The board members came down to shake hands with the candidates. Alice smiled, her heart happy for Red. The vice chair shook Clay's hand. Alice watched Clay nod and say, "Thanks." Grim-jawed, he headed for the hallway. Annette, distressed, tugged his sleeve, whispering. Clay shook his head sharply, shook off

Annette's hand, and moved on through the crowd. Alice followed; she knew Red expected her at the Beer Barn for the after-party and thought she'd head that way. Just ahead she saw Annette catch up to Clay and heard her say, "But darling, just shake her hand."

Clay turned to face his wife. "No one's making a fool of me."

Then he saw Alice, standing behind Annette. He spun on his heel and walked out the front door.

Red caught up with Alice before she made it out the door. "Alice, honey." Red lowered her voice. "The documents you gave me?"

"From New Mexico?"

"Yes. Do you know what those papers mean? If I'm right, matters could really hit the fan next week." But congratulatory voters swarmed around Red before they could discuss it further. So Alice just grinned and headed for her truck.

* * * * *

Wednesday morning, Alice woke restless, cranky, stood on the deck in her robe to drink her coffee, paced through the empty house. No one in John or Ann's room, of course. They'd be home from college for Thanksgiving, and she hoped they were swotting away at midterms. But at the moment, the house felt empty. The living room . . . slightly dusty, wasn't it? She drew her finger over the mail counter by the door. This morning nothing made her happy. She felt a little let down, after the mediation, after the co-op election. She'd had these letdowns before. No big projects awaiting her at the office. One of those mornings when she second-guessed moving her practice to Coffee Creek, second-guessed everything.

Okay, she'd run. Sometimes, like the burros, she just had to take herself for a run. She headed down her gravel driveway and out onto the road.

One and a half miles out she turned and started back, at the gate to the Bellamy ranch, still populated by a motley mix of goats, cows, horses—an old settler ranch, still open pasture and live oak groves. When that ranch finally got subdivided, one of these years, how would she feel? What would she do? "Light out for the territory ahead of the rest," maybe. If Kinsear came with her. If she could afford it after she got the kids through college. But where exactly was the "territory" these days? She briefly envisioned a small house halfway up Rowe Mesa, east of Santa Fe. Or maybe a small cabin in or just outside Estes Park, like Val's? Or a place in Fort Davis, with a porch looking up at the mountains? Well then, what about ocean somewhere? Waves breaking, wooden jetties, oysters? But now she was running back downhill, back down the narrow blacktop, early sunlight in her eyes, a southeast breeze from the Gulf ruffling her hair. This early, the road and the view were all hers: the limestone hill country, pastures, clouds, silence. What had Auden said? This was the landscape she'd be "consistently homesick for."

Half a mile to go. Okay, no oysters, but maybe a breakfast taco from the taco shack just outside town? Yes, with fire-roasted chile sauce. Feeling somewhat more human, she showered and raced to the office, not, however, using any evasive techniques, except to stop at the taco shack. After this run, maybe the week would improve.

* * * * *

Eight a.m.: text from Caswell: "We're here! Do you still have time for us to come by this morning before we go see Files? And also come out later to the ranch? Legal matter to discuss."

She texted back: "Sounds good. I've got a conference call at 1:30 but could drive out afterward."

At midmorning, she glanced out the window and saw, pulling up, a dusty white Subaru hauling a tiny teardrop-shaped silver camper with cheerful striped curtains at the window. Caswell and Davie, dressed identically in cargo shorts, hiking boots, and fleece jackets, jumped out and were at her front door before she could open it. "Surprise!" Davie said, wide eyes hopeful. He was clutching his drone. "We camped out!"

"Yes, and you should see the stars out there," Caswell said. "Mom wasn't too keen on camping; she's over at M.A.'s. She's already seen the house. She wants our take on it—mine and yours."

"Of course!'

When they were settled in the conference room, Davie absorbed in his tablet, Caswell turned to Alice.

"About this Tea Garden house," he said. "Mom and M.A. sneaked over to see it when we were here before. I've set us up an appointment at ten fifteen to see it. What we're hoping is—are you in a position to help us apply for permits and get the kitchen approved and all that? And perhaps get a license to sell wine?"

"Absolutely." Her imagination soared at the thought of Val's food, in Coffee Creek.

Caswell went on. "She and M.A. want to surprise people. Not shock, but surprise and delight. And of course they have this urge to teach young people to cook. I really like their idea for the first installment."

"Which is?"

"Cuisine of poverty! Appropriate for high schoolers. Mom and M.A. decided every high school student needs to know how to produce nourishing food on a minimal budget. Beans and rice, whether Cajun, Mexican, New Mexican. Caldo verde, jambalaya, flavored—but not busting—with a little sausage or chicken. Oh, yeah, they've got ideas for those kids."

Alice was impressed. Her John could cook scrambled eggs. Ann could make cream puffs, but only with whipped cream filling; she hadn't bothered to learn custard. Neither had dived into real cooking. She'd always wondered what they'd do when they had to cook for themselves.

"But the restaurant—is that all the restaurant will serve?" Alice didn't think beans and rice would cut it for long in Coffee Creek.

"Oh, no. Mom told you some of the menu, didn't she? On weekends the restaurant will serve some of her own specialties, paired with some good wines, if we can find them."

"I'm sure we can find some wines," Alice said. She looked at her watch. Just after ten. "Okay, we'd better go meet your real estate broker. Then we can walk over at noon to show Mr. Files what Davie's got."

Davie looked up, face quiet, eyes anxious. A born worrier. Alice could relate to that.

One last task. Alice called Files. "Your drone request?" said Alice. "My clients are here from Colorado. But before we walk over to your office, I've got to hear again from you that nothing's changed. Neither one is a suspect, person of interest, or anything but a citizen helping the police, right?"

"Right. Plenty of people saw them flying the drone during the time we're interested in."

"Great. We'll see you at noon."

Now, time for the Tea Garden house. The sun was out, the air smelled of fall; someone was burning leaves somewhere. Alice, Caswell, and Davie walked out her front door, turned left on Live Oak and crossed the street to the courthouse square. They turned right and walked the block along the west side of the courthouse, then crossed the street again. There before them stood the Tea Garden house, on two lots, one entirely a garden with a gazebo and paths. The house itself, tall and Victorian, reportedly built of cypress, was now painted a soft gray. It sat proudly on a limestone foundation, with a stone porch stretching across the front and along the side facing the garden.

The real estate broker, middle-aged, freckled, perfectly coiffed, met them at the front door. "Joyce Avery," she said, handing them cards. She grinned at Davie and admired his drone, then walked them into the large square entrance hall, with its broad wooden staircase. "Dramatic for brides, you know. Original cypress, too."

Alice always—whether she wanted to or not—evaluated a house by its smell. She inhaled cautiously. Wood polish. The house smelled friendly enough. She grinned to herself when she noticed Caswell doing the same thing, his eyes traveling around the hall, his nostrils flared. No warning smells here. No dead mice, no wood rot . . .

They peeked into the long dining area, which opened off the left side of the entrance hall and ran all the way to the back of the house. The real estate broker pointed to the other side of the entrance hall, where, beneath the soaring front hall staircase, French doors opened out to the side porch. "I've always thought it would be nice to sit out on that porch and have a drink before dinner." She watched their faces. "I know you're interested in the kitchen, so let's check it out."

The kitchen took up the rear quarter of the ground floor. Bright yellow; white cabinetry; checkerboard tile floor; big commercial cook-tops; a bank of ovens; giant island for prep work. Big windows above the sinks and dishwashers, looking out the back.

"Good lighting," Caswell said.

"This is important," said Joyce Avery. She pointed to the last Health Department inspection certificate, posted on a wall. "They got a ninety-eight, before they closed last August. Tells you at least it's possible to get decent inspection numbers here."

Alice nodded. She'd worried about a commercial kitchen in an old house: would it meet code?

"Back here's the refrigeration area and pantry," Avery continued, "this big area around the corner. Huge refrigerators. Well-lighted storage. Okay, ready to go upstairs? Lead the way, Davie." Back to the stairs they marched.

Alice stroked the cypress banisters, admired the impressionistic Western landscape hanging at the top of the stairs.

"They're leaving that painting. Too big to move," said Avery.

She pointed at the doors opening off the upstairs hall. "Two bedrooms up here and two baths, and then two separate apartments." They peeked into each bedroom. In the first, tall ceilings, Victorian furniture. Davie goggled at the four-poster bed. "This is the Bride's Room, with the big mirrors and plenty of space for bridesmaids too," said Avery. "Of course its bathroom is the biggest." Alice investigated the bathroom. Heavens, what lights, what mirrors.

Joyce Avery was moving on. "Here's the Groom's Room." She waved them into a paneled room with a triple mirror, Victorian couch, easy chairs, a coffee table and fireplace. "And here's its bathroom."

Back in the hall she pointed to French doors on the front of the house. "Those open out onto the wonderful screened porch that looks out toward the courthouse. Bride and groom can toast out there, take pictures, and so on."

"Nice!" said Caswell.

"Now, here's the first apartment." She unlocked the door just at the top of the stairs. They entered a long bedroom with tall Victorian windows overlooking the garden, and another door opening onto a screened porch, also overlooking the garden. The bathroom held a small clawfoot tub.

Alice heard Davie say softly, "I like this room, Dad."

"The second apartment's not as fancy." Avery unlocked the last door. This bedroom looked both comfortable and, unlike the others, well used; a modern double bed, good reading lights, a small twin bed in the corner, a utilitarian bathroom with shower. Caswell nodded slowly.

Finally, they trooped downstairs and out through the side porch into the garden, dominated by an enormous live oak. Lights were wound onto its branches. "This looks gorgeous at night, like a tree full of fireflies," said Avery. "There's space for tables, chairs, and of course weddings, with the gazebo."

Caswell shook hands with Avery, thanked her, said, "We'll be in touch." She said her goodbyes and drove off. Alice, Caswell, and Davie started down the sidewalk toward the courthouse. "I'm thinking that place would work," Caswell said to Alice. "Mom could stay upstairs when she's here, and the kitchen looks decent, don't you think? What do you think about the price?"

"It's right at the appraised value. What would you do when the restaurant's not open?"

"Maybe get someone to live upstairs and manage events, like weddings. Listen, do we have time for a quick coffee at the Camellia Diner?" Caswell asked. "Davie, remember the chocolate pie?"

They found a corner booth in the diner, and Alice and Caswell discussed a possible offer while Davie licked meringue from his spoon.

Chapter Twenty-Seven

Show Me What You've Got

At high noon Davie, Caswell, and Alice walked into the Sheriff's Office annex. Files, with his tired brown eyes and a pleasant smile, was waiting inside. "Hey, Alice." She introduced Caswell and Davie. Files shook hands with Caswell, leaned down to shake Davie's hand, then walked them all back to his small office. He pointed at the three sturdy chairs in front of his battered wooden desk.

"Can we ask how many of the other drone fliers have come in already?" Alice asked.

"Both of the two I've heard about."

Caswell nodded. "Two is all I recall. They already had their drones up when Davie and I got there. We went over to check in with them, so we wouldn't get in each other's way. I don't remember seeing another drone. Do you, Davie?" Davie shook his head no.

Files focused on Davie. "Want to show me what you've got?"

Silent, white-faced, Davie took a deep breath. His small hands wriggled the microcard from the slot beneath his drone and gently inserted it into his adapter. Then he offered the adapter to Files, who plugged it into his computer's USB port. Files looked at the menu on the screen. "This one?" he asked, indicating a folder titled "Fireworks." Davie nodded. "Is this the only video you took that night?"

Davie nodded again, then said, "I shot some in the afternoon, to show Gran's rig."

"Can you just keep everything else—all your pictures—from the weekend?" Files asked.

Davie nodded.

"Okay. Let's take a look." Files adjusted the computer screen so all four of them could see. Then he said, "Can you drive, Davie?"

Davie scooted close to the computer and took possession of the mouse.

The screen was dark, then Alice could see people below, arranging blankets, faces lit by the stage lights around the gazebo, and by the streetlights around the park. In the gazebo, the two piano players were attacking their keyboards. The drone moved slowly across the front of the audience, heading toward the west, then turned and slowly came back. Alice saw flowered shoulders standing in front of the gazebo.

"Hey!" she said. "I think that's M.A."

The screen froze. George Files checked the time on the video. "Eight fifty-two." He consulted his notebook, then said, "Okay, start it again."

Now the drone was moving toward the food trucks. Alice peered at the screen, wondering if her own head would appear, standing in line. She didn't see herself. The drone hovered above the street and slowly circled the crowd. A row of heads bobbed in front of the taco truck. The drone climbed higher, still above the food truck area, then moved west again, but this time across the extreme rear of the audience.

"Stop right there," Files said. Davie froze the screen. "See that guy in the ball cap heading into the grove? That could be Pine, maybe. Pretty fuzzy, though. Okay, start it again."

Davie complied. Half the screen showed people, lolling, sitting; the other half showed tops of the live oaks in Founders' Grove. In the lower corner of the screen Alice saw one figure disappear beneath some branches.

"Did you see that?" she asked.

"Davie?" said Files. "Back up and zoom in a bit."

Davie did.

"Slow it down," Files said.

The four of them stared at the screen. Just a glimpse of white head and sleeves, black shoulders, then nothing but leaves.

"The drone's too high to get much. Maybe whoever it is has on a black-and-white windbreaker. Can't see the face at all," Files commented. He looked down at his notepad, then at the video. "Eight fifty-four."

The drone moved back above the crowd toward the bandstand at the gazebo. "There's the mayor, grabbing the mike," Alice said.

"Eight fifty-eight," said Files, again looking at the notepad.

"And there goes M.A," Alice said. The flowered shoulders vanished in an upper corner of the screen.

"Eight fifty-nine," Files said.

Now Davie had sent his drone hovering even higher above the trees, to get a better view of the first fireworks going off behind the bandstand.

"Mmm," Alice murmured, as a red star blossomed below the drone. "Beautiful."

"Nine-oh-one," said Files.

"Wait till you see the finale!" Davie said. "I turned off the camera for a while to save power. Here's the final burst." The fireworks exploded almost under the drone, opening like flowers, gold, orange, green, streaming out in beautiful waving fronds like aeronautical sea creatures, seeking, seeking.

"Then after the fireworks I took it higher," Davie said. And the trees and people grew smaller; the drone could see almost the entire park. Then it moved lower, above the food trucks, scanning the people walking home, walking to their cars, toting coolers, blankets, children. Then it zoomed back—swoosh—to Davie's uptilted face and the screen went dark.

"Go back to the beginning for a sec," Files said.

Davie reversed the video, found a spot early on, paused it. "There's Dad." He pointed to a figure just off center, looking up toward the drone. Cargo shorts, fleece jacket, ball cap. "I'm just over here." He pointed at a small head, hands out in front with the controls.

"Where were the other drone fliers?" asked Files.

Davie pointed at the screen. "One was over behind the bandstand. He was flying pretty high, trying for the fireworks." Then he pointed to the west side of the park. "Another one was over there closer to Gran when he started, but he moved around some, toward the sausage people."

"Do you have their films?" Alice asked Files.

"Yes, but it's helpful for Davie to get me situated."

"Did this tell you anything?"

"I've got a better feel for the layout," Files answered. "And we saw the one guy go under the trees."

"I saw him," Davie volunteered. "That man you wanted to stop the picture for."

"You saw him?" Files focused on Davie. "What made you notice him?"

"He looked toward me, or maybe at the controller. He looked like

226

a sheriff. But then I had to watch the drone."

"Had you seen him before?"

Davie shook his head no. Files looked at Caswell.

"I don't remember him," Caswell said.

"Do you have another shot of John Pine going into the trees?" Alice asked Files.

"We think so. From another drone. We need to match the timing." He looked at Davie. "Thank you, young man. May I save this to my computer?"

Davie nodded.

"I also need to keep your card for a while. I'll copy what's on it onto another card and send it to you. Okay?"

Davie looked at his dad, who shrugged and said to Davie, "Sounds okay." Then to Files: "Will he get the original back some day?"

Files stretched his closed lips into an ambiguous frog-mouth frown. "If and when we get this solved." He stood up and shook hands with Caswell and Davie.

"I'm staying for a moment," Alice told them.

"We'll give you a buzz later, then," Caswell said. "Come on, Davie, let's head for the ranch!"

Clutching drone and controller, Davie followed him out.

Alice turned to Files.

"Okay, George, what's the time frame? When did Pine die? Surely this clears M.A.?"

"Maybe, assuming we confirm a few things. You remember Pine's fitness watch?"

"Right. I asked you about it." She'd thought Pine wore it as part of his "who I am" statement: *Hey, I'm a writer, I'm a jock too, don't mess with me.*

"Yes, you did. We got the results back. His watch says when he died."

Alice cringed, thinking of a small device noting precisely the moment when John Pine's heart . . .

"At least, it says when his heart stopped beating. So we're talking seconds here," Files went on.

"When was it?"

"About eight fifty-five."

"When M.A. was still standing in front of the piano players in her flowered shirt. So she's off the hook."

"Well, assuming we can confirm that that is M.A. in her flowered shirt. Plus we'll have to make sure the times all sync, the drones and Pine's watch. But assuming they're within a minute of each other, and assuming we confirm that's M.A. in the flowered shirt, I agree with you."

He glanced up at Alice from his notebook. "And you're okay, since Pine's heart probably stopped just after you ran into the mayor. About seven minutes before you fell over him and called 911. Lucky for you."

Indeed. She shook her head, closed her eyes. Who'd been there before her? Was that person—she remembered footsteps—standing in the dark shadows watching her? A chill ran down her back.

"I'll call M.A.," said Files.

"Thanks."

* * * * *

Her 1:30 conference call finally drew to a close. Sitting at her desk, Alice felt her pocket vibrate, pulled out the phone. Text from Caswell.

"Alice, we're at the ranch. Davie's excited about showing you the new project we need you for. How soon can you get here?"

A new project that wasn't the Tea Garden house? Caswell's "How soon can you get here?" sounded more urgent than she'd expected. She texted back, "I can make it by three thirty. What if I bring early supper?"

Immediate response: "Excellent."

So on her way out of town she stopped at Shade Tree for takeout. Chips, three chopped barbecue sandwiches, pickles, onions, slaw, extra sauce, and therefore extra paper napkins, and three banana puddings. On second thought, she doubled the order, envisioning the two campers enjoying banana pudding and barbecue sandwiches for breakfast. "Oh gosh! Also two iced teas and a lemonade, please."

In the truck she plugged in her phone and listened to Kinsear's instructive boogie-woogie playlist: Pete Johnson, some Meade "Lux"

Lewis, some Albert Ammons, then the haunting Freddie Slack theme, "Strange Cargo." That tune stuck in her mind. No lyrics. She kept hitting Repeat, playing it over and over, trying to figure out what made it stick. And what did Freddie Slack mean by "strange cargo"?

She crossed the county line into Llano County. On this quiet afternoon, she moderated her speed in case the Llano County Sheriff's Office was prowling the highway. Nearing the turnoff she got a call from Caswell. "Hey!" he said. "On your way in, could you check out the guy parked on the road? Maybe get his license plate?"

Hmm. Alice slowed, watching for the turn off the highway onto the gravel road that led past the Bond and Black ranches, facing each other on opposite sides of the road, and then to the green gate at the end of the road that marked the entrance to Tindall ranch. Alice looked up the long drive toward Clay and Annette's ranch house, glimpsing a big white truck under a tree.

Between Clay Black's mailbox and the Tindall gate sat a small silver sedan, rear end toward her. She slowed down, repeated the license plate number into her phone. The male driver appeared to be studying a large map, and buried his face in it as Alice passed, blocking her view of all but the back of his head. Dark hair.

She got out at the Tindall gate, propped it open. Walking back to her driver's seat she noticed that the silver sedan had turned around and now was parked on Val's side of the road, facing back out toward the highway. Odd.

She drove onto the Tindall ranch—rolling pastures here by the gate, with tawny native grasses punctuated by bronze towers of bushy bluestem. Ahead of her, Quartz Creek glittered in the sun, on its way from the slopes of Turkey Ridge in the west, past the Tindalls' hilltop that so vexed Clay Black, then across the ranch pastures. Alice followed the gravel drive as it turned right, running alongside the creek, and began the uphill climb. She rolled down her window and slowed, listening to the soft song of the water. In the thick shade of the live oak grove on the right she saw the white Subaru and the tiny silver camper where Caswell had suggested they meet. She pulled off the road and hopped down from the truck and looked around. She saw no one.

But right there was Quartz Creek. One shouldn't resist water,

Alice thought. She crossed the road and stepped carefully down the creek bank, mesmerized by the clear water, the sparkling white of the quartz pebbles, the crushed reddish-pink granite.

Suddenly she became aware of a buzz, the same buzz she'd heard above her pole barn a few weeks ago as she hung out laundry. She looked up to see a drone. It veered out over the creek and circled back toward the far side of the hilltop, where the Tindalls' house had stood.

Looking upstream she saw Caswell thump across the pasture and start down the road toward her, Davie following. Why was Caswell wearing such a bulging backpack? And a front-pack? And goggles and headphones wired into the front pack? And over all that, a voluminous rain jacket with a hood?

Davie, pink and joyful, outstripped his dad. He raced up to Alice. "It . . . Dad says"—then he closed his mouth, eyes wide, and looked at his father.

Caswell tugged off the rain jacket, then the headphones. He removed the goggles, leaving circles indented around his eyes. He stopped under the trees by the camper, shrugged off and carefully lowered to the ground the entire assembly, wiring, goggles, headphones, backpack, and front-pack. "Alice! Come have a tour," he said, gesturing toward the camper.

Alice ducked her head as she entered the tiny camper, then grinned at the boatlike neatness: everything tied down, everything in its place, just like in her favorite Little Golden Book from childhood, *The Sailor Dog*. A hook for this, a hook for that. She flattened herself against the minuscule kitchen counter as Caswell lugged his peculiar equipment to the back, locking it in an equipment locker that he slid back under the bed. Davie looked expectantly at his father.

"Okay, okay," Caswell said. "Davie wants me to tell you what we're doing."

Davie nodded.

"We're trying out my invention," Caswell said.

Alice looked back and forth between the two. "Which is?"

"Can't you guess?"

"No. Are you diving for dry land fish?"

He laughed. "No, but I like morels. No, Alice, it's a type of audio-magnetotelluric device, gussied up a bit. I've had a couple of patents in the area."

She asked him to tell her just enough about audio-magnetotellurics to grasp what he was doing at the ranch. He did. Then he said, "And you know how unique the Llano uplift is, right?"

"I just know it's pink granite, magma from deep below."

"Right. Well, you often find other minerals near granite uplifts like this."

Other minerals? He'd insisted on all the mineral rights, hadn't he?

He went on. "In the past, miners have found some cool minerals around the uplift here. Did you know there was once a silver run in Llano County? Back in the 1880s?"

She remembered the upcoming article by Lloyd Neighbors. "I've heard something about that."

"It didn't amount to much. Didn't you ever wonder how Silver Mine Creek got its name?" asked Caswell.

She had to admit she hadn't.

"But we're not looking for silver, are we, Davie?" Davie shook his head no, his eyes round, his pink face utterly delighted.

"We are looking for—drumroll, please—*gold!*"

Gold? Were they serious?

He laughed at her open mouth. "Hey, just little dabs of gold. We're not talking about veins and nuggets. We've found some smidgens, haven't we, Davie boy? Tiny bits, about as much as a baby's fingernail. I just wanted to check whether this new prototype could dial in to a specific metal, in this case gold, found fairly near the surface in small amounts. Checking sensitivity, you see."

"And that's that—that thing you stowed? With the goggles?"

"The goggles let you see the display without having to look down at it. That's why we call it the Gog. You just turn your head, let the display adjust, and there you are."

"Okay," said Alice. "That's why you wanted this specific property with this specific creek, which lays bare the granite and the quartz and so on."

"Right," said Caswell. "Well, other reasons too, of course, but I thought it'd be perfect to practice on. Not too many people out here watching. In contrast to Colorado or California—I can't go anywhere out there without someone trailing me, trying to see what I'm up to."

"Hey, I saw a drone out there just now. That *was* Davie's, right?" Even as she spoke Alice realized Davie wasn't carrying his drone.

"Nope. That drone belongs to the guy down the road, if he's still there."

"Oh, yeah. The little silver car? The guy sitting there pretending to read a map? Who the heck is that?"

Heavy sigh. "My constant companions, always stalking—Deep Metal LLC. But they can't see what's under my rain jacket and so far as I know their drone can't pick up my AMT signal. It's encrypted. At least I sure as hell hope it is. They're racing me to try to bring out a similar device but so far, I *think* I'm way ahead. It's kinda fun."

"You don't mind being followed by that drone? What they're doing is against the law!"

He looked up, face intent. "Is that right?"

"Most certainly! It's taking pictures of you on your property without your consent! That's prohibited under the Texas Use of Unmanned Aircraft law! And what about trying to steal trade secrets?"

"Well, well! Maybe tomorrow we could capture Drone Spy in flagrante delicto and send a demand letter to his bosses!"

"Why tomorrow?" Alice asked.

"By then we could come up with a plan, right, Davie?" Caswell said.

Davie nodded. "I'd film him," he said. "From up high."

"Let's don't wait," Alice said. "He's there now. Can you get your drone up without his noticing, Davie? You see if you can film him filming your dad. And I'll see if I can catch his face this time."

Chapter Twenty - Eight

How'm
I Gonna Get
Home?

Alice waited as Caswell strapped himself into the Gog again and began plodding back toward the creek. Then she drove at a leisurely pace out the gate and down the gravel road, peering ahead for the silver sedan and Drone Spy. Sure enough, there he was, still parked this side of the entrance to Clay Black's ranch, but on the other side of the road and facing out toward the highway.

Alice slowed down, thumbing her phone into camera mode, passing the silver sedan without looking at it. Then, fifty yards past, she threw the truck into reverse, backed up at high speed toward the silver sedan, swung the wheel and parked sideways in the road. She jumped out, phone on video, filming the shocked face of a thirtysomething with glasses, thinning black hair and a skimpy goatee. She moved to the front, taking pictures of the license plate and keeping a stern eye on the driver. He looked this way and that, started his engine, backed up a few feet, saw he couldn't get around her truck, backed up again, stopped. Alice strolled over and tapped on his window, filming the whole time, while he held his hands in front of his face. He'd laid the drone controller on the passenger seat; Alice saw him reach over and punch a button with one finger. Trying to get it back?

She squinted up at the sky above the Tindall ranch. Yes, there it was; he'd told the drone to return to him. But what was he planning now? He couldn't get out of the car unless he—ah. He threw the sedan into reverse and backed up fast in the direction of the Tindall gate.

Alice jumped back in her truck, threw it into forward in hot pursuit, braking to a stop twenty feet from the sedan. Again she left her truck in the dead center of the road, at an angle that left him no room to pass on either side. The driver jumped out just as the drone dived toward his outstretched hands. Alice started another video and captured Drone Spy grabbing his drone, scuttling back into the silver sedan, and slamming the door. Surely he wouldn't try to squeeze past her truck? And he struck her as gutless; she calculated he wouldn't even try, afraid of dinging his car. Again she slid down out of the truck, strode to the silver sedan, and banged on the driver's-side window.

Drone Spy stared straight ahead. "Deep Metal LLC?" she yelled. That got a wide-eyed reaction. He hadn't dreamed she'd know the company name. "Open your window. If you don't talk right now, I'm calling the sheriff."

"You can't make me!" he yelled, staring straight ahead, tugging at the visor so it shielded his face.

"Too late, buddy. I've got video of you retrieving your drone from my client's property!"

"Your client?" He rolled the window down an inch.

"My client. Dr. Caswell Bond. I'd say you're on your way to see the judge."

"I did nothing!"

"You violated the Texas Use of Unmanned Aircraft law. And you're engaged in theft or attempted theft of trade secrets. Do you have a lawyer?"

He shook his head no, white hands gripping the steering wheel.

"Does Deep Metal Whatever have a lawyer?"

He shrugged.

"Of course they do. You'd better call that lawyer and tell him or her to call me right away, and I mean in the next ten minutes."

He rolled up the window and sat rigid.

"Here's my number." She held out her business card.

Something was bothering her about this whole situation. She banged on the window again. Finally he rolled it down a quarter inch and she shoved her business card inside, dusted her hands, and yelled, "Ten minutes!"

But as she stood there she realized that if he left with the drone . . . with the evidence of what Caswell was doing—even if later Deep Metal Whatever destroyed the evidence—Caswell's secrets would be out. Plan B? Plan B: she'd block his escape.

She climbed back into her truck, backed up a bit, chose a particularly narrow stretch of the gravel road and parked perpendicularly across it. Now he definitely couldn't leave unless he crashed through Clay Black's fence or Val's fence. She walked back to the silver sedan, thinking all the way. Then she stopped ten feet away. Drone Spy stared mutinously at her through the windshield. She called Caswell.

"What would Deep Metal learn if they get his drone video?"

"Good question," Caswell said. "Can we put the genie back in the bottle, once they've seen his pictures? Maybe, maybe not; but I particularly didn't want them to know yet about the goggles. I arranged the raincoat hood so it stuck out over my face today, but he may have gotten images of the goggles before I got my hood fixed. Can we keep him from ever showing his video?"

"I'm going to try," Alice said.

She walked to the window, tapped again. He rolled it down an inch.

"Here's the deal," Alice said. "I'm leaving my truck where it is, locked, in the middle of the road. You can stay here till hell freezes over. No lunch, no dinner, no nada. Because I've got reinforcements, up there." She nodded toward the top of the Tindalls' hill, where the ranch house once stood. "Or."

Ten-second pause. Finally he spoke. "Or?"

"You get to come meet the inventor himself. You eat a delicious barbecue sandwich. You do have to bring the drone and ride with me. Just leave your car where it is for the moment."

"Or?"

"If you don't come with me I'm calling the sheriff—and you *and your drone* will be in the Llano County Courthouse. I'll request a temporary restraining order against you to stop what you're doing, including getting the judge to confiscate your drone for theft of trade secrets or place it in court custody until this gets resolved." She wasn't sure a judge would actually deprive this man of his property, but she thought there was a good chance that trespass by drone would not fly, as it were.

Heavens, he looked like he was actually considering the option she'd offered.

"There's banana pudding, too," she said.

Slowly the door opened and Drone Spy crawled out. He looked at her, then reached back in for the drone and its accoutrements.

"What's your name?" she asked.

He rearranged his awkward armload. "Tony Stolak."

"From?"

"Um, San Jose. California." He turned back to his car. "Let me get my wallet and stuff."

Alice turned and began walking back to her truck; she heard his door slam and his engine roar and she turned, horrified, just in time to see the silver sedan's right fender crash into her hip and send her flying. She landed on the gravel, hands first, and heard a *thud* and a *bang*. Then silence. Alice couldn't breathe; the landing had knocked the breath out of her. Finally, hip aching, she made it to her hands and knees and crawled in a half circle, thinking, If that bastard touched my truck . . .

Finally she stood up and surveyed the damage. The silver sedan's rear stuck up at a rakish angle from the ditch. That put Alice in mind of Cadillac Ranch outside Amarillo and she snorted a laugh, which hurt. Gingerly, she took a couple of steps, picking the gravel out of her wounded palms, and tried putting some weight on the leg with the wounded hip. Still no sound from the sedan.

She limped over to the sedan, scrutinizing the front of her Toyota truck. Nope, no new scrapes. She peered through the sedan's passenger window. Drone Spy thrashed ineffectively behind the deployed airbags. After a moment Alice decided mercy was in order.

She found a forgotten paring knife in her glove box. She pulled open the sedan's passenger door and said, "Hold still." She could barely see his eyes—the airbag had cracked his glasses and bloodied his nose.

She waved the knife. His eyes widened. She poked the airbag with the knife and the big bag slowly deflated, leaving an odd smell in the air. She held a fold of the bag and hacked enough away that Drone Spy, puffing and wheezing, blood and snot running down his chin, could squeeze his rear end over the console and into the passenger seat. She grabbed him under his armpits and hauled him backward far enough that he could pull his legs over the console.

She noticed that the drone and controller lay on the floor on the passenger side. She backed away, hands on hips, and watched Drone Spy struggle. Then she pulled her phone out of her pocket. Miraculously, the screen was not cracked. She filmed him pushing backward up into the tilted passenger seat, laboriously hauling first one, then the other foot over the console, grabbing the car roof and, finally, extricating himself. He turned, a sorry sight, to face her phone.

She turned it off.

They stared at each other.

"I didn't mean to hit you," he said. He wiped his nose on his sleeve and looked in horror at the blood.

Alice considered the matter. "I may turn you in," she said. "Depends on what happens right now. You don't have a lot of choices." She walked around to the front of his sedan and bent over to peer at the left front tire. Mostly buried in the ditch—but she could see it was flat. He couldn't leave without a tow truck.

Why hadn't he called his bosses? she wondered. But what the hell would he say? "Um, I wrecked the car while engaged in vehicular assault on the lawyer for our opposition."

And, she wondered, what would he say about his drone footage? Because, guess what, she was gonna confiscate the drone.

"Tony, if that's your real name, here's the deal. First, show me your driver's license."

Reluctantly, he held it out to her. She took a picture of it. Then she said, "I'm taking your drone. That's the price of freedom."

His face contracted in pain. "My drone?"

"Yep."

He sighed. "Okay. I don't see much choice."

"There's none." She reached into the sedan, got the drone and controller, and shoved them behind her truck seat. "Hop in," she said. Face resigned, he climbed in next to her. She started the truck, backed up carefully, and turned toward the Tindall gate.

"So, Tony, what's your title at Deep Metal?"

"Um, I'm not really an employee. They just hired me for this."

"Independent contractor?"

"Yeah."

"You do this kind of thing often?" She wouldn't accuse him of industrial espionage just yet.

"Well, I'm new at it. But I insisted on a written agreement."

Whoops, Alice thought. I'd like to see a copy of that, and I will, too. "So they don't pay you until you deliver the goods?"

"Well, sort of, but they're also supposed to be paying my expenses."

"I thought you'd be on the phone with the lawyers by now," Alice commented.

He sighed. "Left my phone charger in the motel."

Amateur hour, she thought. But also, he was just an independent contractor. Deep Metal would abandon him, say he violated the agreement, which no doubt their lawyers had drafted. But they'd still hire him a lawyer, one who'd be on their payroll.

"This is a far, far better approach," Alice told him. "I mean, you've fucked up, but now you're about to meet some excellent barbecue."

The truck had slowly filled with the aroma of Big John's brisket, a brisket that had enjoyed hours of careful tending over plumes of oak and hickory smoke, a brisket covered with Shade Tree's secret rub and anointed (Alice suspected but was not sure) with judicious amounts of Big John's secret mop. Despite herself Alice was salivating. She glanced at Tony. Yep, he was breathing deeply. And who knew what he'd reveal about his bosses once he got a few bites of brisket into his sorry gut.

* * * * *

Alice did not want Drone Spy to see anything Caswell didn't want him to. Since she didn't know what Caswell was doing at the moment, she called him. "I've got someone with me out here at your gate I'd like you to meet," she said. "Where's the best place?"

Pause. Very softly he said, "Up by where the house was? Not the creek and not the camper." He stopped. "Sit him where he's looking off the back of the hill away from the camper."

"Got it."

"We'll picnic up there," she told Drone Spy, pointing up the hill. "Great view." She noticed his eyes swiveling left and right as the truck made its way up the drive. And when she got the truck parked at the top, she handed him the cardboard box heaped with bulging barbecue sandwiches wrapped in greasy paper and Styrofoam cups full of sides. She made him carry it past the ruined house to the picnic table at the western edge of what had been the Tindalls' backyard. She took a cautious sniff as they walked past the concrete slab, still littered with wreckage. She could still smell the acrid aftermath of burnt furniture, burnt flooring, burnt cushions.

"What happened there?" he asked.

"Someone torched it. Was it you?"

He looked at her, horrified. "Burn down a *house?*"

Maybe not. But Alice's hip still ached. In relief she reached the picnic table, and Drone Spy set down the barbecue box. To the west rose the dark green ridges, topped by Turkey Ridge, which rose above the pink granite uplift and looked down onto the Tindall ranch, as well as the Black and Bond properties. Downhill to her right she could see the roof of Clay Black's ranch house through the trees. She couldn't see the white truck now. Nothing moved over there. She tugged her phone from her pocket and called Caswell again.

"I'm thirty seconds away," he said. She heard the Subaru starting up the drive. He emerged without Davie and strode to the picnic table, grinning. No backpack, no equipment, just the bright-eyed, inquisitive look of a curious squirrel.

"Caswell, meet Tony Stolak, who was spying on you for Deep Metal LLC. Tony, meet the inventor."

The two men nodded. Neither offered to shake hands.

Caswell pointed to the driveway side of the picnic table, looking toward the bigger peaks. "Tony, come sit here. The view's better to the west."

Alice raised her eyebrows, questioning. But Tony dutifully slid onto the bench where Caswell pointed.

"Davie's taking a short cut," Caswell said. "He'll be here in a few. But let's go ahead."

"Good," Alice said. "I'm starving." She passed out paper plates while Caswell lined up the sides—beans, potato salad, coleslaw, pickles, onions. They unwrapped the greasy paper from buns overflowing with chopped brisket. Alice noted Tony's intense focus on his bun and the ineffable smell of hickory, oak, and smoked meat rising from their plates. Maybe Deep Metal was slow pay on travel expenses.

"Tony," she said, "the drill is, decorate your sandwich however you like. Personally, I'm partial to coleslaw and pickles. And don't forget to choose your vegetable of the day." She pointed at multicolored bags of kettle-fried potato chips—jalapeño, salt and vinegar, classic.

"Speaking personally, I'd include onions with the pickles and coleslaw," Caswell said.

"What about the sauce?" Tony asked.

Silence. But he was a foreigner, from beyond the Red River. "Well, they give it to you, if you ask. But proper brisket does not need, or even tolerate, sauce," Alice retorted.

Tony dithered, then cautiously inserted some dill slices into his bun and took a bite. An involuntary "Mmm" escaped. He sneaked a little sauce into the bun.

"Like it?" Caswell grinned at Tony, who lifted his face and nodded at him, just as a drone rose to the west behind Caswell, zoomed to a stop two yards from Tony's startled face, then rose out of reach, hovering over the picnic table.

"What the hell!" sputtered Tony. Too late, he lowered his head, hid his face, staring down at the chips on his paper plate.

"Gotcha on camera," Caswell said calmly. "Consorting with the enemy. Deep Metal will love that."

Davie came scrambling up the west side of the hill, controller in his hand, huge smile on his face, brown eyes shining. He called the drone home, grabbed it, set it carefully on the picnic table, and clambered onto the bench next to his father. Caswell patted his back. "Great work, son."

"Nice unit," Tony said, nodding at Davie's drone. "I had one like that. Mine had a big upgrade on the camera, though."

"What happened to it?" Alice demanded. She still wanted to know about the drone above her pole barn.

"Oh, I wanted a new one, with more features." And he took another bite. As he finished his brisket, Alice asked Tony again whether he wanted to go ahead and contact Deep Metal's lawyers.

"You gonna charge me for hitting you with the car?"

Caswell's head jerked up. "What?"

"Not if you play ball with us," Alice said to Tony. "But first you have to confirm to both of us that you don't want Deep Metal's lawyers to sit in on this conversation."

He shook his head no. "Not after the brisket. I've made up my mind."

The afternoon was wearing on, sun slanting across the dry fall grass, air turning chilly. Alice and Caswell hurried to extract information about Deep Metal's instructions to Tony. Alice scribbled in her notebook as Tony talked.

"I was to get the shape of the device, and all attachments," he said, toying with a pickle slice, staring at his plate. "I was especially to focus on the detection device and how it transmitted to the system. And I was to get sufficient info to determine the weight of the unit. That was big."

"Why?" asked Caswell.

"I think—I don't know, but I think—maybe Deep Metal's having trouble with size," he offered. "Miniaturization, I mean. Theirs is too heavy to wear for long."

Caswell permitted himself a tiny smile.

"Don't tell us about Deep Metal's device," Alice ordered Tony. "I don't want any of Deep Metal's information. I just want to hear what you were supposed to do out here."

At the end of an hour Tony was talked out. Before he shut up entirely Alice insisted on hearing the names of all the people at Deep Metal who'd met with or talked to Tony. Finally she put down her pen.

"That'll work," she said.

"How'm I gonna get home?"

Oh yeah, his phone was dead.

Alice called AAA and gave detailed directions.

She said goodbye to Caswell and Davie. "We're camping out two more nights!" Davie told her.

Then she dropped off Tony at the crippled silver sedan, its rear end still pointed up into the clear blue fall air, and left him to wait for the tow truck.

Chapter Twenty-Nine

Bad Day at Black Rock

Alice's hip hurt all the way home. The burros stood waiting at the pole barn. She eased off the seat and grabbed three treat cookies from the workshop by the pole barn. The burros came crowding up to her. She offered each a treat, stroking their necks. "Burros, who killed John Pine? And why? Do you know?"

No answer, just steady munching. Sometimes the burros offered a soothing effect, but not tonight. She limped into the house, heading for a hot bubble bath. Message light blinking: Kinsear. "Call me. Bad day at Black Rock."

She called. "What happened?"

"My day began with a call from the school. Daughter number two got busted for honor code violations at the Latin Club convention." Daughter number two was a junior at a well-regarded Austin boarding school.

"Uh-oh," Alice said, instantly recalling similar moments from John and Ann's high school days.

"Yep. Beer and curfew violations with her buddies. So she can't get into Honor Society until next year. At least she didn't get kicked out. I feel highly inadequate as a parent."

"We've all been there. She'll grow up, Ben."

"That's not all. On my way back from Austin I had a call from the ranch and had to get Javier to the hospital." Javier had worked as his ranch manager for years. "He was trying to load a bull into the trailer and the bull hit the trailer gate so hard it practically dented Javier's skull. He's got forty stitches and he's seeing double with concussion."

"Yikes!"

"But wait, there's more! Then I got a jail call from his cousin Enrique, who'd gone to Monterrey to see his sick mama. Even though he's got a green card he got arrested at the border coming back. So I had to scout out an immigration lawyer for him. He's scared. I hate that."

"That sucks."

"Yeah." Silence. "I could use some refuge tomorrow night, Alice. What if I grill us steaks with the famous Kinsear steak rub? Would you accept?"

"I would," Alice said, "except I was thinking of offering dinner to M.A. and Val and Caswell and Davie before they head back to Colorado. I thought Davie might like to meet the burros. Deal 'em in? What do you think?"

"Steaks all around. Tell 'em I'm cooking," Kinsear said. "I miss you. Don't get into any more trouble before dinner tomorrow night, okay? No bodies, right?" He hung up.

She realized she hadn't mentioned Drone Spy. Well, that tale could wait until dinner tomorrow. Worried now about her own children, Alice called John. "Got your Thanksgiving tickets home?" Yes, he had. Yes, midterms went okay. But why had he ever signed up to write a senior thesis? And could she mail him his hiking boots?

"You'll get it done. Yes, I'll send the boots," Alice said, groaning inwardly at the cost of postage.

Next she called Ann.

"Mama!" Ann's voice always cheered her.

"Everything okay?"

"Pretty much. Got a babysitting gig for extra money, two afternoons a week. And I'm singing this Friday night at the campus grill."

"Wonderful! And in your spare time are you taking any classes?" Alice sometimes thought Ann's college experience was mainly extracurricular.

Ann giggled. "They're fine, Mom. Gotta go. Can't wait for Thanksgiving. Love you."

Alice shook her head. Parenthood. At least her kids were in another time zone, another area code, and most of the time she, happily, was buffered from whatever mischief they were up to. Unlike poor Kinsear.

She sent a text inviting Caswell, M.A., and Val for Kinsear's steaks the next night. All accepted.

* * * * *

Friday morning. Alice made the early yoga class but had zero success in "setting an intention for her practice." Too much monkey mind today.

The phone was ringing when she unlocked the office: Red. "Hey, Alice! The co-op just posted the agenda for my first meeting next Tuesday. Guess what's up first? Quote: 'Auditor's request for additional time to complete audit.' My CPA heart beats in eager anticipation! Second item on the agenda: 'Wally Phifer retirement.' The word is Wally's decided to retire sooner than December."

"Really! Should be quite a meeting," Alice said.

Red laughed. "Watch this space!" She hung up.

Second phone call: M.A. "Alice! I'm vindicated!" Her voice rang with its old assurance. "Did you see the *Caller* this morning? It says the sheriff's office is still investigating the Pine murder but the owner of the murder weapon has been cleared. It also says drone footage may provide new leads." Alice was surprised at that last bit. Why leak the drone info?

Third phone call: Eddie LaFarge. "Alice, I want to thank you. I got a call from your friend Val about her new venture. I've heard of her," Eddie said. "I'd be honored to help her out with some Raptor Cellars wines. So, thanks."

"Of course."

"Listen, Alice. I'm wondering if you'd help me on a legal matter. I need to dissolve this partnership I'm in, buy out my current partner at the vineyard. Can you help?"

"Yes, depending on conflicts," Alice said. "Who's the partner?"

"I'll send you all the partnership details." Eddie paused, then said, "Okay, one more thing. I had a call from Leo. He's worried. He overheard Mikey on the phone and swears he heard Mikey say something like, 'Look, I'm not gonna be third on the match. And I don't do kids.' Mikey wouldn't tell Leo who he was talking to and also wouldn't tell him what 'third on the match' meant. So, Alice, I just want to be sure you're staying clear of Mikey."

"'I don't do kids'? What in God's name does that mean?"

"I can't think of anything good. Just—you stay away from him."

"Okay, thanks." Thoughtfully, she put down the phone.

Third on the match? Alice wondered if Mikey was turning down someone for a third gig.

Maybe the first involved fire, and the second involved a rocky slope?

What was the third?

Silla brought her the Austin paper. "Hey, look at this. Lloyd Neighbors has a piece on the 1880s silver rush in Llano County." Alice scanned the article. "Even today," Neighbors had written, "people speculate that traces of gold and other minerals can still be found, perhaps in the streams running off the granite uplift."

Fourth phone call: unexpectedly, Annette Black. Alice couldn't remember ever getting a call from Annette before. She waited for something about the library. Instead, Annette began, her voice wavering, "Alice, I'm just wondering. Have you heard any more about that poor Pine boy? We read this morning in the *Caller* that there are more leads. Drone footage. Do you know if that means they've found the murderer?"

"I don't, Annette," Alice said.

Silence. "There's another thing I'm wondering," Annette said. "Is —are there minerals at the Tindall ranch? We also saw this article in the Austin paper about mineral finds in Llano County. Silver and even gold. And we didn't even know the Tindalls were planning to sell. Clay's still upset about that."

Disjointed thinking, but telling, Alice thought. "Sorry, can't help you on that either, Annette."

"Oh. Well, what I really called about is this," Annette said. "Clay told me he saw a drone flying at the Tindall ranch yesterday. He's very concerned it was looking at him, at our property. I mentioned Caswell's son had one but—surely he wouldn't fly it over us. If—if it's little Davie's, I wondered if you could talk to Caswell about it?"

"Annette, Davie can of course fly his drone out at the Tindall ranch. He won't spy on you. Caswell will be sure of that," Alice said. "But I happen to know about the drone Clay saw yesterday, because we caught the guy flying it. He's an industrial spy, spying on Caswell, trying to learn about an invention Caswell's working on." She paused. Annette said nothing. Alice went on: "I'm sure that drone wasn't aiming at your place. Can you let Clay know, so he won't worry?"

"I can't get him," Annette said after a pause, her voice trembly. "He's left, and he's not at the office. No one there knows where he is. I'm worried."

"When did he leave?"

"An hour ago. I've called and called. He's not answering. He—he got upset about—oh, just everything, today. And then to make matters worse, Wally Phifer called and made Clay so angry."

"Why?" Alice asked.

"Something about the co-op. I heard Clay tell Wally, 'You can't retire now, there's too much at stake.' Then Clay slammed down the phone and left. I couldn't get him to tell me where he was going. And he's not answering his phone." Alice waited for more. She heard Annette swallow. "Thanks, Alice. Sorry to bother you." Before Alice could answer, Annette had quietly hung up.

Alice put down the phone. She felt her heart pounding, her temples pounding. That's three, she thought. Three pieces of a puzzle. First, the co-op: Clay knows the audit's deepening, meaning Phifer's loan from Cowman's could become public; the co-op might then yank its accounts from Cowman's. Second, she suspected Clay would be enraged if Caswell found precious metals on the Tindall property, right next to his property. Surely by now he knew that Caswell was a metals researcher. Clay would be humiliated if he'd missed the opportunity to own the gold right next door to his ranch.

But what made her hair stand on end was the third piece of the puzzle: that Clay now knew that the police, still searching for Pine's murderer, were looking at drone footage. And that Davie flew drones. Had he guessed the drone footage was Davie's? If so, what else might he remember about the little boy with the drone?

Alice dialed Caswell's cell phone. It rang and rang, then went to voicemail. She called again. Same result.

Silla stood at her door. "What's up? Are you going to the probate bar lunch?"

Wild-eyed, Alice stared, voices whirling in her head: *I prefer stalking. Clay's a superb shot. I don't do kids.*

She grabbed her keys. "I've gotta go. The Tindall ranch."

Silla moved out of the way. Alice ran to her truck, backed out, and floored it. Her tires squealed on the curves. Just let me be in time, she prayed, and let there be no sheriff on the road. She raced north toward Llano. Now the pink granite domes of granite flashed by. Tight uphill right turn; she braked, pulled the wheel left, then right. The truck fishtailed and leaped into the curve. Miles sped by. Finally the left turn onto the gravel road. No Drone Spy parked alongside the road, no one on the road, no one at all.

The Tindalls' green gate, wide open. Alice skidded around the driveway curve by the creek and pulled over at the silver camper and white Subaru. No one in sight. The birds stopped singing as she jumped out of the truck and ran to the camper. "Caswell? Davie?" She turned the door handle, peered in. No one. Silence. The equipment locker gaped open, empty.

They must be prospecting up or down Quartz Creek, she thought. Which way? If she drove to the hilltop she could see in all directions. Back to the truck. She drove up the drive, glancing toward Clay's house, now visible. Nothing moved there; a large white truck stood by the house.

Alice parked by the wreckage of the Tindalls' burnt-down house and pulled binoculars from her glove box. If I walk to the edge of the hilltop, she thought, I'll be able to see up and down the creek.

On the hilltop, silence. Nothing moved. A trio of vultures circled lazily above Turkey Ridge, then suddenly wheeled and moved south. Alice walked along the fence around the Tindall yard—the fenced "acre" that appraisal districts assigned to rural homes to separate them from the agricultural acres. Outside the fence she walked a deer trail under ancient live oaks toward the wide sky that loomed beyond the trees.

At the hill's edge, the land dropped steeply toward the creek. Standing in the shade of the last oak, Alice saw nothing moving below. She turned to face Turkey Ridge. Wait, had she seen movement? This side of Turkey Ridge faced full east. The morning sun had gleamed briefly on something, something not cedar, not oak, not grass, not limestone. Alice moved further back beneath her tree, lifting the binoculars to her eyes. She twiddled the focus knob. What about close to that rock formation? She adjusted the focus. Cedar scrub grew thick on Turkey Ridge. Nothing; she saw nothing. Then, next to the rock formation, a cedar branch moved. Just one branch. There's no wind, she realized. She didn't move a muscle. Slowly he came into focus, the hunter in camo, face hidden, still as a statue. The rifle glinted once in the sun, then disappeared again.

He was waiting.

But where were his prey?

From her vantage point she couldn't see anyone down in Quartz Creek. To see more, she'd need to look into the creek where it circled this end of the hill, then headed out to the pastures. Alice looked down with dismay at her white shirt and polished cowgirl boots. No camo here. She stuck close to the oaks as she crept toward the side of the ridgetop that faced away from Turkey Ridge. Just then she heard a clunk. She looked over the edge. There was Davie, putting up his drone, and Caswell, adjusting goggles, decked out in all the Gog equipment. They'd been standing behind a large boulder, screened from her and from Turkey Ridge by the curve in the creek. They were only six feet from the point where the creek turned in full view of Turkey Ridge. Alice yelled: "Davie! Davie!"

The small face turned up, smiled, waved, looking so like her son John at nine. Caswell, headphones on, seemed oblivious. He kept turning knobs on the device tethered to his chest. He motioned for Davie to move around in front of him.

Davie darted in front of his dad, holding the controller. His drone rose to eye level with Alice and kept rising, a perfect location give-away for the rifleman. Davie again waved happily at her and started forward. Caswell began walking, staring at his screen. They'd already started around the curve.

"Davie!" shrieked Alice.

Too late. Now he couldn't see her. No help for it. Alice plunged over the edge, trying to stay vertical, and skidded down the rocky incline, too steep to walk down. She dug in her boot heels, slaloming down the scree, grabbing at the few cedar saplings, trying to reach Davie before he was fully in view of the rifle. She sent down a shower of crumbled limestone, old seabed. "Davie!" she yelled. "Caswell!" She tried but failed to miss a cactus, which embedded spines in her thigh. She lost her balance and tumbled sideways, out of control. *Crack!* Rock splinters flew up from the rocky slope, some hitting her in the scalp. But the rifle had missed. Alice grabbed for but missed the last scraggly bush on the slope, plunged over the edge of the creek bank and fell heavily on Davie, just as a second shot hit the boulder next to him. The binoculars twisted around Alice's neck smacked Davie's nose.

Caswell pushed up his goggles and stared at her. "Get down!" she gasped. "Get back!" Alice and Caswell tugged Davie back around the curve. Alice peered back at Turkey Ridge. Now she couldn't see the rock formation where she'd seen the rifleman. So maybe he couldn't see them. She looked at Davie, who had a bloody nose and a cut on his forehead. Davie stared mournfully at his smashed controller.

"Who's shooting?" said Caswell. "Hunting season hasn't started yet!"

"I think it's Clay," she said.

"Clay? Shooting at us?"

"Yes. Davie saw him the night of the fireworks," she said. "And he knows it. We've gotta get out of here. You two get out of the creek bed," she told Caswell. "I'm going for the truck."

Alice clambered out of the creek bed and climbed, gasping, back up the side of the hill. She hurried to her truck and drove it down the drive, even with the curve in the creek, then bounced across the pasture to Caswell and Davie. She leaned over and shoved open the door. "Get in!"

Caswell threw Davie in the front seat and stuffed the Gog and all his equipment in the back seat. They accelerated down the drive and out the gate, not stopping to lock it.

Alice dug in her pocket for her phone, handed it to Caswell. Her hands were sweaty on the wheel. The sweat stung the cuts on her palms. She turned off the gravel drive onto the highway, headed for Coffee Creek.

"Call George Files and hold up the phone," she ordered. Caswell obeyed, put it on speaker.

"It's Alice Greer," she panted. "Someone shot at us out at Tindall ranch. At Davie and Caswell and me. We're in my truck heading for

Coffee Creek. We need help!"

"Got it. Did you call the Llano sheriff's office?" asked Files.

"No. No time. Listen, I think it was Clay Black." She looked in her rearview mirror. Large white truck, gaining fast. "He's following us. We need help now! Please hurry!"

For the first time, she longed for a bigger engine, for more power. Clay was gaining fast on this hill.

Alice tried to visualize the next mile. Ahead lay the straightaway along the side of the hill, with a big drop-off that left the right lane exposed to a beautiful view, where you could see much of Llano County—if you didn't miscalculate and run off the cliff. Then the road turned left through a road cut at the top of the hill, then curved right again and ran straight on till morning.

Clay was going to try to pass her going uphill, was going to try to knock her truck off the right lane and into infinity. She knew it. The left lane nestled against the cliff, while the right dropped sharply away. She had to hang on, make it through the rock cut at the top. In her head she heard Eddie's voice: "Alice, remember this if you ever have to take a turn fast." In her rearview she could see Clay moving left, getting ready to sideswipe her. Alice moved left in front of him, crossing the centerline, driving along the cliff and praying for no oncoming traffic. Clay swerved back into the right lane; she swerved ahead of him. He crashed into her tailgate. Alice bounced forward into the left curve through the rock cut at the top of the hill, staying in the right lane, then steered left across the centerline and started tapping her brakes for the right curve just as the big white truck crashed again into her tailgate. He'd hit her hard, but too late. She yanked the wheel right, feeling the little truck fishtail, and shot straight into and around the right curve, tires squealing. Behind, they heard a metallic crunch, then a scraping sound.

Caswell, left hand gripping the seat back, peered back through the rear window. "He ran off the road and scraped the cliff," he said. Alice gripped the wheel, focused on the downhill straightaway. Caswell craned his neck, still looking back. "I don't see him."

Alice took a deep breath and slowed to sixty. "Whoo." The back end of her truck was shimmying in a new way.

"Wow," said Davie. "No one at school will believe this."

"Nope," said his dad, hugging him. "Don't tell Mom."

"Keep watching," Alice ordered Caswell. He did.

Ten miles outside Coffee Creek they met sirens and three Coffee County Sheriff's Office SUVs, lights flashing. They flagged Alice down. She pulled over and stopped, hands shaking. Davie was mesmerized by the flashing lights, the uniforms. "They aren't going to give us a ticket, are they?" he asked his dad.

"No, son."

The first SUV had barely stopped before Files unfolded his legs and climbed out, moving faster than Alice had ever seen him move. She rolled down her window. "We're okay," she said. "But Clay Black may still be back there in his truck. He hit the inside of the cliff on that last turn. He was trying to run us off the curve at the overlook."

"Hold on a moment," said Files. He walked over and spoke to the driver of one of the SUVs, who gunned his engine and raced off toward the scene of the truck crash. Files walked back to Alice's window. "Okay, go on."

"We—I steered left and he hit my rear end. Then we made the curve right and he didn't."

Files walked around and stared at her smashed tailgate, then walked back. "You're sure it was Clay Black?" Files asked.

"I didn't get a good look," Alice said, "but it looked like his truck. And the truck was on our tail pretty quick after we left the ranch."

"I think it was Clay," Caswell said, "but I've only seen some old pictures of him since we left Texas." Alice stared at him. Could that be true? And another puzzle piece fell into place. When Clay had encountered Val at M.A.'s rig, Caswell and Davie had already left. When Clay asked if Caswell was at the park, Val had said yes, but had never mentioned Davie. Annette, but not Clay, had seen Caswell and Davie at the drone competition. When the barbecue winners were announced, Annette had been there, but Alice hadn't seen Clay in the crowd.

Which meant that since Caswell returned to Coffee Creek, Clay hadn't laid eyes on him before Pine's murder. No, she was wrong; he said he'd seen someone in a T-shirt and a ball cap roaming the Tindall ranch on Thursday before the Friday closing. But that was apparently as close as Clay had gotten.

The last puzzle piece fell into place. And she felt sick, thinking about it.

"Tell me again why you think it was Clay Black shooting at you?" Files asked.

"It's a guess," Alice said. "The shooter was on Turkey Ridge. I saw the white truck, like the one Clay drives, by his house when I got to the ranch. Then a white truck followed us. It looked like the same truck."

"We're sending a couple of cars out there now," Files said. "But why was he shooting at you?"

"Because Davie can identify him. He's the man in the drone footage."

Files stared. "Clay Black?"

"Yes."

Long pause. "Come on, let's get you back to Coffee Creek. I'll meet you at my office."

Then he took out his phone and turned away. Alice heard him say, "Start drafting a search warrant for Clay Black's house and ranch, in connection with a reported shooting and—in connection with John Pine's murder. Yeah, you should coordinate with the Llano County Sheriff's Office. I'll be back in the office in about twenty minutes."

The parade—law enforcement vehicles and Alice's battered truck —wound back toward Coffee Creek. On the way, Caswell called his mother at M.A.'s, where the two entrepreneurs were working on a budget for the Tea Garden house. "We're fine," he said, after giving her the short version of the story. "We'll be back soon."

"Fine?" Alice thought. Maybe. John Pine's face rose before her.

* * * * *

Alice parked at the courthouse. She, Davie, and Caswell climbed out of the truck. Alice's hip still hurt. The palms of her hands were cut and battered. She looked remorsefully down at her boots, at the torn knees of her jeans. Files was waiting at the entry.

"Let me talk to these guys first," Files said, beckoning to Caswell and Davie. Alice waited outside his office, arranging puzzle pieces in her mind.

After a while, Files took Caswell and Davie to the break room for drinks and doughnuts, and it was Alice's turn. She sank onto the chair by his desk.

"Why, Alice?" asked Files. "Walk me through it all."

"Why was Clay shooting at us?" she said. "Several reasons. For one, he needed to silence Davie."

"Davie? I need to hear again why you think that."

"The paper mentioned you were looking at drone footage. Davie's the only person who actually saw Clay going back under the trees in the park that night. Remember how Davie told us the man he saw looking back at him looked like a sheriff? Davie's been watching *High Noon*. It wasn't a black-and-white windbreaker we saw on the computer. What we were looking at was a man in a white shirt and a black vest. That's what Clay was wearing in that drone video."

"Clay Black was following John Pine?"

"Yes. And he could've picked up M.A.'s thermometer when he stopped by her rig on Friday night. We were distracted."

"But what motive did Clay Black have for killing John Pine?"

"None. But he did have a motive for killing his nephew, Caswell Bond. Unfortunately for Pine, Clay thought Pine was Caswell." She was remembering the remark Clay had made that night about hunting: *If an opportunity knocks, you zero in for the kill.* Then she said, "As far as I know, Clay hadn't met Pine, hadn't seen Pine except maybe when I was talking to him at the taco truck. I'll bet he thought I was talking to my client, Caswell. The lights might have fooled him, too. The streetlights. And you remember how Caswell told us he only thought it was Clay, that he'd only seen some old pictures since he left Texas?"

Files nodded.

"I just realized, when Caswell said that, that Clay also hadn't had a close-up look at Caswell. He'd only seen him from a distance when Caswell was looking at the Tindall ranch last Thursday."

"They didn't run into each other at the barbecue competition?"

"I don't think so. Ask Caswell."

Files nodded. "Okay, I see. But—" Files paused, his forehead puckered. "Why would Clay Black try to kill his own nephew?"

"That's a long story. A long, old, sad story. Clay's nephew, Caswell, had to watch his own dad, Clay's brother, bleed to death. By the time Caswell's mother got home that day, Caswell's dad—Clay's brother — was gone. I think Clay believed his nephew, Caswell, might have seen him—Clay—watching as his own brother died."

"You're not saying Clay killed his own brother?"

"Not . . . not directly," Alice said. "He might have hoped that the post-hole auger he lent his brother would kill him, and it did. Clay told everyone he hadn't seen that happen. But when Caswell and his mother showed up here and bought the Tindall ranch last month, Clay was afraid they might be coming home to Coffee Creek, and that eventually everyone in town would hear their version of his brother's death." She remembered Val's face as she stood on her Colorado porch, remembering that she thought she'd seen Clay . . . watching.

Alice went on: "Plus everything else was coming down on Clay at once. The golden parachute from his bank? Toast, if the co-op moves its deposits out of Cowman's. His reputation? Also potentially toast, depending on what else happens at the co-op."

Files raised inquiring eyebrows.

She told him about the documents she'd given Red. "Ask Red Griffin about the co-op audit and Wally Phifer retiring early," she said. "I should also tell you Annette Black called me this morning, worried about Clay. Ask her how angry Clay was, telling Wally he couldn't retire yet."

"We've got someone talking to her," Files said. His phone rang. He listened, said "Thanks." He looked up at Alice. "Well, they found Clay at the ranch. He was just sitting in his living room, staring into space. Didn't react, just sat like a zombie."

Alice said nothing for a moment. "Did you arrest him? Did you get the rifle?"

"Yes to both."

"Someone's finding the two bullets at Tindall ranch? I can show you where they hit."

"We're on it. I don't think we'll need you." He studied her face. "You're afraid to have him walking around loose, right?"

"Davie and Caswell are in mortal danger from that man."

"And now you could be. You were there." Files picked up his notebook. "Okay, shifting gears. Tell me a little more about this apparatus Caswell says he was wearing when the shooter got after you and Davie? What's with the goggles and headphones?"

"An experimental invention," Alice said. "Caswell calls it the Gog, short for goggles. Caswell's got a number of patents. He's trying to get the Gog—this item—ready for production. I think it zeroes in on specific minerals via some sort of audio-magnetotelluric, or AMT, device, whatever the hell that is." She frowned. "Listen, it's confidential. It's a valuable trade secret. I must ask you to protect the information on the Gog, or I'll have to get a temporary restraining order. A California company sent a guy out just to spy on him this week. The spy used a drone."

Files's eyebrows shot halfway up his forehead. "A drone?"

Alice told some of that tale.

"Give me Tony Stolak's contact info," said Files.

She nodded, showed him her picture of Stolak's license, sent it to him. Then she said, "Will you protect the confidential information on the Gog?"

Files agreed.

"And also, can we keep Davie out of this as much as possible?"

"I'll try." He looked again at his notebook, scowled at the end of his pencil. Then he said, "Caswell tells me you saved Davie."

"Well, I landed on him," Alice said. "I was trying to get downhill to the creek fast enough to warn Davie and Caswell. I tripped and fell when the shooter first fired and missed. Davie was coming around the corner in the creek bed when I landed on him. Another shot hit the boulder right by us. Rock shards everywhere." She blinked and looked away, again seeing the splinters of shattered limestone flying past.

"So, two shots?"

Alice nodded. "Caswell hauled us back behind that boulder." She sat silent, remembering hurtling down the rocky cliff. She looked at her scraped hands, at her precious Goodson Kells boots, toes and heels scratched, perhaps beyond repair. Maybe she'd get on the list for a new pair next year. Right now she was beginning to feel giddy, wanting a glass of wine, wanting to go home and pat her burros.

"Okay, Alice. You look about done. What are you staring at?"

"These boots."

"Yeah, yeah. Go on home."

"First I need to know if Clay's going to be out on bail or not. Davie and Caswell will still be in town tonight. I want them safe."

"I doubt he'll be out. I'll call you if he is."

"I should hope so."

Chapter   Thirty

Loyalty's a Fine Thing

On the way out of the building she saw Caswell sitting on a bench on the courthouse lawn. Davie, nearby, was reading the legends on the war memorial. She sat down and they watched Davie together. After a moment, Caswell asked, "What set him off?" Alice told him about the bank sale, the co-op, Phifer's loan, and Clay's face when he realized he'd killed Pine. Caswell was uncharacteristically still. Davie was swinging on the lowest branch of a Spanish oak out on the courthouse lawn.

Finally she asked, "Caswell, did you ever wonder if it would drive Clay nuts having you next door?"

He glanced up, eyes wide, then looked down, twisting his wedding band. "No. Not that. All my life I've most desperately wanted to come back, to lay claim again to our ranch and buy the Tindalls' place with the creek. That's been my dream. Maybe I thought it would keep me closer to my dad, honor him in some way." He paused. "But it's true I've had this picture in my mind of Clay up on his hill watching my dad, down by our fence, and I've always wondered if I really remembered that or just imagined it. I don't know how I thought getting the Tindalls' place would answer that question."

He turned to her. "Alice—if I'd known that Clay would kill Pine —my God. I don't know if I can stand it, to tell you the truth. Poor John Pine. And if Clay had killed Davie, or you?" His eyes filled with horror.

"Or you?" said Alice. "If it had been you, dead under those live oaks, Davie and Anna would be without their dad."

Davie had managed to scramble up onto the branch. Alice realized that Kinsear was probably en route to her house, ready to cook.

"Caswell, do you still feel like dinner tonight out at my place?"

He looked at her sweat-stained face, abraded hands.

"Oh, I'm not the one cooking," she reminded him.

"To tell the truth, I'd like us all to be together, if you're still up for it," he said.

They sat companionably for a minute. Presently she said, "Are you going to say, 'Don't tell Bonnie?'"

"Fat chance," Caswell said. "She kept saying Pine's death was a danger sign. I didn't see it."

* * * * *

M.A. sautéed the mushrooms. Val opened the wine. Caswell mashed the new potatoes. Davie set the table and got to light the candles. Alice made salad. Kinsear's steak rub had M.A. asking for the recipe. Since Kinsear was usually the recipe hound, he was deeply tickled.

Around the candlelit table Davie and Caswell recounted again the events of the day. Kinsear's looked at Alice with horror. "Can't you just practice law in your office?" he said.

Davie surprised her. He stood up at the table and said, "But Mr. Kinsear, she saved me. She was very brave. Even if she broke my controller. But that was an accident." Then he sat back down and dug into his mashed potatoes.

That night when they were finally alone, she poured Kinsear a last glass of wine. In the darkened living room his face looked—not sad, exactly, but resigned. Alice sat down and scooted close. Suddenly she felt great tenderness for this man, who'd dragged her out of the slough of despond, who roused her to passion, who made her laugh. She liked his hands, long-fingered, strong, restful. He never bored. He cared deeply. So, indubitably, did she. She ran her hand over his forehead, ruffled his hair, moved closer to his warmth.

"I'm sorry about Honor Society and Javier's concussion and Enrique getting arrested," she said.

"I'm sorry you nearly got killed at least twice today," Kinsear said. "Every time I think we're through with your experiments in narrow escape, you try another one."

"I really don't mean to," said Alice. "But when I looked down the hill at Davie, he looked so much like my John I couldn't stand not to get to him."

She looked sternly at Kinsear. "And admit it, you'd have done exactly the same thing, except maybe not slide into the cactus."

He nodded. "Also I owe some thanks to Eddie LaFarge, sounds like."

"Yes. I do too." She leaned over and kissed him, then kissed him again, looking into the brown eyes under the black brows now flecked with white. He put his hands on her shoulders, pulled her a little closer, kissed her very seriously.

"Listen," Alice said, finally. "You want me to teach you that Scandinavian flick?"

* * * * *

The next morning, Files called. "We found the black vest, at Clay's house. Believe it or not, it was hanging out in the garage where Clay had left it. Annette said she was about to send it to the cleaners."

"And?"

"Bloodstains, Alice. Tiny, but a little spatter of blood by one of the buttons. I guess Clay missed that."

"And?" Alice held her breath.

"Preliminary only—but the blood matches Pine's."

"Ah." Then she asked, "What does Clay say?"

"Not talking. Still not talking."

* * * * *

That afternoon she called Eddie LaFarge to say thank you.

"I already heard. George Files told me you pretty much mastered the Scandinavian flick." Alice blushed. She hoped he meant the evasive driving technique.

"Yes. Thank you, Eddie. Caswell and his son, Davie, and I would've been toast—flying off the road down the hill—if you hadn't offered to teach me a few things."

"How's the truck?"

She admitted it had a new shimmy.

"Told you it was time to consider a new ride," he said.

"I hate change."

"You can keep the truck for ranch work, of course," Eddie said. "You can afford a second car. Just use your truck to haul hay. That shimmy sounds expensive." He paused. "Okay, Alice, assuming you had to get a new ride, what would you get?"

Alice was stumped. Silent. Her mind went blank.

"Okay, I'll give it a little thought," Eddie said. "You need something with a little room and a lot of speed. No, I mean it."

* * * * *

Two days later, Eddie called back. "Okay, Alice. I got something for you to look at. No obligation. Just come on out. Bring your boyfriend."

Boyfriend?

"You know, that Kinsear guy," he continued. "Your friend Val mentioned him. Says he likes wine. Bring him out."

So Kinsear got his wish. Alice took his picture with Eddie LaFarge in front of the vat of Mourvèdre. And right after that, Eddie said, "Okay, Alice. Come out back."

Behind the winery sat a used forest-green Land Rover Discovery. Alice walked slowly toward it, peered inside.

He told her the price. "Dealer let me bring it out here. I told him otherwise he'd never get you out to his lot."

Not bad, she thought.

"I thought about a Defender," Eddie said. "But you'll need ongoing repairs. Then I thought about a convertible, like that Fiat from 1980. Very cute. But ridiculous for summer. Thought about a Jeep. No, not Alice. Thought about a Land Cruiser. Too much, since you have a truck, and a little top-heavy for, um, evasive driving. Thought about a Mustang convertible. Again, there's the Texas summer. Thought about a Porsche."

Alice stiffened.

"Yeah, yeah, you aren't self-indulgent enough, Alice. You really might like a Porsche. We'll see."

"We won't see. I keep my cars as long as I can."

"Whatever," Eddie said. "Try this one out."

Cautiously she opened the door, slid into the seat, looked around. It wasn't her truck. It was glossier. It had more bells. More whistles. But her truck—she had to admit it still had that disconcerting shimmy, ever since Clay rammed it on the highway. This felt solid. It did not yet feel hers. She started the engine, listened. She rolled down the driver's-side window, lifted an eyebrow, smiled a cautious smile at the two men.

"Reach under the seat," Eddie commanded.

She groped beneath the driver's seat, felt soft plastic, pulled it out. An emergency signal pack, with flare gun and five flares. Kinsear was grinning ear to ear. The boys had plotted this.

She burst into tears.

"Maybe it'll work," she said, wiping her nose with a tissue. "If it comes with the flare gun."

"She's a hard woman," Kinsear said. "She loves that truck though."

"Loyalty's a fine thing," Eddie said.

Chapter Thirty-One

Humans
and
Velociraptors

The insurance company finally paid on the fire damage to the Tindall house. The fire marshal, though suspicious, could not confirm that the fire was deliberately set. Besides, Caswell and Val had been miles away.

Alice was pleased for Caswell. Still, she wondered about the black truck with the maroon paw print decal, and the rock river on Audubon, and the man sitting at the next table at Twin Owls.

So, angling for answers, she delivered her shimmying truck to Leo at the central garage for its next oil change and an estimate on shimmy repairs. She took a seat on the dinette chair by the cash window, watching the mechanics and waiting for Leo. To her surprise, Mikey was working in the last bay. He gave her a quick look, then dived back under the car he was working on.

Leo came out, shaking his head. "How far you going to drive this truck now that you've got that little Discovery? Just back and forth from home to the feed store?"

"Yes."

"You promise?"

She laughed. "Yes."

"Because I can't fix that shimmy for less than the truck is worth. And I can't guarantee you can drive it without winding up in the ditch somewhere."

"Okay. Listen, Leo, can I talk to Mikey for just a minute?"

He looked unhappy, then uncertain, then resigned. "One minute." Face set, Leo walked over and spoke to Mikey. Mikey set down his tools and walked up, his frown set in concrete.

"Can we go outside?" Alice said.

Mikey hesitated, then followed her to the front parking lot.

"I understand you don't do kids," Alice said.

His eyes widened.

"I'm awfully glad you don't," Alice said.

He just looked at her.

"What else did Clay Black say?" Alice asked.

He stood for a moment, considering. "Whoever it was, and I ain't sayin' who, I told him no. Apparently you already heard that. But if anyone else asks me about it I ain't sayin' a word. So don't try to get me called at his trial. But"—he looked at his grimy fingernails, and then directly at Alice—"I *don't* do kids."

She thought for a moment. "I'm not promising. That was you up on Audubon, wasn't it? Starting the rock river?"

"No idea what you're talking about." He turned to go. She thought she heard him whisper, *"But you all looked mighty funny dancing around."*

"What?" Alice demanded.

He turned and looked back at her. "I didn't say a thing." He strode off.

Leo, watching from the open garage doors, shrugged with his hands in the air.

Alice got it. She called George Files and told him her suspicion that Mikey had been in Estes Park and had started the rock river. "You didn't see his license plate?" he asked.

"No."

"You couldn't identify the guy at the top of the mountain?"

"No."

"You didn't get a good look at the guy at the restaurant either, or anywhere else?"

"No," she admitted.

Later that day, Files called Alice at her office. "The prosecutor's already got Clay's phone records, trying to pin down where he was and when. We looked at Mikey's too. A cell tower in Estes Park shows a call to Clay the day before you went up there. From Mikey's phone."

Alice waited.

"So we can put him there, Alice, but that's all. Unless you've got more."

She thought for a long minute. "I don't." So, she concluded, he'll walk. Maybe he'd been sent to Colorado to watch Val or Caswell, or maybe he'd learned from Jana that Red would be there. Maybe opportunity just knocked, up there on the mountain. A chance at two birds with one stone. But still, he'll walk.

* * * * *

Life, so far, had taught Alice to pay attention to death. If you didn't attend the funeral, you hadn't been fully human about that person. Whatever that meant. So she went to John Pine's memorial service in Westlake, at St. John Neumann. M.A. asked to come with her.

Alice shook hands with his parents. His mother had the drained face, the stiff courage, of a mother who'd lost her only child.

M.A., not Pine's mother, was the one who cried first. Tears slid silently down M.A.'s face as she told Pine's mother that at the barbecue competition, she'd asked John Pine to come back the next morning to hear M.A. explain how she knew when brisket was done. "I looked forward to it," M.A. said. "I enjoyed the boy. He was a promising child."

The mother wept.

To Alice's surprise, the program listed Travis Poole as a participant. Wasn't he the football player Pine had taunted at the barbecue competition? The one who laughed at Pine and said, "You never change"? A broad-shouldered young man walked to the front of the sanctuary during the eulogies. He cleared his throat. "We all envied John; he was so smart," said Poole. "Yes, and a smart-ass. One of the smarter smart-asses." The congregation chuckled. "But I'll tell you this," Poole went on. "I read all his columns. And I ate at all the places he wrote about. I don't know why—he ragged on me all the time. Maybe I was just checking to see if he would make a mistake. But you know what?"

The congregation waited.

"He was right every time. Yep, got it dead right every time. So here's to you, John Pine: you had an edge, a sharp edge, but it was an accurate edge. And you will be missed. Hear me?" Poole looked up toward the high sanctuary ceiling and waved a clenched fist. "You will be missed." Face pink, he walked back down to his pew.

Alice's eyes filled. Why, why, she asked, did one person think he was so privileged he could kill another? Could snatch away the life of another human?

Maybe he was frightened that people would see him for what he was: a man who let his brother bleed out in a sunny pasture, alone, without going to his aid.

That wasn't enough.

Alice shook her head in despair at the nature of the species. Her own species. She too had felt what it was like to attack someone, knowing her attack might kill that person. No, she had not yet learned to turn the other cheek, not enough to accept death at another's hands. This species! Well, she thought, thank God, if appropriate, for the rule of law, which she served. Sometimes she thought that the stone tablets and their modern counterparts were the only thing separating humans and velociraptors.

* * * * *

In furtherance of the rule of law, she sent a demand letter to Deep Metal LLC, threatening damages. She attached the draft lawsuit. Counsel for Deep Metal responded with a confused denial of liability and request for mediation. She filed the lawsuit and served discovery. Caswell said, "This will be fun."

* * * * *

With Val, Caswell, and Davie back in Colorado, Alice drove north one Saturday morning to meet the wildlife-management consultant at the Tindall ranch. November: high blue sky, brown grass, still sunny but with a line of gray clouds looming on the horizon to the north. When she and the consultant finished checking over the tax application and he left, Alice locked the Tindalls' gate and started back down the gravel road in her truck.

As she approached Val's half of the Black ranch, she slowed. On impulse, she parked and climbed over the gate. A few Angus heifers snorted, backed away, returned to their stolid grazing. Alice walked through the fall grass close to the fence, then back, wondering where exactly Caswell Black had "bled out, right there in the field." Shouldn't the spot be marked, somehow? Maybe indelible memories in the heads of his wife and child were enough.

Sighing, she walked up the grass-grown driveway to the grove where the roofless house stood inside a tumbledown fence. A jackrabbit bounded away. A tangled rosebush still clung to the wall by the old front door. The door, paintless and buckling, stood slightly ajar, caught on the stone lintel. Alice peered past it into the house. So small, she thought. No furniture inside. No pictures. On the chimney mantel, a small dusty bottle holding a couple of dried flowers.

She heard footsteps and turned.

Annette Black watched her. She looked different. Ah, Alice thought. No makeup. The fixed smile had vanished.

"Hi, Annette," Alice said. She couldn't help it—she glanced up toward Clay's hilltop.

"Don't worry, Alice," Annette said. "He's not there. He's under house arrest in Coffee Creek, awaiting trial."

She paused.

"I'm living up here now. Till it's over."

That surprised Alice. The devoted wife no more? "Let's get in the sun, Annette," said Alice, feeling chilly in the shade of the trees by the house.

The two women walked back down the drive toward the gate.

"I was trying to figure out where Caswell Black died," Alice said. "You were here that day, right?"

Annette nodded. "I came home from work and the ambulance was already there in the driveway." She pointed. "Right there. They'd loaded the body, were going to at least take the body to the hospital. Val and little Caswell were going to follow them in their truck. There was nothing I could do. I knew I needed to call Clay and let him know." She looked across the road and up the hill. "So I got back in my car and drove up to the house. I thought he'd still be at the bank. But there was his truck, parked right behind the house. And there he was inside, sitting in the big chair by the fireplace.

"I couldn't believe it. I told him Caswell was dead, dead from that damn auger. 'Didn't you hear anything?' I asked. He swore he'd seen nothing, heard nothing. And I knew the ambulance didn't use its siren. Val had told them Caswell was already gone."

Annette surveyed the grassy area by the gate. "Clay never changed his story. It's exactly what he told Val. But that day I found him, sitting in the big chair, he had a distant look about him. And his black shoes, the ones he wore to the bank every day, had mud on them. When I took the trash out that afternoon I saw his footprints in the dirt, coming around the corner of the house."

She looked at Alice. "What should I have done? He'd helped it happen. He'd watched it happen. He'd let his own brother die. Is that murder? What is it? I didn't know. I've lived with it all these years." Then she said, bitterly, "One thing I did know: he wasn't going to let anyone change his story."

* * * * *

Halloween, then November. All Saints' Day, El Día de los Muertos. Death and remembrance. Not Alice's favorite holiday.

Alice could hardly wait instead for the cheer of Thanksgiving, for Ann and John to be home, chopping celery for cornbread stuffing, letting her sneak up and hug them over and over.

Val was staying with M.A. So far as Alice knew, Val still had not traveled out to the Tindall ranch; that was definitely Caswell's project. This was hers. The Tea Garden house bustled with deliveries of china, tablecloths, kitchen equipment. The high school class, scheduled for Christmas break, filled immediately.

In a week the restaurant would open, serving dinner Thursday through Saturday evenings. M.A. taped the first menu to the front door. "We're full the first two weekends," she reported proudly. "Holy cow, Alice, what have we gotten into?"

Alice snorted. "It's exactly what you wanted."

At the office, the rancher who'd worried that Alice was "anti-realtor" called for another appointment. Silla called the bank VP, arranged for him to sign his will, and shamed him into paying his bill. The mayor hinted that the contracts project might be back on.

Kinsear sat Alice down for a talk, one she wasn't ready for. "When can you meet my daughters? I want them to know the woman I'm hanging out with."

"When they let you know they're ready to meet me," Alice said.

"Are you chicken?"

"No," she countered. "But I don't need their approval either."

"Very true," he said. "Actually, neither do I. Not for what we've got."

Still, she knew a day was coming.

* * * * *

The morning John and Ann were due in for Thanksgiving break, Alice headed well ahead of time to the Austin airport. She always stood at the top of the escalator—never would she simply wait in the cell phone lot for her children.

Her phone went *ping!* Had they landed? No.

Instead, she saw a new email. From: "Tony." Subject: "Pistol Packin' Mama." Message: "Alice, I tried to scrub this from any server at you-know-where. I think you suspected me—you were right. I had instructions to check out counsel for the subject. Thanks for the brisket. Best wishes. Tony. P.S. Don't try to find me. I've set this message to delete itself five minutes after opening so save the video somewhere if you want to enjoy it. P.P.S. Despite the brisket, I'm not coming back to Texas." Tony Stolak, she thought—last seen by the side of the road, waiting for AAA.

She saved the attached video. Then she opened it. In grainy color, she saw herself dancing around the clothesline in her nightie, gripping the orange plastic flare gun in two outstretched hands, with such indignation on her face. Then the sound went *blam!* and the screen went white.

Alice giggled. It made her think of Robert Burns—"O wad some Power the giftie gie us / To see oursels as others see us."

She looked up the phrase "Pistol Packin' Mama" and found it was a 1943 Al Dexter hit, with a boogie version by Albert Ammons, Pete Johnson, and Meade "Lux" Lewis. Maybe she'd just call this little video of herself, madly dancing around in her nightie, the Flare Gun Boogie. That would mightily please Kinsear, the boogie guy—if she told him.

And from the corner of her eye she spied John and Ann racing toward the escalator.

THE END

ABOUT THE AUTHOR

Helen Currie Foster writes the Alice MacDonald Greer Mystery series. She lives north of Dripping Springs, Texas, supervised by three burros. She is drawn to the compelling landscape and quirky characters of the Texas Hill Country. She's also deeply curious about our human history and how, uninvited, the past keeps crashing the party.

Find her on Facebook or at www.helencurriefoster.com

HEARING FROM YOU

Thanks for reading *Ghost Next Door!* If you enjoyed it, please consider rating it or putting a short review on Amazon. When readers take the time to review books, they can and do make a difference in the success of a series.

If you have comments, questions or suggestions, drop a note to thealicemysteries@gmail.com.

You can find out more about Alice and her adventures at www.helencurriefoster.com, and subscribe to the mailing list there, for updates and news about upcoming books.

THANKS AND MORE THANKS

This book would not have taken shape without the collaboration of Larry Foster, Sydney Foster Schneider, Drew Foster, and Grace Currie Bradshaw, nor hatched without valuable comments and critiques from Carol Arnold, Ann Barker, Dr. Megan Biesele, Diana Borden, Elizabeth Christian, Ann Ciccolella, Keith Clemson, Sue Cleveland, Floyd Domino, Dixie Lee Evatt, Kathy Gresham, Fran Paino, Suzanne Wofford, and Stephenie Yearwood. Thanks to Claudia Irwin for the inspiring meeting with mountaineer Jean Warner, and to the Heart of Texas Chapter of Sisters in Crime. All have my heartfelt thanks. Any errors are mine.

For superb advice from Aaron Hierholzer (editor nonpareil) and for Bill Carson's cover, design, layout, and sheer professional brio, thanks and more thanks.

27936076R00167

Made in the USA
Columbia, SC
02 October 2018